JOHN ELLSWORTH

THE MENTAL CASE

ＶＩＮＣＩ
BOOKS

Vinci Books

vinci-books.com

Published by Vinci Books Ltd in 2024

1

A CIP catalogue record for this book is available from the British Library.

Paperback ISBN: 9781036700188

Printed and bound in Great Britain by Clays Ltd, Elcograf S.p.A.

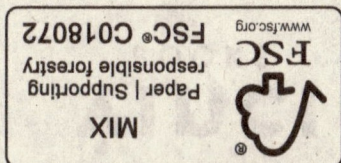

By John Ellsworth

THE THADDEUS MURFEE LEGAL THRILLERS

The Defendants

Beyond a Reasonable Death

Attorney at Large

Chase, the Bad Baby

Defending Turquoise

The Mental Case

The Girl Who Wrote The New York Times Bestseller

The Trial Lawyer

The Near Death Experience

Flagstaff Station

The Crime

La Jolla Law

The Post Office

The Contract Lawyer

THE MICHAEL GRESHAM THRILLERS

The Lawyer

The Defendant's Father

The Law Partners

Carlos the Ant

Sakharov the Bear

Annie's Verdict

Dead Lawyer on Aisle 11

30 Days of Justis

The Fifth Justice

Lies She Never Told Me

Girl, Under Oath

Lawyers in Gray

SISTERS IN LAW

Court Order

Hellfire

The District Attorney

Justice in Time

Chapter 1

There was a girl to be saved. She was nine. She lived in Nogales, Sonora. He had never met her, had never seen a picture of her, and had never spoken to her. Yet, he felt he knew her. He felt he knew her because he knew about kids' hearts. He knew how fully they trusted and how easily they were broken. He couldn't let that happen. Not to Maria of Sonora.

He chose a Toyota Camry for the trip. It was beige, several years old, bookended with brick-red Arizona plates. The license plates would only make sense, crossing at Nogales, Arizona, into Nogales, Sonora. *Gringo* coming into Mexico--everyday it happened tens of thousands of times.

Border station rising up out of the desert, gull wings in flight. Two giant concrete spans, northbound, southbound passing below each wing. The sign looming in the quivering heat: PUERTO FRONTERIZO SON MEXICO. Too late to turn back now, inching ahead with the long lines, six abreast, souls floating into Mexico. On the hills ahead,

1

stunted saguaros, all but dead from the assaults of angry, aimless children of Mexico.

Thaddeus wet his lips. Truth-telling time was just about here. He was hiding a handgun up under the dash. He planned on saying nothing about it to the officers up ahead. Glock 26, pocket holster--your best friend in a fix. He would need it below the border.

He nosed up to the yellow stop line and cracked a window. Cold air out, oven air in.

The border guards carefully looked him over. Motioned him to step out. They made him open the trunk. They raised the lid and unzipped his single blue bag. They flipped through its contents. Blue jeans, three tee-shirts (Suns, Cardinals, NAU Lumberjack Football), Jockeys, Teva sandals, three balls of white athletic socks, navy RL wind-breaker, toiletries, and a folding knife with four inch blade.

"*Señor*?" said the agent, a Federale wearing the navy uniform of Mexican customs. The man's eyebrows met in the center, but the eyes--blue and piercing—missed nothing.

Thaddeus looked at the knife and nodded. "Don't want to get mugged down here. It's for self-defense. My apologies if it's a proscribed item."

"Yes, *Señor*," said the agent. He opened and closed the blade. "It's a proscribed item. I could put you in jail but I won't. You don't look dangerous, just uninformed. We'll keep it here for you."

"I can pick it up when I return?"

"*Si*," said the border agent.

Thaddeus nodded. The knife was a ruse. It was to make them feel like they had found something and done their jobs correctly. All the while failing to discover the gun taped under the Toyota's dash. The Glock was not only proscribed, it was a felony to possess a gun in Mexico, a crime punishable by thirty years in a Mexican prison. Thaddeus felt the sweat break out across his shoulders. Even six months in a Mexican prison was impossible. It was a death sentence for an American.

He shook his head as if injured. "I was hoping I could bring my knife in," he told the agent. "But I guess you're just doing your job."

All innocence. He shrugged. The agent went for it. Or did he?

"Show me your driver's license."

Thaddeus complied.

"I write your name on this knife."

"Thanks. I would like it back when I leave."

"You can pass through now, *Señor*," the agent replied. "And don't forget to pick up your knife on the way back. We will leave it with ICE on the other side."

He meant the U.S. customs agents. He was telling Thaddeus he would turn the knife over to them so that they could return to Thaddeus when he came through northbound. Fat chance of that ever happening, thought Thaddeus. But the hand had been played. They waved him through, gun and all.

Now he was free to do what he had come for. Which was to meet Hermano Sanchez and escort him and his family to Mexico City, away from Sonora.

Hermano Sanchez had been a drug client in Flagstaff. He had been arrested when he was linked to a suitcase filled with fifty pounds of marijuana. Hermano's reason for becoming a dope mule was simple: the cartel would pay him $1000 on delivery in Flagstaff. Otherwise they would make his nine-year-old smuggle drugs. So he went to try to save his baby girl. With $1000, he could move his family far away from the cartel. But he was caught in the US. Thaddeus had represented him until his bail was paid and Hermano fled back to Mexico. That had seemed to be the end of it.

Then Hermano had called. The cartel was going to take Maria if he didn't pay them for the marijuana he lost to the police seizure of the drugs.

"I don't know anything about dealing with the cartel," Thaddeus had told him. "I wouldn't even know where to start."

"*Señor* Murfee, they are coming for Maria in one week. They will take her from me if I don't have their money."

"Look, I'll come and meet with you. I can help you get moved the hell out of Nogales. What about Mexico City for you? Does that make sense?"

"*Si*, that makes sense. I pray you to do it."

"I'm on my way," Thaddeus had said. "Give me one day and we'll meet."

"There's a pharmacy, Roberto's *Farmacia*, where we can meet. At the counter."

"I'll be there tomorrow at five p.m. Meet me."

They had hung up and Thaddeus had made arrangements to journey to Mexico.

Thaddeus had long regretted he hadn't been able to do more for Hermano. Hermano's daughter was in jeopardy. The kids would smuggle drugs in walk-bys--passing from Mexico into the U.S. with a backpack full of drugs, posing as students. After a few times of this the kids became useless because the border agents got to know them and got suspicious. Bags got searched, drugs got seized, and the kids were held. At that point the cartel rescued them, only to pimp them in the red light district.

That haunted Thaddeus.

He had lost countless hours of sleep fearing for Maria.

His own daughter had been kidnapped. He couldn't stand to let it happen to some other child.

"We stop this insanity one kid at a time," he told Katy, his wife. Then, the more he had thought about it, the more it seemed like Hermano's help must come from Thaddeus. There just wasn't anyone else.

The gun was protection against the cartel's plans for the girl. It probably wouldn't be needed. But if it were, there it was. So the gun made the trip.

"Proceed, *Señor!*" The Mexican border guard tossed off his best military salute and looked Thaddeus directly in the eye. Thaddeus nodded and was just about to apply the gas, when, "*¡Alto!* Halt!"

His foot jammed on the brake. He waited.

The guard returned to the driver's window. He made a rolling motion with his hand. Thaddeus complied, again lowering the window. "Did I do something wrong?"

"Yes, you looked guilty."

"What?" It was said in amazement. How could someone *look* guilty?

"Twenty years I have studied faces. Yours has a guilty look. Step outside, please."

The agent's drug dog glowered, straining to sniff inside. He would have the gun in five seconds. Yes, border dogs knew guns all too well. It was cake for them.

Thaddeus quickly debated offering a bribe. He decided he had nothing to lose at that point. Reaching inside the breast pocket of his shirt he displayed the top-half of a $100 bill, USD. The guard's eyes fastened on the move.

"*Señor*, do I look like a thief to you?"

Thaddeus shook his head. "Not at all."

The man tilted his head. A querulous expression formed on his face. "So why treat me like one?"

"It didn't mean anything--"

"Oh, yes. It meant something, *señor*. It meant you are guilty of something. It is my job to find out what that something is now. Go to the windows and have a seat on the bench."

Thaddeus shrugged, climbed out, and inched around the dog. He crossed four lanes of hopscotch traffic. A cement bench was indicated and he plopped down. Great, he thought. If they find that gun--

The guard was advancing, holding the holstered pistol before him as one would carry a dangerous snake. The dog was on a short leash. He appeared to be prancing. Almost rejoicing at his find.

"*Señor*, this is very bad. Follow me inside, please."

"Should I move my car first?"

"We will take care of the car, *señor*. Just follow me, please."

Inside the station, air conditioning was beating back the desert heat although it was still early morning. On overload, ice sprouted from the window AC's vents, wheezing and choking off every few minutes. It was then Thaddeus knew: this wasn't the United States where a federal maintenance crew stood poised to repair air conditioning units. This was the other side of the world, the Third World. Here when the air shuts off, brother, it stays off. Maybe for days, maybe forever. He knew way more about it than he wished. He had heard the stories and he had experienced some of Mexico during his trials and travels. But now he was in it for the close-up, the money shot, the minute his life had been waiting for: he had tried to smuggle a gun and he had been caught. Thirty years loomed as he was pushed against a wall and his photograph taken by a remote camera. They were booking him!

"*Señor*, please come with me," a tall Mexican man wearing a white shirt and bolo tie and natty dress slacks said. He crooked a finger at Thaddeus, who fell in behind.

Down a short hallway, then to the right. He knew it.

A holding cell. Maybe twelve-by-twelve. A stinking gutter at the back wall, two cement benches. Unlighted. Reeking of urine and despair. He was amazed at what he didn't see: toilet paper. There was no toilet paper in the cell and he would have bet everything they didn't allow restroom breaks. Images passed through his mind, erratic and useless. He had to admit: he was scared.

Two angry-looking Mexicans were there before him. They watched as the guard clicked a keypad and the cell door sprang to life. Then he felt a push at his back and--just like that! He was in. The cell door whooshed behind him and clanked into place. A metal maw awaiting its next delicacy. White meat from *Los Estados Unidos*, Thaddeus thought.

The two Mexican inmates stood and softly began clapping.

Chapter 2

January of that year in Chicago, the hawk was flying.

Winds whipped up from the lake. Gusts at forty miles per hour lashed the streets, leaving office habitués to plunge like Chicago Bears running backs. But for Ansel Largent, partnership in the city's premier law firm overrode the power of Lake Michigan's blast and made placid his way. Partners scored underground parking in the eighty story Citibank Building.

He nosed his black Escalade between the lines at the headstone marked LARGENT. Nearby was the elevator, heated and tucked away from the outside bluster of winds and commerce.

He checked himself in the rearview. Neat, graying hair, wings on the side, straight back on top, gray eyes. He turned his head and admitted that Libby was right: the profile was hawkish. He bobbed his head in the mirror and caught up to the inner beat that only he heard. Ta-ta-TAT, it went, Ta-ta-TAT.

Not actually hearing things. Not actually *not* hearing things.

He timed the elevator from basement to seventy-eighth floor.

Exactly three-minutes-ten-seconds without stopping.

The elevator didn't stop because there was no one else out and about at 6:20 a.m. Which was lucky, because Ansel Largent vomited up his raisin-bagel and salmon cream cheese on the elevator deck. Withdrawing his pocket square, he wiped it all up. No trash receptacles there, so he stored the mess in a side pocket. Breakfast lost to a bad case of nerves came as no surprise. That morning, Ansel Largent would announce the terrible news to his partners. They were broke. And he was headed for jail.

Or worse.

What could be worse?

Ninety-nine lawyers gunning for you. Definitely worse.

It was simple math: when he logged out Friday night the ending trust account balance tipped the scale at $200 million. Over the weekend a rather large withdrawal had been made. Leaving home that morning, he checked the account online. One-hundred-and-sixteen dollars remained.

Ansel had been a partner in the 820 lawyer firm long enough to know that it wouldn't look kindly on lawyers who stole from its trust account. Like the *Bible*, trust accounts are sacrosanct. Trust accounts are the lawyer's solemn promise to guard a client's money like Brink's. The trust account at MacDevon Largent Law had been tapped and bled dry. All eyes would be on Ansel. Which meant they would be looking in the right direction.

The actual withdrawal had been made by someone near and dear to him. The afternoon *Chicago Tribune* would report the theft on page one of the business section. Right above

Promotions and Awards. The press would learn all about it because Ansel was beholden to turn in the thief. Which would bring down the FBI because the account was federally insured.

Ansel knew that turning someone in did nothing toward recovering the funds. But it would reveal the name of the thief. Which would astonish all hands because the wrongdoer was one of them. The wrongdoer was a guy who knew the secret handshake, who wore the right suits and pissed in the carpeted john, who could write a personal check for $500,000, who knew the login and password to the trust account.

The elevator door whooshed open. He stepped into the pastel-and-gray reception area. Water-lattice sculpture twelve feet in height in the center of the room, receptionist station constructed like a hotel front desk, nine separate islands of expensive seating (everyone there had secrets), a tennis court's worth of hardwood flooring at $32 per, and modern art straight from the Art Institute faculty show of 2014--all creating the sense of an oasis of calm and trust. Ansel hurried through, looking neither right nor left, head bobbing to the internal drum track.

He made coffee in his office. He settled into the ergochair and took stock as he sipped.

The questions the FBI would ask were predictable:

1) What was Ansel's role in the embezzlement? He had entrusted the guy with full administrative access to the client trust account and its bounty of $200 million.

2) How close was Ansel to the thief? Truth be told, Ansel loved the guy like a son. In fact, Ansel believed the thief *was* his son. David, newly-minted multimillionaire, was a junior partner.

David had been given trust account access when Ansel

was out of town and David needed trust funds to settle a simple auto accident case. The firm was holding the insurance company's reserve; $100,000 was needed to pay the other driver for her back injury. Ansel's solution? Give David the user name and password. Let him login, issue the funds, close the case. Business as usual, so why not? Ansel believed that David, for whatever reason, hadn't stopped at $100,000. David hadn't stopped at $100 million. David had stopped only when he had cleaned them out to the tune of $200 million. All of it except for $116. He had left them enough to pay the wire transfer fee. The wire transfer used to move the money to Zurich, then to Africa, then to Antigua, back to the Caribbean, vaulting north to Mexico City, where the trail ended.

3) What about prosecuting the thief? Ansel believed that David had fled as soon as the money was wired out of the country. Ansel suspected he knew David's ultimate location. But Ansel wasn't telling. Tracking him down--that would come later.

4) Who would be legally responsible for the theft? Ansel and his ninety-nine partners were responsible for making good on that hole in the air. The math was first grade easy. Each owed $2 million. Every last dime.

TWO HOURS LATER, rather than greet the FBI, Ansel remained hidden away in his corner office. The receptionists were to say he wasn't in yet. His curtains were wide open onto the blustery Chicago sky and the possibility of an airborne solution that might flap up against his windows. A solution was sorely needed; he was fresh out of ideas.

He considered the angles. David had violated Ansel's

trust. But if Ansel turned him in, the partners would literally send hit men. That's how enraged they would be when he told them in fifteen minutes at Partners' Monday.

Just as he was considering a free fall from the seventy-eighth-floor, his desk phone flashed. He already knew who. The caller would have been informed by Accounting and immediately buzzed Ansel. And Ansel, in his role of managing partner, would be looked to for a simple remediation of the fiscal outflow. The partners would expect a solution to spring from his brain into the room and jump onto the electronic records of the accounting system and induce a great healing. They would actually expect him to replace the funds with brain power. Not to be.

"Ansel speaking. Let me guess, JM?"

The voice was depleted of hope. "We've got problems, Anse. My office, three minutes."

He hung up without waiting for confirmation. It was a given, it was assumed, that the managing partner would drop whatever lay before him and proceed without dalliance to JM's corner office at the far end of the galaxy.

It lit up again.

Melinda.

"Have you heard, Mr. Largent?" Her tone was breathless.

"I have heard from Accounting. Was that what you mean?"

"Suzanne Fairmont! She's in her office, dead! Cops are pouring in and putting up their yellow tape. A SWAT team grabbed an elevator and won't let anyone else ride it. We're being invaded!"

"Say again, slowly."

"She's dead!"

He felt his pulse race. Too coincidental. His son stole

$200 million of their funds and a full partner had been shot in her office? Connected? Was David seeing her? What else might he not know about this flesh of his flesh?

"All right," he began slowly. "Tell me what you know, Mel."

"I'm coming in."

She hadn't asked to come into his throne room. She had announced it. There was no holding back all that was about to happen to Ansel, his family, and his law firm. She was just the first of it. He drew a deep breath and mentally fastened his seatbelt. It was all about to come undone.

Melinda entered. She clutched a forgotten box of donuts in one hand, a blossom of tissue in the other.

She attached herself to the window-side client chair, one of four spread before him like angels awaiting new souls.

She was tall and leggy, brunette hair parted down the middle, violet eyes that sometimes pursued him and sometimes recoiled from him.

She held a master's in psych. But she preferred toiling away at legal research that she fashioned into pleadings and points-of-law.

Her reasons for her under-employment were simple: he paid her double what she might earn in private practice as "a couch mouse," eavesdropping on patient woes at $150 per. Besides, there were no after-hours calls and no patient suicides. No wonder she'd opted to stay with him the past five years.

Plus there was the other thing.

The thing between them.

That thing always gathered and loomed whenever they inhabited the same space—office or hotel suite. It was large, like the Hindenburg, hanging voraciously upon the air, aflame, threatening to crash down around them and make the *Law Journal* gossip column. Another managing partner enjoying yet another romantic drive-by. But neither of them was willing to let it go. So they maintained its tether and refused to let it go. But that was just Ansel's view. He didn't much ask her views anymore.

Her eyes were moist and the tissue looked damp. Mel cried easily and of course the Suzanne Fairmont death would be torturous. As for him, he was a realist. Suzanne Fairmont had hated the law since her first day in law school and had never tried to cover up her hatred of her job. The fact that she had committed suicide came as no surprise to him and was a development that he, the Managing Partner, would handle with reserve lacing his voice as the facts of Suzanne's professional life were told to police officials and the press.

Mel's face was twisted with more than grief, however, and he caught her meaning. They read each other as if their facial emotions were Times New Roman. Who wouldn't, after five years outside the bed and three years in?

Ansel was proceeding slowly with the breaking news.

There was one bothersome aspect to Suzanne and suicide. Just last Wednesday she had staged a press conference in the main conference room (royal purple chairs and drapes--Ansel's pick) and announced her candidacy for District Attorney. Primary election nearing, time to make her move.

Yes, their Suzanne had tossed her hat in the ring to vie for the job of top cop. Having done that, why, less than a week later, would she kill herself? The implausibility of the act frightened him, its implications running wild in his mind insofar as David's possible involvement.

"So what do you want me to do first?"

He responded with his thoughtful-lawyer-look.

In a blink, the death of Suzanne Fairmont would focus on him as managing partner as he would be the firm member responsible for aiding the investigation. It set him on edge and threatened his normal public certitude that, whatever might be said outside their firm, those who inhabited and toiled in its guts knew that their firm was always right. That they always owned the high ground. That the law firms and companies that opposed them were simply wrong-minded. That the death of Suzanne Fairmont hadn't happened on their watch and in their enfoldment. It just didn't make sense. They rejected it.

Ansel's mind was already hardening reflexively. Lawyers are good at that, rejecting reality. The trick was to get buy-in.

"What should you do first? Have a donut, I'd say."

"Suicide is so horrible," moaned Melinda. She dabbed her eyes.

"Suicide?" he asked.

"Nobody's saying. I'm only assuming. Suzanne's always so down on everything."

"Was there a gun?"

"Ambrose didn't tell me. He unlocked Suzanne's office with his passkey when Suzanne's husband called and reported she never returned from the office last night."

"Sunday night. She was diligent, if not happy."

"Our maintenance guy lets himself in and finds Suzanne slumped in her chair. There's blood on her head. Ambrose feels for a pulse and backs out. He calls 911 and stands guard until the cops show up."

"Was there a gun?"

"I don't think so."

"Why don't you think so?"

"Because I asked Ambrose what he saw in there."

"Sounds like you."

"Well--part of my job is to know what's going on. You're Managing Partner and I work for you. I *should* know."

"Long story short, did Ambrose see a gun in Suzanne's office? In her hand? Answer me, please."

"Short answer, I didn't ask. Whether he mentioned it, I don't know. I'm sorry. Want me to go ask him?"

"Yes. Go. Snoop. Ask around, ask the cops for what they know. There had to be a gun. Tell them you work for me and I'm Managing Partner. Also point them my way for their questions. Pass the word to all staff that they should avoid comments to both the police and press. No one makes public statements today but me. Got all that?"

"I'll put it on the phone tree."

"Yes, voice calls. Don't use email."

"Of course not."

"Go, my child."

She stood up but didn't leave immediately.

"We need to talk later. Don't try to duck out today without giving me ten minutes. Promise?"

He lifted his oath hand. "Promise."

"Good. I'll be calling you at home if you forget."

"You wouldn't dare."

"Wouldn't I? Do you need to test me on that?"

"I'll make sure we talk. Now go. Please, Melinda."

Chapter 3

Two hours later, his watch said 11:14 AM.

Thaddeus lifted his eyes and considered the jail cell.

Each prisoner had been allotted a bottle of water. The cement floor was actually hot underfoot. It had turned out that, while the office up front was air conditioned, the holding cell was not. The Toyota's outside temp gauge had been punching up around 105 F when Thaddeus last saw it —unseasonably hot for January in Sonora. He was guessing the temperature inside the cell was every bit of that. Maybe more.

He had sweated through his clothes. His blue jeans were damp and clinging. His tee-shirt was soaked; both underarms and even the breast pocket where he still had the $100 bill tucked away was wet. All skin surfaces were beaded and sweat was rolling down his face.

The two Mexican inmates sat side-by-side on the right side of the cell; Thaddeus had the left bench to himself.

He had arrived just after breakfast, when he was asked

to exit the Toyota. He would soon want food again. And another water. But nobody had come around and said anything about food or toilet paper or any of the barest necessities for the cell's occupants.

Then at 11:29 another victim appeared outside the door and was ushered inside.

He was white, probably late teens, Thaddeus guessed. He had a tricolor eagle tattoo on his bicep and was wearing cutoffs to his knees and a wife-beater shirt that said "GO!" across the front. His face was riddled with angry acne and a wispy beard mapped out the cheeks and chin. There was little growth on the upper lip but Thaddeus gave him a "C" for effort.

He was amused by the youngster, whose first move was to take a seat next to Thaddeus and then fasten his eyes on the floor. Clearly scared to death. No wonder, either, his boundaries were flattened by his fear, leaving him vulnerable. In a word, he looked tasty.

The Mexicans wasted no time.

"You got dollars?" they asked the newcomer. He resisted making eye contact and Thaddeus thought that wise.

"Hey, man," the taller Mexican said, his voice notched. "You hear *mi amigo*? You got dollars or what, *cabron*?"

The eyes ventured a look. "Twenty bucks is all. Just gas money."

"I give you gas," said the smaller of the two Mexicans. "I pump you full, *chico*."

The taller one stood and approached. The American shot a sideways look at Thaddeus. "Hey, man, I'm Burton. Can you help me here?"

"Give the man the twenty," said Thaddeus. "I'll make it up to you."

Burton pulled a crumpled twenty dollar bill from his

pocket. He two-fingered it to the man, who took it and put it in his own pocket. But he didn't move away.

"Thas all? It costs forty dollars to stay here, man."

"That's all there is," said Burton. "My girlfriend is making some calls. Maybe I can get more."

"I need it now. Pay before play," said the taller man. He reached and put a paw on Burton's shoulder. "Now listen up, *gringo*. I don't like you already. I don't like your tattoo and I don't like your face. You got pimples. You too ugly for here. You should go back to USA."

Burton was bewildered. He dropped his eyes to the floor. The Mexican inmate moved his hand to a chokehold at the young man's throat. He began applying pressure, his knuckles white. The young man jerked away but the choke-hold tightened.

"Hey," said Thaddeus. "You need to go sit down."

The tall man shifted his eyes. Thaddeus Murfee was thirty years old, heavily muscled from afternoons at the Flagstaff Athletic Club where he was bench-pressing 325 and looked buff enough. Still, the man was committed and didn't dare back down or the roof might fall in on him, making him the new boy toy.

"You can talk when I talk to you," the man said. He held a finger to his lips. "Sssh."

"Not good," said Thaddeus. "Burton here is with me. We don't like being here anymore than you do. So, please return to your seat." Thaddeus pointed at the opposite bench and made a passing gesture with his hand. He was waving the man away.

"I sit where I want, when I want. I told you, sssshhh."

"Not good," said Thaddeus again. "You need to sit down now. Please don't make it worse than it is."

The man moved in front of Thaddeus. He laid his hand

on Thaddeus' shoulder, where it was immediately knocked away. The man reached for Thaddeus' throat and Thaddeus seized his arm and pulled the man to him, while sweeping his right leg against the man's left leg. The man swept down to his knees, his chin hit the bench, and he crumpled forward. Thaddeus stood and forced his foot against the man's skinny neck. "Not good, I told you. Now are you ready to go sit down on your own side of this shithole?"

"*Sí.*"

"I'm going to let you up. But if you bother either of us again, I'm going to hurt you. *Comprende*?"

"*Sí.*"

"*Bien.* Now sit down. Please."

The man pushed himself to his knees and clumsily found his footing. Shoulders slumped, he backed away, keeping a hand behind. His hand touched the wall and he sat straight down, never taking his eyes from Thaddeus.

"You goan be sorry for that, man," the tall Mexican muttered. "You'll see."

Thaddeus stood. "Then come on back over here. Let's just get it done right now."

"Not yet. I'll say when."

"You do that. But be advised, *compadre*, I will hurt you next time. I will break something."

"We see about that."

"Sure. We'll see."

Thaddeus turned to his bench mate.

"Now, what are you in here for?"

Chapter 4

Ansel shrugged into his suit coat, buttoned the top two, and began the trek down the hallway. He was at one end; the office of senior partner James MacDevon was at the other. JM, as he preferred, was a rangy six-footer with arms too long for his body. Plastic Man, the associates were said to whisper. He once pitched for the Cubs AAA ball club but watched his career crash and burn after an unsuccessful Tommy Johns surgery. Anymore his elbow gave him fits, and that day he had resorted to a nylon splint. Ansel wondered whether the rain forecast had anything to do with it. They nodded and it meant nothing except: Here we are again. JM waved the managing partner over to his circular table and ordered two coffees from Nedra. She poured and the men waited for the door to close behind her.

JM plopped two sugar cubes into his creamy drink.

"Accounting call you?"

"Yes. I heard. I was just dialing you when you buzzed."

"Two hundred million. And change."

JM's hands shook and the coffee cup slid across the saucer.

"So I heard."

"How do we get it back?"

"We make it up on our own. Immediately. Not a check bounces, not one payment gets delayed. Business as usual."

"Ansel, we don't *have* two hundred million among the partners. We'll all wind up in jail."

Ansel fixed him with his eyes. "Let's talk about that. Who would be going to jail?"

JM looked at the desktop. He shrugged. "Haven't really researched it yet. Probably those of us who can sign on the trust account."

"There's four of us can sign. Me, you--"

"Nedra, with my countersign, and Louis Rammelkamp."

"So how were the funds accessed?" Ansel thought he knew the answer, but asked anyway.

"Wire transfer. The bank's working on it. And the FBI, since it was FDIC insured. All we know so far is the money hit Zurich just before nine last night, then to Zaire--"

"Africa?"

"Africa. Then Antigua. Then it vanishes. Poof!"

"They're going to have to do better than that."

"Agree. No way we can get it back if we don't know where it wound up."

Ansel took a sip of black coffee. Now *his* cup jiggled in the saucer and he tightened up. JM didn't seem to notice. The shake--slight, but telling. But JM never played poker, never learned to read a tell. Said he had no interest in wagering. *Well, he's wagered this time*, Ansel thought, and a flood washed through his mind. *Wagered by allowing my son access to the trust account--oh wait, that was me. I'm the one who gave*

David access. So he could write the checks on an accident case last week when I was in Dallas for depositions. I gave David my passcode. I can't believe I even did that. But I did. Who's at the head of the go-directly-to-jail line? Why is everyone looking at me? What conspiracy, detective? You're making this up as you go, correct?

"So where do we start?" Ansel asked. He was going to make it up as it went along. He had been a thespian in college. He'd played Oberon in *A Midsummer Night's Dream*. The king of the fairies.

Ansel's mind raced along. *But it was foretelling, my role as the fairy king, because David Largent, my son, is gay. David is twenty-seven years old, unmarried but in a long-term relationship with an oncologist I've met several times who seems right for David. You've come a long way, baby, when a guy your age can allow that another man is "right for your son." My own father's hatreds, so carefully passed along to me, are fallen away. David is gay and so what? That's my and David's attitude. That's his friend Scott's attitude too. Near as I can read Scott.*

"We let the FBI do its thing," JM said. He finger-stirred his coffee and sucked. "We let the FBI do its thing and we hire a group I'm looking at out of Washington. They're ex-FBI and don't bother with little things like search warrants."

"Got a name? I'll call them."

"XFBI."

"Brilliant."

"I'll have Nedra text you a number. Call them and get them moving like yesterday."

Ansel was the Managing Partner--at least by title. But truth be told, JM bossed Ansel around. As senior partner, that was his prerogative. Within bounds. According to the firm charter Ansel actually outranked him. But in reality, Ansel deferred. JM was smart and death to anyone who crossed him. Ansel's David was in his crosshairs right then.

Out of focus and ranging off-field, but that would come. Then who would call the shots? JM? Ansel? Ansel shuddered and JM noticed that time.

"Cold? You shivered."

"Cold coming on, I think."

"Okay, so that's number one, calling the ex-FBI boys. Now what the hell is this about Suzanne shooting herself? Why pick our office to do herself in? How absolutely thoughtless. Leaves her mess for us to clean up."

Now that. That was sounding more like JM. JM as he sounded when not on the ropes for $200 million dollars. JM as he sounded when the bell rang and he came off the stool to stalk you around the ring. David was doomed, truth be told. Only David didn't know it yet. Ansel knew it and there was nothing he could do.

But he was going to try.

The phone chirped. JM took it.

As JM listened to the incoming call, Ansel mouth-mimed to him, "There's something I need to tell you. About my son."

JM watched Ansel's expression, watched the lips move, but offered no response. Someone on the other end had his ear and had his cognition.

Then Ansel realized: JM didn't get his mime. Which meant his secret was still safe. Which meant David was one step further away than he was when Ansel came in with every intention of blowing his cover.

Ansel's resolve dissipated like smoke. Go David, go! He wanted to cheer. Who wouldn't? It was his son, for the love of God.

The feeling of love for David overwhelmed Ansel's duty to the firm. He decided in that instant that he was not going to tell JM about David. At least not then.

But hold on, he thought, that would be a cover-up, right? Well, not if I didn't know. Which came down to the note Ansel found on his laptop, which read:

Dad, by the time you read this I will have broken your heart. And mom's heart. There's a certain group that helps kids who would otherwise die. It needs help. So I've embezzled the trust funds. All of them. May God guide my journey as I obey His commands. May you somehow find it in your heart to forgive me. But most of all, may you and your partners come to understand how your funds have touched so many little lives. God bless you, Dad. D.

Ansel had printed out the note and left it centered on his own desk in his office where it couldn't be missed. The note was Exhibit 1.

When he turned his son in--that time would come--his computer would become evidentiary. Everything on it would be studied by the police and FBI and insurance companies whose funds were gone. Ansel's hundreds--thousands?--of emails back and forth with Melinda all those years past, would become common knowledge. As would certain pictures that she presented Ansel at those times when he was traveling and aching for her body. Yes, they had those moments when nothing else would do but flesh. At least, pictures of. While Ansel knew he could erase all of it, like all good trial lawyers he also knew the forensics. Anything erased wasn't really erased and could be recovered. Which made it look like someone had something to hide. Which he did, as far as he and Melinda went. His mind was spinning and he still had to get through the partners' meeting.

JM finally hung up the phone, but not before saying into the mouthpiece, "Tell them I'm reviewing the numbers. Tell them the checks will issue today." Pause. "Yes, today. Yes, I'm sure."

JM removed his eyeglasses and pinched the sweet spot between the eyes. "God," he moaned, "what did I do to deserve this?"

"What did *we* do?" Ansel added.

"We're needed in the purple room. Partners' Monday."

"Lead the way."

They ferried cups and saucers to the wet sink.

JM held out a hand. Ansel went first.

Chapter 5

Burton shook his hands in the hot cell air, alarmed and frightened.

He turned to Thaddeus.

"Man, you saved me from that guy. I owe you big."

"No, you don't. One *gringo* to another, that's all."

"What'd they get you for?"

"Gun."

"They busted me for an ounce of pot. It was under the floor mat. I forgot I even had it."

He shook his hands in the air again, as if exorcising kinetic demons. He slumped back against the wall and shut his eyes.

"Man, I am so screwed," he said to anyone listening. "Man, oh man."

"What's your story?" Thaddeus said. He watched the two men across the cell, whispering and shooting looks his way. He might need backup next time.

"I'm going to Hermosillo to get married."

"Who's the lucky girl?"

"Girl I met online."

"That sounds promising."

"Plus Arizona's after me."

"For what?"

"Prison. I was supposed to report and do six years."

"And you didn't."

"Man, I can't do six years. I don't want those guys raping me."

"Well, you're in a mess. Drugs are a serious crime down here. You'll probably wind up in prison along with me."

"Could we partner up?"

"I'm not looking for a partner. Find someone else."

"I'm just saying, man."

Thaddeus gave him a hard look. "And I'm saying no. You don't bring anything to the party, Burton. You're one big plate of need."

"I got one thing you might want."

"Such as?"

"I know my way around Mexico. My old man crossed cattle for forty years. I worked this side of the border for him. I know the language and I know the towns. I know the good places and the bad places. And I know the cartel guys, lots of them."

Thaddeus looked at him. "What about the cartel guys? What do you know about them?"

"I know they're death on guys like us in Mexican prison. We're goners if we end up staying."

"You're probably right. So you know how to find someone down here?"

He was thinking of Hermano Sanchez. Which was looking more and more impossible the longer they were being ignored by the guys out front.

"I can find anyone. That's my specialty."

"Your specialty."

"It is. We have contacts all over Sonora. Who you looking for?"

"We can talk about that later. First thing, we need to see a judge and get out of here."

"Good luck with that."

"It's not about luck, it's always about money. We've got plenty of that."

Two hours later a different man appeared from the front office. He was barrel-chested and wore his blue Federale jumpsuit unzipped neck to navel. He was hot despite the air conditioning up front. His bulk was too much for the AC.

"Can you open the door in between here and your office?" Thaddeus said as the man bellied up to the cell. "Let some cool air in here?"

"You have the right to remain silent," the thick man laughed. "And you got the right to roast in peace."

"Seriously. When do we get to see a judge?"

"What for you want to see a judge?"

"Determine conditions of release. Bail."

"Six weeks probably."

Thaddeus stepped closer to the bars. "Can we make that happen faster than six weeks?"

"Maybe yes, maybe no. How much you got?"

"One thousand dollars."

"*Señor*, everybody got one thousand dollars. Is no good. *Mas--mas*."

"Five thousand. Take me to a judge before night and I'll give you five thousand dollars, American dollars."

"I don't know. But that's closer. I'll ask."

The man pointed at the smaller Mexican man.

"You come over here."

The smaller man got up, blinking and unsteady on his feet.

"You sober up?"

"Si."

"*Boracho?*"

"No."

"Gonna drink if we let you go?"

"No."

"Not gonna come round here begging no more?"

"No."

The jailer worked the keypad and the cell door opened.

"You come out. You going home."

"Hey, what about us?" Thaddeus said.

"Mr. Five Thousand can wait. I'll ask up front."

"Good going," Burton said, once the jailer had left with his newly sober charge. "Will that include me?"

"We can see about that," Thaddeus said. "Right now I do need someone who knows someone. That just might be you."

"I can find anyone."

"Sure you can."

Chapter 6

When Ansel was a kid, his Uncle Jan asked if he would like to be a barber someday (like him). Ansel violently shook his head and vowed he would be a lawyer. Which was unheard-of in Ansel's blue collar home.

His father excavated water lines and strung plumbing in the three-bedroom eyesores of the western 'burbs.

College? Why college, when you had an in with the pipe fitters' union?

His mother had learned early on how to beat a type-writer to death at 100 wpm and excelled at her legal secretary métier. But she was also carrying on affairs with a dance card of lawyers--a fact which became known to Ansel in his early high school years. That solidified his commitment to lawyering: he wanted desperately to kick some bar association ass. He hated those sons-of-bitches for taking advantage of his mother (as he perceived it) and wanted to get back at as many as he could. This was back in the day before you could buy an AR-15 and shop the local mall for payback. This was back in the day when payback took exertion.

Law school followed college and he exerted and passed the Illinois bar exam the first time around. Following that he began to practice his hatred of lawyers on anyone with a law license who crossed his path. And there were plenty. DA's, insurance whores, bankruptcy slime, divorce denizens, real estate scammers, criminal counsel, and especially the blue-noses from the silk-stocking firms where he couldn't even score an interview upon graduation. He mowed those guys down.

And he did the next best thing: he hung out his own shingle.

Then JM happened along and a partnership bloomed when Ansel found nothing about him that he hated.

Then a third partner happened by. At the same time, Ansel was mellowing, as the math of having others earn and give him a piece of their action settled over him like Scrooge McDuck's MBA. He told them, 'You earn one hundred and kickback seventy to me and I continue to make rain and bring in more and more clients by my TV Five courtroom highlights. That's our formula."

In six years they were one-hundred strong and two years later they agreed to cap it at two-hundred attorneys.

They went back on this, JM and Ansel. They added a few more here and there--gunslingers they couldn't pass up--and became a two-hundred-twenty-lawyer firm. Teeny, by national standards, small by Chicago standards, but large enough to litigate with any firm anywhere in the world. They even tried a Washington office for eighteen months. It eventually closed when Bush was handed the White House by the Supremes and the firm lost its ins with bureaucrats as the Republicans stirred the pot and sent Democrats home.

Mostly the firm litigated in the Midwest. It strained to grow. It was a struggle to maintain a stasis of two-hundred-twenty, as law firms—like zombies at large—tend to replicate unless carefully corralled. This became Ansel's job, the management of the firm, since that had been his role from the first day anyway. He relaxed the reins and in five years they were eight-hundred strong and counting. "So much for keeping it simple," he told JM.

Which was where they were when JM and Ansel marched into Partners' Monday the day after Ansel's kid ran the table.

The purple room was anchored by a forty-foot conference table around which all fifty-five full partners clustered. JM took up the Visitors' goal; Ansel the Home. As soon as Ansel sat down, the conversations drifted away and eyes rested on him.

"We're going to dispense with the reading of last week's minutes," he began. His voice, even and steady, evinced no alarm.

All attendees settled back. Some patted at breast pockets for the cigarettes that were banished from the building. Habits, thought Ansel. Habits like adoring my son, easy to consciously avoid; impossible, subconsciously, to give up. And he realized in that moment that he had no idea what he was going to say there that morning. He realized that he was probably unable to tell the truth, the whole truth, and nothing but the truth, so help him God. Probably he would have to settle for half the truth. An evanescent stream of truth flitted in and out of his brain like barn swallows at dusk.

"Gentlemen, it is my sad duty to inform you that we have been embezzled. Our trust funds are gone."

Pandemonium.

Fists banged and howls went up.

Eyeglasses were adjusted and shirt-cuffs tugged.

Eyes met, horrors acknowledged, and eyes flitted to other eyes for more of the same.

One hundred-ten ears immediately on alert.

The transformation was instantaneous, like electricity charging headlong down a wire, flipping negative ions to positive, without thought, without the need for reflection, for everyone knew and understood to their marrow one inalienable truth: they were jointly and severally on the hook. This base knowledge came as naturally as the *ex tempore* act of taking the next breath. *Presto*, the financial grim reaper was come.

And they knew it.

Now to cut the losses. All eyes were on him. They waited, there would be a way around this, Ansel had never let down the firm.

"As of this moment we are less than one hour into this. JM and I have met and talked and we've already contacted agents to recover our funds. The FBI is in the building as we speak."

There, he'd made it sound like they were but one step behind the perp, that a collar was imminent. A sigh of relief swept the crowd. Bulging neck veins were seen to relax. Clenched hands paused with the hope that the firm's leaders had the situation under control. Ansel nodded with the reassurance the parent offers the child when fears of the dark are dismissed.

JM cleared his throat as if throwing a rope to a floundering lifeboat.

"We don't know who has our money," he said from the Visitor's goal. "But we have a very good idea who it might be. And we think we can mitigate our losses at around ninety percent."

Always the numbers guy, JM was making it sound like the partners might be out a couple million bucks, give or take, a figure they could make happen. It wouldn't be pretty, but they could make it happen. Fact was, personal credit lines should carry the day. Everyone would chip in a small amount, he said. He looked from face to face. Lips were pursed as internal calculators did the math.

Bill Gerard, one of twelve among them who held a CPA designation, raised a hand and asked, "How was the trust account accessed? Check? Wire transfer?"

Shock was easing up. Now the questions.

They were inquisitors, the partner bunch.

Ansel clutched the creases in his trousers to steady his hands.

"Wire," Ansel answered, and everyone nodded; yes, that's how they would have done it too. Enough wire transfers bouncing around the Caribbean and you had a mess. Hard to trace, impossible to untangle, especially from a distance. Someone, Ansel said, would have to go there. They looked at him. By default he would be the one to go there. Which was when it first occurred to him. He just might have a play here, after all. It might just be a way to buy some time. He announced he would be the one to make the trip and right the wrong. But go where? He thought he knew, but wasn't certain. Most important, what he thought he knew, he didn't tell them.

But the CPA hadn't finished. This time, without raising the hand, Bill Gerard lurched ahead, "Who had access to make wire transfers?"

He was asking for the list of suspects, those who had the credentials to initiate a wire transfer.

JM nodded Ansel's way. The ball was punted.

"The list consists of me, JM, Louis, and Nedra with JM's countersign for checks, no access for wires. Not for her."

"So that leaves three of you. Not much of a field," Stan Morehouse III stated.

Stan was their mandatory African-American civil rights litigator. He had more black clients than Johnny Cochran and possessed the phone numbers for all members of the Congressional Black Caucus. Ansel sized him up. His guess was Stan was smarter than the rest of them, but Stan had never been known to lord that over anyone. Among their firm he was quick to defer and always willing to take the losing end of an argument if it meant keeping a friend--especially a white one. Ansel was aware that black people, even in the age of enlightenment, most often took that higher road of letting the lesser mind win, were it white, out of necessity. It was a damn poor commentary on race relations in the U.S., but there you were. It was what it was. You didn't make the rules. You could only hope to make them more fair and that, in Ansel's view, would come only when a thousand years of intermarriage produced the same mahogany hue among all men. Ansel's take.

Ansel looked at Stan and nodded. "That's right. That leaves three of us."

Stan continued. "And what do the network administrators tell us about which of you logged in to make the wire? We all know those credentials events are stored on the servers. The transaction has an electronic signature attached." He said "electronic" with a full emphasis on each syllable, much like the witnesses of Alexander Graham Bell's era might have said it: E-LEC-TRON-IC.

Stan swallowed and said it again, but differently, the

cross-examiner coming back around for a second bite. "And the electronic signature belonged to which of you?"

JM and Ansel exchanged a look. A key clue overlooked. Maybe they were too rattled. Or maybe one of them had just avoided it. Thank you, Stan, for that.

Ansel unstuck his hands from his trouser seams. He should depart the place, and now. Because any minute, when the FBI obtained the name of the login, that person could very well be taken into federal custody and confined to a six-by-nine in the Federal Detention Center while the evidentiary egg-gathering proceeded.

"We're going to keep it short, this morning," Ansel abruptly announced, totally ignoring Stan's perfect question. "JM and I are needed back at the ranch to assist the investigation."

Ansel found his feet and steadied himself. He then turned and fled into the hallway, where he headed north, toward his office. There he would close the doors and segregate himself from the mob that would be only too happy to lynch a wrongdoer. And if it became known that Ansel had turned over the kingdom's keys to his son--set him loose in the trust fund vault--Ansel's lynching would be fiscally indicated, of that he was certain. Those men out there were acquired from Ansel's own mold; should one pilfer the whole, they would see him swing. Now it was only a matter of time, moments maybe, before they appeared at his door with a coil of rope.

Time to run.

In his office then out the other end. Luck was with him: Melinda was in the ladies' room.

Seventy-eight flights of stairs and he reached the airlock and stepped onto the sidewalk. There were no cries behind him. Not yet.

The crush of Chicagoans frantic to get to the next important moment in their lives surrounded him and bore him south toward Madison Street. There, he started looking for cabs. They darted and glided toward him, closest lane then furthest, then closest again, and finally one swung to the curb and hit its flasher.

He swung in, surrendered to the momentum of entry, and prostrated himself in the rear seat.

"Evanston," was all he could choke out. It was like a giant hand was encircling his throat. He watched buildings glide by out the top of the rear window. He recognized none of them and why would he--he'd never looked up before. How odd, he thought. He told himself to grab hold. Take a deep breath and hold... hold. Release slowly, now another.

They moved with the traffic in the direction of Lake Michigan. He sat upright and his OCD kicked in, the compulsion to freight the meaningless with meaning. He found there was a count of one-to-fifteen for each city block of travel followed by a count of one-to-fifty for each red light. There was a metric, a poetry in his travel, and in considering that he caught himself and realized he was losing his mind, that it was running downhill much faster than he would have predicted for himself. Had the pills been downed that morning? No image leapt to mind.

First off, he needed money. Lots of money. To make his escape.

Then he considered Libby. They had been together beginning senior year in Ithaca twenty-five years ago. They had mostly been true to each other. As a practical matter they never divorced even when he or she held the moral high ground and had every right. In the end, divorce was just too predictable and it was small. They considered themselves and their lives and their kids' lives larger than divorce. So they stayed together.

He would definitely take her along.

David would listen to her.

Who?

David, damn it, David.

Chapter 7

Vice President of New Wealth, Banco Nacionale, was the title on the business cards he handed out all over Mexico City.

His name was Enrico Rodriguez, Jr. and he was a third generation grad of the Wharton School, and a third generation officer in Banco Nacionale. His great-great-grandfather had served twenty-two years on the bank's original board of directors. Except for his father, all his forebears had held high positions there.

His own father was a dreamer, a graphic artist who was responsible for the monthly exploits of four Mexican Super-heroes in the gaudy Mexican monthly comic *Revista de Super-heroes*. His father earned millions with his comics and it was his artistry and renown that had introduced him to the Tijuana Cartel's leader's son, Juan Carlos Hermeda Ordañez.

Ordañez was one of four sons, the eldest, and he was in awe of the superheroes penned by Enrico Rodriguez Senior, so much so that the two families became connected.

As a result, Enrico was connected, albeit distantly, to the Tijuana Cartel. So, when the $200 million USD flowed into his bank and flagged him with a screen alert, his astonishment at the size of the new account was without measure and his first thought was larcenous. He had the credentials and knew how to move the money with a single login. His second thought was Juan Carlos' father, Miguel Ordañez, who, for a fee, would wash the funds and bank them offshore, perhaps in Asia. Enrico Rodriguez would be set for life, the life of all his kids, and the life of his kids' kids. Hong Kong? Maybe. Shanghai? A strong contender. Most favored: Dubai, Abu Dhabi. He could fashion a lifestyle in Dubai that rivaled that of the oil sheiks.

They met on a trawler in the Pacific Ocean, off La Misión. The meeting location was Ordañez' requirement. Enrico was taken there on a smaller boat and transferred to Juan Carlos Ordañez' boat in three foot seas. Juan Carlos greeted him and they went below decks. An angry looking black man searched him, roughing him up in the process. Ordañez watched all this with little regard. Then, in the boat's galley, they were served coffee and glazed donuts, Ordañez' preferred conference refreshments.

"I have access to two hundred million USD," Enrico said.

Ordañez' expression never changed. He was young-- early twenties--and worked for his father in the Tijuana Cartel. He was dark complexioned with a sweet face that perhaps would look less surprising at the front of church leading Mass instead of working for a father who headed up a multibillion dollar crime family that killed, looted and exploited fearlessly and without boundaries.

Coffee and pastries served, the possibility of making a deal was taken up.

"You have two hundred million to wash," said Juan Carlos between mouthfuls of donut.

"Yes. It came in unexpectedly."

"Who did it belong to?"

"That's just it. A single individual. A name none of my contacts seems to be able to track down."

"Which is?"

"Ansel Largent."

"And what do we know about this man?"

"Very little. There is a man with this name in Chicago. A lawyer. But I don't see how he would have access to such money."

"Why wouldn't he?"

"He works for insurance companies. *Abogado*."

The young criminal's face was contemplative. Then he said, "Really? He must have hit the lottery."

"That's just it. We haven't been able to connect him to any huge verdicts. It's always minor stuff, low millions. And he's never the winner, always the loser. So it doesn't add up."

"Maybe it is money he is holding for someone else."

"I've thought of that," said Enrico. He chewed slowly and seemed lost in thought for several moments. "I think I might know how that would work."

"Go ahead."

"Well, he defends insurance companies, this man. Perhaps the money he transferred wasn't his money at all. Perhaps it was money belonging to insurance companies."

"You mean he's a thief. A thief like you want to be."

"Exactly."

"How much for me?"

"Fifty cents on the dollar."

"My father washes two hundred and keeps one hundred. Is that it?"

"I think that's fair."

"I think we get seventy-five percent, you twenty-five percent. But since our families are friends, we will accept sixty-five."

"And I get thirty-five. Consider it done, Juan Carlos."

There was a handshake and smiles all around.

"Your company will be named Eastern Star Lines, Ltd.," Ordañez told the banker. "Organize under the laws of Canada. The money will be in a bank in Hong Kong under that name. Routing and account details will be provided by four text messages. You must never contact me again."

"Agreed," said Enrico. He felt a tingle of excitement run along his back. He shivered.

"Cold?"

"Excited."

"Excited is good. That means I have been fair with you."

"More than fair," said Enrico. He had hoped for twenty-five. He was going to get that plus another ten. It was beyond imagination. He could only think how much they loved his father, the cartoonist. It all made him giddy.

He ran up the short stairs to the railing. Small seas, big bellyache. Sailors' woes.

But he was happy. Even while he threw up the donuts into the Pacific Ocean.

He was deliriously happy.

Chapter 8

The stroke had done its work.

Libby now talked out the side of her mouth and the mouth and the food drooled and the coffee splashed around as she struggled with enunciation.

It wasn't just her ear for good speech the stroke robbed from her; rather, it was the ability to make the sounds that anymore she could only dream to utter.

Stroke victims are often angry, Ansel had learned, and Libby was no exception. While Ansel might have meant to do it only with the greatest love in his heart, the serving of a simple mug of her favorite Starbucks could make her erupt into a longshoreman's curse. What once created intimacy now created rage all too often.

He was having second thoughts as the cab neared home. Did he dare take her with him when he ran after David? She had her home health aides during the day; she had him at night. Could he handle her alone without the refuge of a job? He honestly didn't know, but he knew that he was not a born caretaker.

With him, it was an acquired skill, not unlike learning to draw freehand, except that his model was always moving, always changing, full of needs that ebbed and flowed and always blurring in unexpected mini-dramas and difficult presentations.

Bottom line: if not him, then who? Who else was there to take care of her? Their youngest, Winston, was away at school in Berkeley. He was clearly out. Besides, he'd given every indication that he had dropped out of the family, as he didn't even bother to return home during summers any more. So, no Winston. And Ansel believed that David was already spoken for by some bankrupt ministry for needy kids in Mexico City.

So if he left--when, rather--it would have to be with Libby in tow. He resigned himself to that. He would be reduced to the role of fugitive-caretaker. There was no romance in any of it.

Those thoughts plagued him as they made their way on Lakeshore Drive, finally arriving at his gated home at 11:20 a.m.

He jumped from the cab, hit the gatehouse button, and announced himself to Libby. Moments later the gate swung open, and they finished the ride. Again he jumped out, this time to pay the cabbie.

At the double doors he repeated the intercom process and Libby finally pushed open the door herself, a streak of orange juice mapping the right side of her face between mouth and chin. She forced a half-smile, literally, and said, "Whersh ya car?"

"Long story," he said, and planted a kiss on her face. She tasted vaguely of OJ and oatmeal. He brushed on by and headed for his office. "I'll explain in a few. First I've got a couple things I must hurry to."

"Ash ushual."

"Thanks, but this time it's really urgent, I'm afraid. I'll explain it all shortly."

Libby's mind was unaffected by the stroke. She would follow exactly the dynamics of the tale he planned to unload on her in a few. But first--first there were financial arrangements to be made.

He reached Jim Decker at Fifth Third Bank on Michigan Avenue. Jim was his college roommate. His official title was regional manager at Fifth Third. He commanded twelve banks and made them profitable. He was a small wiry man who played intramural field hockey in their yahoo days and was the league's top scorer for his foot speed and tenacity.

"Jim, it's Ansel," he said when Jim punched in.

"Anse, old dog. How's tricks down at the ATM?"

He referred to Ansel's law firm as his personal ATM. They went way back, and there was nothing that was off-limits between them.

"All good. We're still making more money than Exxon."

"What about Libby? Recovering?"

"Getting better just about every day. She's a fighter, Libby."

"And your last little bout? You feeling better?"

"Jim, I have no complaints. How about Marianna, have the kids made her a grandma yet?"

"You know, they're trying--they have to be, they're related to me."

"But I hope without your notorious perversions?"

"Still spoken of in hushed tones down at the SAE house."

"Listen, Jimbo, why I'm calling..."

"You found a smaller house? It's just the two of you now isn't it? Ever since David—"

"It is. But I've hit a little snag and need some cash money. Real cash."

"Hot real estate? Want me to drop a few hundred thousand into your personal account?"

"Thanks, but what I really need is cash. I'm wondering-- would it be too much to ask you to send a courier to my house with a couple hundred thousand cash?"

"Whoa! This must mean you've got some poor young thing pregnant!"

"No, nothing like that. I've just had something come up. I'd rather not discuss by phone."

"I don't see why I can't do that for my old roomie. Two hundred thousand? Same home address?"

"Yes and yes."

"Personal signature required. You going to be there to sign?"

"Sure."

"Done, brother. What else can I do you for?"

"That's about it for now. But let me get back to you if I think of anything else."

"We'll just put this on your line of credit and I'll make a note for the examiners that you made a verbal request on today's date."

"Perfect. Thanks, Jim. You know how much I appreciate it."

"Call me some time. Let's catch a Bulls game and get drunk."

"You're on. I'll call in a week and we'll make plans."

"Looking forward."

So they hung up. Ansel crept up to the office window and peeked out the curtains. No black-and-whites, no anonymous white vans from the Fed Fleet. He tried to calm the paranoia rattling through his brain. But again, his hands shook and he gulped air like they were going to stop making it. He'd have a drink to steady things down, but he wasn't allowed. Doctor's orders.

His mobile chimed. JM on the other end. Nervous.

"Hey, JM, I had to scat for a few hours."

"Dammit, man! The cops want to talk to you. Where the hell did you go?"

"I had to run home. It's about Libby."

"But your car's still in the garage. Did you take a cab?"

"Wanted to work on the way. I brought my laptop."

"What time will you be back? We've got two Chicago homicide detectives snorting around for an official statement. You know how pushy those animals are. That's number one. Number two, have you called the XFBI guys yet? We need them online like today. Also I'm looking into FDIC coverage for something like this. I highly doubt there's anything there, but I'm looking."

"No, I don't think FDIC covers situations where the account holder steals from himself. You're barking up the wrong tree."

"Well the FDIC covers $250,000 per depositor, per insured bank. Now I'm wondering if that's cumulative where there are different depositors in one account. I don't know."

"I really don't know about that."

"So what time can we expect you?"

"Let--let me have a talk with Libby. She might need me to run her by the hospital for a scan. I don't know yet."

There was a pause. A meaningful one.

"That's evasive, friend. Should I be worried about you?"

Ansel pressed a fist against his head. It had begun to

throb in back. He told himself it was all the stress. David, JM, Libby, Melinda, Suzanne--it was overwhelming. One thing his doc had insisted: no stress. Plenty of sleep, no stress.

He caught a glimpse of Libby passing by his office door. He whispered, "No need to worry about me. Why, am I a suspect?"

"Tell that to the frigging cops! They're falling all over themselves down here looking for you. One of the FBI jerks wants your home address. I told him I'd have to get back to him on that."

FBI? Really! His throbbing head reacted. A drum pounding. He was thinking he might need one of his pills. Which he tried to avoid during the day, as he needed to be clear-headed.

"Hell no, don't give the FBI my home address. That's all Libby needs is for the FBI to slime up our house. Just tell them I'll get back to them. Say I've got a medical emergency with my wife."

"Do you? Emergency? Really?"

"No, but--you know. Hold them off until I get there. Just stall, JM."

"And I have nothing to worry about with you?"

"Like what? Come on, man. How long have we known each other?"

"Since we were pissing in the wading pool."

"Look, let me deal with Libby's little flare-up and I'll be back in. It might be this afternoon late, it might not be until tomorrow morning. Probably tomorrow, knowing how long we'll have to wait on films at the hospital."

"Brain scan?"

"Something like that."

"Give her my regards. Hope it all goes well."

"See you in the a.m. Peace out, brother."

He ended the call and dropped the phone in his shirt pocket. It was time to get moving. He wants to get them packed so they could leave when the money hit the door. There was no time to waste. He thought he knew right where David had gone and he had to get to him before the authorities ran him to the ground.

Chapter 9

Every year the Defense Counsel Institute held its retreat in the Cayman Islands. The customary haunt was the Marriott Hotel, where the Grand Ballroom would be reserved for the three day soirée, including the capstone Turtle Soup Dance. The Institute's annual joke was that no turtles had actually been harmed in the making of the Dance's table decorations, which were phony sea turtle shells adorned with local *Birds of Paradise* and *Denbrobium Orchid* bouquets.

It was at the 2012 retreat when Ansel had found himself dancing, after midnight, with Suzanne Fairmont. While she was a criminal attorney and did zero insurance defense, she had accompanied a young attorney from the firm of Blasingame and Richards to the retreat. Showing all the customary signs of conservative insurance industry living when he took himself off to bed at midnight, the young attorney was upstairs in their room, asleep, leaving his date alone at the Turtle Soup table, where, like the lovely sea creatures after which the dance was named, she awaited poaching.

Ansel saw her first. He had come to the Caymans alone in the firm airplane. Libby had gone west, out to Berkeley, and was helping their youngest commute to his first year in college, so the customary restraints on a married man's late-night habits were removed. Of course restraint wasn't even necessary, because Ansel was merely coming to the aid of an abandoned woman who looked like she had one more dance in her before she too, took herself off to bed.

An hour later they were on the beach, barefoot, swaying in the moonlight to the dance music wafting outside on the warm air. Her arms were around his neck and his were around her waist, a half-full bottle of Chateau Mouton Rothschild 2000 dangling from between two fingers of his right hand.

"That's cold there," she said of the sweating bottle, and moved a hand behind as if to brush it away.

"That's seven hundred dollars of grape juice you're swatting at, m'love," he whispered.

"That's less than one hour of billable time for you," she laughed.

And the retainer was signed.

They became lovers five minutes later and remained lovers up until the night she was murdered. There was only one rule, as neither wanted a child from the merger: They always used a condom. The flirtation and consummation was meant to be therapeutic only, never productive.

In fact, they had met and made love the night of her death, at the law firm. Afterward, he had gone back to his office "to finish up."

To his great surprise he found Libby in his office, sitting

in his chair, and swinging back and forth as she cried and wiped her tears on the Bears sweatshirt she was wearing.

"How did you get here?" he asked. He was genuinely startled, but then realized an aide must have driven her into the city.

"I know what you're doing," she said through her tears. "I came down and shaw you in there."

"Libby, let me explain what's happened to me since your stroke--"

"Bullroar, Anshel! Itsh been going on a hell of a lot longer than shince I had my stroke!"

He plopped himself down in a client chair and faced her.

"Please," he whispered, "stop crying. Let me get you a towel."

"That would be nice. Wet it."

"Hold on. Be right back."

He headed for the partners' lavatory and the soft stack of towels kept there.

Libby saw something on his desk that abruptly stopped the flow of tears.

Could it be? She leaned closer and moved an envelope to the side.

It was.

She opened the plastic container, hefted herself upright with her cane, and headed back to Suzanne's office.

Chapter 10

Lunch left no doubt about it: they were really and truly in a Mexican jail. The tortillas, beans and rice erased all doubt.

It was served--as it were--on paper plates folded and passed through the bars of the cell. It could then be unfolded, unstuck from the plate, and crudely introduced onto the tortilla, rolled, and eaten. Four more prisoners had arrived, all Hispanic, leaving a pair up against a full house. Two on five, or five on two, depending.

From the get-go it was clear the Mexicans had no use for the two white guys. Not enough seating, there were four Mexicans on one side, one Mexican and two whites on the other. Thaddeus listened as the five amigos did their back-and-forth, tossing glances at Thaddeus and Burton as they spoke. Evidently the new guys were being updated on the two Americans, with particular focus on Thaddeus, the one who had shown he could handle himself.

"Gonna eat all that?" Burton asked.

Thaddeus stopped chewing. "What? You want my lunch?"

"I'm just asking."

"Shut up and eat. Every time you speak, these guys think we're plotting against them. Try not to look threatening."

"How do I do that?" said Burton, who sat upright at the suggestion he might be looking like a threat to anyone.

"It was a joke. Never mind. Just shut up and eat."

Five minutes later the same rotund Federale as before rejoined them and demanded return of the paper plates. Thaddeus took Burton's and passed the two back through the bars. The Mexicans were slower to respond and made a big show of chewing and swallowing the last bites before they would surrender their paper plates. The Federale rolled his eyes. But he was outnumbered and didn't want to make any enemies.

"So," Thaddeus said to the man's back as he was leaving. "Anyone out there looking for an easy five grand?"

"Not yet," said the jailer. He continued on through the door and out.

"Hey man," the original tall man said.

Thaddeus looked at him. "You talking to me?"

"Yes, man. You got a way out of here?"

"I'm working on it."

"You take me with you?"

"I don't think so. I'm a one-man show."

"You taking that loser next to you though, no?"

"We'll have to see. He might have something I need."

"He gonna bend over for you, man?"

Thaddeus smiled. "No need for that, friend. Let's be *amigos*, eh?"

"Chure, man, you take me with you. Then we friends."

"I'm working on it. We'll see how it goes."

"These new guys want you, but I told them you were too strong."

"What's not to want?" Thaddeus laughed. He made a joke, but inside he was praying they would decide to spend their time doing something besides assaulting him.

"That's good, man. That's good."

"Tell you what. I'm going to try to get us all in front of a judge. I can't offer any more than that, but that much I'll try to do."

"It's a deal, hombre. Now you talking."

"Good. Pass the word to your friends."

The tall Mexican said something to the new guys. Their expressions didn't change, although one of them nodded.

At which point the Federale who had searched the Toyota and found Thaddeus' gun appeared in the doorway.

"You want to see a judge?" he said to Thaddeus.

"I do."

"You can afford it?"

"I can."

"Let me see the money. I didn't see no money when we booked you in."

"Let me use your phone. I can have five grand here in five hours."

He knew it would take Christine just five hours from Flagstaff to Nogales. Including a quick stop downstairs, at the Bank of America. He had thirty-five million on deposit with BOA. Five grand shouldn't be too hard.

"Five hours. We can have a judge here five hours from now. But he will need five grand too."

"Done."

"But if you're lying to me, man, you won't see no judge for six months. I promise you."

56

"The money will be here. It's what, one o'clock now? We can do the deal at seven. If you let me use your phone."

They took him up front and, instead of allowing him to use their phone, they gave him access to his mobile. His plan was worldwide, so the call from Mexico to the States went smoothly.

She would be there at seven o'clock with ten thousand dollars. Added to Hermano's money hidden inside the spare tire in the trunk of the Toyota, he would be good to go.

They returned him to the cell. He explained to the Mexican man they would all get to the see the judge. At seven o'clock. They looked placated.

Which meant there would be no attack before then.

But if it went wrong or the judge refused, it could be a very long and painful stay in that cell.

Very painful.

Chapter 11

Ansel couldn't make preparations to flee fast enough.

First there was Libby to collect up.

She was found in the den. She had managed to disarticulate the vacuum cleaner canister from frame. She sat cross-legged on the floor, the skeleton and guts of the machine pulled half up in her lap, the schematic open in her hand, extended at arm's length, reading glasses perched on her forehead but thought by her to be lost. She was frozen in deep thought as she absently spun a small fan with her finger and read. So, Ansel had to take care not to startle her. He knew that the startle response in stroke victims was very unpredictable and could range from being ignored to loss of bowel control to physical assault.

He paused in the doorway and cleared his throat.

"I hear you, Anshel. Pleash ride this down: Libby appears bishy."

"And I didn't want to disturb you for that very reason.

But I'm afraid something unexpected has come up and we need to deal with it immediately."

"Thersh no 'immediately' with a stroke victim, Ansh. Have you not heard the doctorsh?"

"I have heard the doctors. But this is one of those times. We need to leave town for a few days."

"That won't happen. Whatever it ish, you go without me. Pleash."

"I don't have time to argue. Now, what about your passport? Do you remember where it might be?"

She turned her head to him and her reading glasses plunked down on her nose—askew, but located. "I don't need it. I'm not leaving my housh."

"Ah, but you are—we are. We'll discuss it on the way. Now, do I look in the roll-top?"

"Maybe. I don't know."

"Please. Put the vacuum away. We need to change you into travel clothes and get moving."

"I can't put it away like thish. It'sh apart."

"I'll buy you another. Whatever."

"Whatsh it about?"

"Business." Ansel took a seat in the white chair, one of two. He leaned toward his wife and immediately felt like a conspirator offering a bribe. "There's a large sum of money overseas that I have to retrieve for the firm. It's waiting for me to come get it. Pretty simple stuff. A large amount would be yours."

"If itsh so shimple why do you need me?"

"There's a person there who might need to hear certain things from you. That's all I can say right now."

Up to then, he had told her nothing about David, nothing about the missing funds, and nothing about the David note. But he believed he knew where David had gone and he believed he knew the fastest way to retrieve the missing funds and return them to where they belonged. David would dissolve once his mother lit into him. He had never been able to stand up to her. Libby was thus an essential element. She was a must-have, a *sine qua non*.

"Ohhh," she said in a Halloween-scary voice, "big mishtery, have we? Put me down for that. Make me a definite 'yesh,' Ansh."

"Please. Don't ridicule. I stand by *you*, Libby. All I'm asking is you stand by me now."

"Do we need to talk to the doctor before we go?"

"Oh, I'm okay to travel. Okay to work, come and go, fit as a fiddle."

"Right. Where've I heard *that* before?"

"Roll-top?"

"Passport, right hand drawer desktop level."

"Hold on." He crossed to the roll-top and opened the indicated drawer. Below two Chicago roadmaps he laid hands on the passport. Checked the date. Valid until 2017. His own passport he stored in an inside pocket of his overnight bag. That way, it was always on hand even when he had to unexpectedly leave the States. Which had happened, and so now he was always prepared. Managing partner duties and all that.

"Okay, I'm busshted. Hand me my cane and help me up."

He did as she ordered and offered his hand. She gripped it with her left hand, as her right side was still virtually useless. She had enough arm strength to plant the cane and push off as she would go along. Just that feat had taken three months of daily physical therapy.

She began the hobble toward the hall stairs, where she

would sit in her Stair-Assist and ride up to her walk-in closet. He followed her upstairs, into her bedroom.

A glance at his watch. Twelve-thirty. Packing up would eat up a good hour as they quibbled over her selections, then a thirty minute wait once he called for the cab, then two hours to O'Hare because they'd be fighting outbound traffic, then thirty minutes to check-in--he ran the math and decided they had an all-clear window at five o'clock. Fine, so he'd make flight reservations for five or later. Hopefully the Fibbies wouldn't have put him on a no-fly list before then and they would get out of the country.

The thought of the FBI investigation that even then was coiling in on him like a python frightened the hell out of him. He felt his bowels shift deep down and a toilet urgency raced to his brain. The toilet was down a small hall off the bedroom and he headed there to gather his thoughts and un-gather his bowels. The laptop was indicated, so he reversed field and retrieved it from the bed, then reversed field yet again and headed for the promised land.

Libby observed his gyrations, of course, and he could see her trust meter sink to four.

"Lots going on," he offered, and touched the side of his head.

"Uh-huh," she said, and began opening drawers. With Libby it was always underwear in first, then the slacks, then a black dress--good for cocktails or burials--and two sweaters. She would be chilly at night no matter the latitude, so always with the sweaters. Four shoes would make it inside the suitcase, situated north-south-east and west. They were arranged to help absorb the shock of baggage handling as she--probably accurately--imagined it behind the scenes.

Ansel turned back to his toilette.

Ansel was no sooner planted on the porcelain and the

first deposit of sub-stratum laid down than his cell phone chimed. JM.

"Ansel. What's up?"

The panic was marked in his voice. "Did you call the XFBI people?"

"Yes," Ansel fabricated. "They're already on it."

Ansel didn't want them "on it." Not yet, not until he was clear of the U.S.

"Any feedback? What do they think?"

"Think? They think we've been embezzled is what they think."

"Who's our contact there?"

"Can't give that out." He made something up. "They want clean margins around the investigation," he said, making it sound like surgery to remove a tumor. "They only want one contact point with the firm. And that's me. You understand."

"No, I don't understand. But if you say so."

"Well, that's just the way they want it. If it was me, I'd say whatever. But it's not. Now, what about Suzanne? Have they found a gun?"

"No, but I did get the medical examiner's guy to talk to me a minute."

"Oh? What did he have to say?"

"He doesn't believe it was a suicide. No powder burns."

Ansel remembered something from some forensic evidence class he was forced to take somewhere along the way, probably a Continuing Legal Education credit to satisfy some damn bar requirement. Something about gunpowder burns and the absence of.

If the gunshot wound is self-inflicted there will be powder burns left behind on the skin of the victim, as they're unable to hold the gun far enough away from the head not to leave gunshot residue.

So JM had the inside story: a third hand fired the fatal shot. Which meant they were looking for a killer. It sounded very bad.

Immediately his fear quotient for David skyrocketed. It was just too coincidental. But why would David shoot Suzanne? Did she get in his way? But he was on a ministry, a mission to save kids. Last time Ansel looked, ministries didn't commit murder to obtain funding. In fact, neither did they commit embezzlement. But that was a conversation for another day. Maybe even later that day--that night--once he found David and ordered a sit-down.

"So no suicide. Any leads?"

Ansel wasn't a criminal lawyer. But he'd seen enough TV and movies to know it was a reasonable question to pose.

"No, no leads. But that's the other thing. The dicks want your home address. I held them off like the FBI. But Anse, everyone here is pissed. I mean really pissed. They'll need to speak with you personally in the next hour. How's it going at the hospital? You are at the hospital?"

He looked around the bathroom.

"Yes, I'm in the waiting room. They took her to Xray. I have no idea what's up. Scans or something."

"Is her neurologist there?"

"Neurologist and psychiatrist."

And I'm sending out for a phrenologist for myself, he thought with sudden glee. Examine the lumps on my own head.

JM was a considerate soul.

"Jeez. Poor kid. You don't need all this at the same time, either. Not with your deal."

"Believe me, I know. But I'm fine. It's just my world that's collapsing."

At which point Libby called in, "Do I have an unopened pantyhose?"

He barely got the phone shoved down a pant leg before she finished. Tentatively he returned the phone to his ear. "Libby's calling. They need me. I'll get back to you, JM."

"Thought I heard Libby. All right, you go take care of her. Give her my love. Esme and I are thinking about her."

"Will do. Talk in a while."

"How long should I tell the dicks?"

"Tell them two hours. Text me their number and tell them I'll call them in two."

"Got it. Anse, one other thing."

"Yes?"

"I don't need to be worried about you, do I?"

"Of course not, JM. I'm here, it's me, buddy. Relax."

"I'll try. I'll try."

They ended it.

"I'm not in charge of your pantyhose!" he called back to Libby.

But he might as well be. For the first few months he had been responsible even for wiping her ass. Literally, usually at 3 a.m. when she crapped the bed in the middle of the night. He knew that until you had cared for a stroke victim, you wouldn't know what he was talking about. So it was only natural for her to think he might have also taken up pantyhose inventory control, as well.

He joined her at her open middle drawer.

"Where are we?"

She clenched her fists. "Don't rush me, dammit. Pleash!"

"We'll be gone three days--four, max. So you need four undies, four T-shirts, two slacks, two pair of shoes, flip-flops for the beach, and two sweaters. Always with the sweaters."

"Then I need two more T-shirts."

"How about the one says 'Cal Golden Bears.'? It's young."

"Okay. What elsh?"

"This one," he said, riffling through the neat stack. "This pink jobbie. I like this on you, tan skin, happy eyes, running to me across the sand--"

"You mean struggling to sh-stand with my cane. Running was two years ago. This is now. Old lady with cane."

"You're not old, my sweet," he told her. He touched her shoulder gently and she brushed up against him.

"I'm forties. Thash a short leap to fifty and that ish old."

"Nuts to that. You'll never age, Libby. You're a sprite, beautiful and ageless."

"You're shweet, Ansh."

"Come on now. Let's toss this in and get things zipped. We don't want to be late."

"Where are we going, exactly?"

He had been wondering how long he could avoid saying.

"Mexico. We have business in Mexico City."

"Ish it someone I know?"

"Oh, you know this person very well."

"Well?"

"I can't tell you. I'd have to kill you if I told you."

"Ansh! Come on!"

"Let's make it a surprise. You are going to be very happy. In fact, I predict tears of joy."

"Only seeing--"

"Never mind. Let's see if this thing will zip."

She flattened one edge of the suitcase, forcing her cane along the horizontal flap. It worked remarkably well and just like that, they were zipped.

"Excellent. Now let me grab a few things and we're off."

"Lesh eat first. Hungry."

"You go fish something out of the fridge. I'll grab some things and be right down."

"Okay."

She plunged the cane to the hardwood and bravely headed for the door.

"I'm not making you anything," she called back. "You'll eat on the plane."

"Fine, fine."

He quickly filled his overnighter with a few items and exchanged a used razor for new, and he was ready. His meds--good there. When you got to be fifty you started needing more than a small space on a shelf to hold your meds. Anymore his took up almost half of one shelf--and counting. Statin for cholesterol, antihistamine for allergies, blood-pressure--all fifties knew the drill.

Chapter 12

Juan Carlos Ordañez was sent by his father to put the squeeze on Hermano Sanchez. There was the matter of the suitcase of marijuana lost by Sanchez to the Drug Task Force in Flagstaff. The cartel wanted Sanchez to repay the value of the lost pot, $150,000.

To Juan Carlos' father, head of the Tijuana Cartel, it was a matter of principle that Sanchez pay up or be hurt. If he failed to enforce against a mule like Sanchez his business would quickly unravel. Drug smuggling would abruptly cease if the mules thought any less than their very lives was at stake when they were hauling the kingpin's drugs across the international boundaries. Sanchez would either pay up or--there was one other way. Sanchez had a daughter. Juan Carlos knew her name was Maria and that she was nine or ten. He would threaten to take her away. That would motivate the mule to get their money.

He pulled into Nogales driving a battered white Toyota Highlander. Among the other old cars along the street, it was invisible and that's the way the family wanted it.

Ordañez parked one block from Canal Street, the infamous red light district of Nogales. At the corner of Canal Street and Dulcea Avenue he ducked inside El Camino, a whore house that was huge in the sex tourism business. El Camino's popularity was legendary because of the underage prostitutes available.

He found his contact, Efrain, who worked for Juan Carlos' father in the whore house. Efrain's job was to inter-cept men at the border and promote the strip and massage clubs along Canal Street. The clubs featured young—twelve- and even ten-years-old--hookers. It was into El Camino that Juan Carlos would place Maria if the $150,000 wasn't forthcoming in three days.

"Have you seen our man Sanchez?" Juan Carlos asked the employee over a *Dos Equis* beer. *Dos Equis* was brewed by Heineken--with whom the senior Ordañez also had a deal for distribution in Sonora, and the first sip was satisfying to the younger Ordañez, for it was good to keep business within the family. Even the beer in the saloons belonged to his father, and that made him very proud and made him feel very strong, even invincible.

"Yes, he is at home with his wife and kids."

"And Maria is still with him?"

"Last I know she was."

"Has he come in to talk about the money he owes?"

"He was here two nights ago. He said he was working on it."

"Sure he is. We are going to take his daughter. Tell him that."

"How long?"

"Three days. In three days I come for her."

"I will tell him."

"Good. Now who do you got for me tonight? I am looking for someone twelve."

"Girl or boy?"

"Either one."

"I have just the *puta* for you."

"Let's finish our beer and then I will go to my room in back. You don't let no one else use it?"

"Not since you said."

"I said. It's for me only."

"It's clean. No one else dares to go inside."

"Good. Now send me a chicken. Not too plump, not too skinny. In the middle."

"As you wish."

Chapter 13

Five minutes later, Ansel headed downstairs with his bag. She was in the kitchen; he smelled the onion soup heating. So he ducked into his office.

On his laptop he located a travel site and paid round-trip air fare to Mexico City. Return in three days. They would have the trust money back in hand by then and they could fly home.

Of course they would have to spend a day with David and listen to his pitch for his kids or whatever he was up to. Ansel would probably make a sizable gift. "Largesse Largent," his friends called him at the office. Because the firm's largesse was well-known to his partners and the several charities he considered deserving.

Thus, David had come by his proclivity for giving naturally; Ansel wondered that maybe it was even genetic, for his own father's obsessive tithing kept the family constantly poor as the proverbial church mice. His giving became Ansel's became David's. There were worse character traits, he didn't doubt, and they had done well in order to do well. David's own career had been astonishing to Ansel.

"Then we're ready?" she called. He envisioned her spooning soup to the good side.

"Just about," he called back. "One last item."

The money hadn't arrived. Two hundred thousand dollars. It would be no easy trick to smuggle that much cash out of the country. Failure to declare over ten thousand was a crime. A very serious crime, and he knew that, and he knew that he could be sent to prison for up to ten years and fined up to $500,000. Still, the money was a must, and no one could know about it. Not even Libby.

At just that moment the front gate buzzed.

Ansel checked the video and confirmed it was the courier, as he'd expected.

He buzzed him up the drive and hurried to the front door to intercept the delivery. There would be a valise and there would be a bank note to sign, and a receipt. And he would be ready.

He was at the front door, stretching out his signing hand so that the encounter was a quick one, when his cell phone chimed yet again.

Melinda calling. He already knew she was hopping mad because he had ducked out without first having the talk that she was demanding. His mistake. Big mistake. For all he knew her next call might be to Libby. He didn't think that would happen but with Melinda you never knew. After all, she was young and impulsive. The mother of three middle-schoolers and wife to Ramin Singh,

Melinda was all Indian grace, hallowed brown skin that always left him panting for more, large breasts that, despite filling three voracious newborn appetites over the years yet retained their newness, their pout, their upward tilt and gravity-defying protrusion.

Ansel hated to share with Ramin even though the husband held the deed. She knew better than to ever remind Ansel that she still was, at times, finding it necessary to satisfy her husband sexually. No matter that she was foresworn to Ansel and his love. She indulged Ramin as one might indulge a high school flame ten years down the road when, at the first reunion, he copped a gratuitous feel. Old times went down hard, old feelings could be fanned, histories shifted and tilted as in tectonic plate hydraulics where one forgot one was now ten years older and no longer enfolded in the high school status equivalency of "engaged."

All he asked of her was that if there was to be a cop and feel that he didn't hear about it. If he didn't hear, it didn't exist.

Thus he survived the reality of her other life and wifely duty.

"Where the heck did you go?" she said when he accepted the call.

"I had to get away. It's impossible to explain right now."

"Does this have anything to do with Suzanne's death--wait, don't just answer and tell me 'no.' First remember that I love you and you can tell me anything and my lips are sealed. Having laid that foundation, did you bolting off have anything to do with Suzanne?"

"Yes and no. Yes because I didn't have time for the police. No because I had nothing to do with her death."

"You're sure about that?"

"Which?"

"The police part. You're too small to kill anyone."

"Well, thanks." Anything more would have required

arguing he wasn't too small to kill someone. He yielded the point.

"What about talking to the cops? They want your number immediately."

"Listen, I can't talk just this minute, a courier just pulled up at my front door. I'll have to call you back."

"Brother, you've got ten minutes. Then I'm escalating."

"Escalating? What the hell does escalating mean?"

"Do I have to spell it out?"

"Yes, please."

"Ansel, you won't hear what I have to say. It won't wait. It involves our spouses. So if you won't hear me out you leave me no choice but to take it up with them."

"Don't go postal on me here, Mel. I'm not dodging you. Life implodes sometimes. I'm in the midst of a meltdown--"

"Do we need to call Dr. Starkey?"

"No, it's not like that."

"You're sure?"

"I'm certain. No, this is real life stuff that's happening. I want to bring you up to speed about it. You more than anyone. Let me answer the door. The bell's ringing. Then I'll lock myself in my office and call you back. I promise."

"Ten minutes, Ansel. I'm not kidding around."

"I know you're not. Ten minutes."

"Be safe."

"I will."

She had to add an admonition because she not only loved Ansel, she also knew him.

"And call Dr. Starkey if you need to."

"Please."

The front door buzzed a third time. It sounded angry and final. He quickly pulled it open before Libby came.

The driver held a zippered pouch that he held back as he pushed an electronic clipboard forward.

"Sign here," he said, which Ansel did, and he punched the face of the machine and said again, "sign here," which Ansel did. He appeared to study the signature, but then dropped the machine, which was tethered to him by a belt band. Then he handed Ansel the zippered pouch and tossed off a mock salute. "Enjoy," he laughed.

The door quickly shut behind him and Ansel headed for his office, making it inside and locking the door behind him before Libby noticed. Or so he thought.

No sooner had he unzipped the pouch and begun counting than she knocked.

"Busy, Lib," he called out. "Important and confidential law firm business."

"Jush open the damn door, Ansh!"

"Libby, come on! We both have our boundaries! That's important. And I'm not letting you in."

"Then I'm not going."

Great. She had him, and she knew she had him, because he wouldn't leave her there without him. Great.

So he stuffed the banded money back inside the zipped bag.

She was just about to knock again when he jerked it open.

"What?"

She looked beyond him, determined to see what he was up to. He stood aside and swept his arm wide.

"As you can see, I have nothing to hide. I need to make a few firm calls. That's all I'm doing."

"Ansh," she laughed and brushed past. "When have I ever given up your shecrets? Heaven forbid I would do that!"

"Please. This is different. Give me some space here, Libby."

"Oh, pshaw," she said, using an expression her mother once used in his presence.

"So what do you need right now that can't wait until I make my calls?"

"Nothing. I'm jush being nosy. Thash what wives do. Were you on the phone with Melinda? Did I hear you whispering to her?"

"I was speaking to Melinda, yes, but it was business."

"You're shtill shtupping her, aren't you."

It wasn't a question and he didn't know where she got the expression. It came out of nowhere. They were Methodists. They didn't say "shtupping."

"You are. I can see it in your eyes."

He took her hand and led her outside his office, cane and all. She resisted, but not violently. She didn't have the strength to violently resist and had to lift-plop her cane in stutter-step to keep up.

"Now. You fix yourself a nice cup of coffee and give me ten minutes. That's all. No more, no less."

"'Kay."

"Thank you."

He closed the door and locked it. He got back to counting. At one-hundred-fifty-thousand he lost count and thought *screw this* and began forming a half-size human skeleton with the bills, which were banded in stacks of thousands.

How was he going to smuggle two-hundred of those? Tape was the obvious answer. He figured he could tape ten to each arm, twenty thousand. Twenty to each leg, which would be forty. The rest would have to encircle chest and abdomen. Plus he could throw another fifty in his travel bag and pray they didn't ask him to open it. In the inside pocket, the dirty-clothes sleeve. Fair enough.

Off came the suit coat, shirt; off came the T-shirt and down went the pants and off came the shoes. Wearing only his boxers, he began the tape job.

Ten minutes later he resembled the Michelin Man. His mid-section had gone from his svelte thirty-four to something resembling a fifty inch paunch. His chest looked, like it was protected by the same body armor police employ, and his arms--he could just barely bend his arms. And he'd made one huge mistake. Nothing fit. The pants wouldn't slide back on and the shirt sleeve wouldn't pass down over his swollen biceps and wouldn't button up the front anyway. Great.

As in other times of pure stymie in his life when he had run out of all good ideas, he was saved by serendipity. He heard the washing machine begin running water. And it was in the basement and he knew it was running water because it made the pipes pound in the walls of his office. Libby was running a load.

Without a second thought he dashed out of his office and raced upstairs two-at-a-time. Then he was locked in his bedroom.

Quickly he shrugged into his Bears sweatshirt, which dropped easily over his balloon arms and torso as it was an XXXL. And his fishing pants, huge as they were to allow comfort in the boat, passed with no small tugging and coaxing up his legs and around his waist. They snapped closed but only after he shifted fifty-thousand from waist height up a notch to kidney height. Sideways in the mirror he look distorted and bloated and strangely dressed for someone about to fly out of the states to a foreign country.

Sweatshirt and fishing pants? Are you kidding me, he thought? Customs would have him face-down on the ground in a flash.

Just in time to confirm his insanity, Libby said from behind, "Why are you wearing that get-up? I thought we were flying?"

Evidently the lock failed.

"Don't know. Just wanted something comfortable."

"You don't look comfortable. You look swollen. What the hell you got on under there?"

Before he could stop her she pulled up his sweatshirt and visualized the first-level tape job, the kidney belt of fifty grand.

"Ansh, what the hell do we have here?"

"I know. This is part of my firm secret. It's for the law practice, I swear it."

"Cash money? Lawyers don't use cash money. Try again."

"Okay. It's part of my surprise for you, but you caught me. Feel better? Do you feel better now that you ruined part of the surprise I have for you?"

Lawyers also attacked when run to the ground and mauled by lions.

"Really? I didn't mean to ruin my shurprise."

"Well just drop it. I can still make most of it a surprise for you."

"Well. I'm getting lots of money. I can't see anything wrong with that. When are we going?"

"Right now. I just have to call a cab. Now give me five minutes alone, please."

He was about to dial Melinda's number when he heard a voice over the front gate intercom. All he could make out was "FBI," followed by the sound of Libby hitting the gate unlock.

The FBI had officially arrived.

Chapter 14

Libby ushered them right inside, right into the living room, and then called upstairs. "FBI, Ansh! Come down, pleash!"

She tried to make it sing-song but failed. Her voice was plaintive and frightened. Which told the FBI they were on the right track. All this before hands had even been shaken and intros made.

"Coming!"

He took care coming down the stairs so as not to trip and spill two hundred thousand dollars out of his clothes.

The agents stood when he walked in. Both had been waiting on the couch, and both extended their badges over their wrists, like waiters offering the bottle.

The taller, black male went first. "Special Agent Freyer Smothers, FBI."

The shorter, thick male followed, "Special Agent Kip Honeycomb, FBI. You must be Mr. Largent."

"I am. Call me Ansel. Sit, please."

"Coffee?" Libby called in.

Both refused. Always with the business-first drama.

"How can I help?" Ansel asked, rubbing his hands together briskly in the universal 'let's get to work' sign language.

"We've asked around, down at the firm. You're the one trust account signatory we haven't spoken with yet," said Agent Smothers. He was very black with very Caucasian features. Ansel figured he hailed from one of the islands. Which meant he could read nothing into him. He would have to tread lightly with the guy.

"I am a trust account signatory. There's James MacDevon, Nedra, and Louis Rammelkamp."

He spoke up, Agent Honeycomb. "Rammelkamp was removed from the account two weeks ago. By you."

"Louis was? I must have forgotten."

"Recall why you took him off?"

He shrugged. "I must have had my reasons."

"Being what?" Agent Smothers asked. There was no tell about him, no reading him.

"Louis hasn't been well. We--I--just thought it would be best to remove him."

"Would that have anything to do with his real estate venture going belly-up?"

"It would."

Louis had invested in a five-acre-horse-farms venture near Barrington. Zoning had failed although the proper payoffs to board members had been made, so Ansel took Louis off the trust account. You couldn't be too careful, was his slant at the time.

"How would that be necessary?"

"His real estate investment plan fell through. JM and I talked it over and thought it best to remove Louis."

Smothers steepled his fingers. He was wearing a gigantic

class ring on his left hand, a ring with a huge ruby stone. The stone tossed a laser of red light at Ansel's face. He blinked, hard. And pulled his face to the side like one dodging mirrored sunlight. Smothers smiled, just barely, but he smiled.

"So when the money went missing, only you and James MacDevon had access to the account?"

"Far as I know, that would be correct. Plus--"

"Yes?"

"Well, my son had--"

"This would be your son away at school?"

He shook his head. "No, that would be his brother, David."

The agents traded a look. "And where is David? If he had access to the account we'll need to talk to him, too."

"David is out of town, business."

"Where?"

"He was supposed to be in the air on his way home. Should be back late tonight."

Whereupon, Libby called in from the kitchen, "Are we going, or what?"

Agent Honeycomb smiled. A tease had been tossed his way. He accepted. "Going? Where are you going? Are we keeping you?"

"No--Yes. We're having to visit someone who's ill. We're about to leave for the hospital."

"Sorry about that," said Smothers. "Who is ill?"

"That would be confidential."

"Well, that wouldn't be David, would it? Is David having problems we might need to be made aware of? Mental problems?"

"No, no, no, nothing like that. No, it's not David, anyway. Family member. Family friend."

"Sorry for that. We both are."

They both nodded solemnly. They traded a look. Which didn't surprise Ansel one bit. He was being evasive, unsure, all the things you don't want to be with the FBI.

He half-stood. "Well, then, we really need--"

Agent Honeycomb raised his pudgy hand. "You know what? This might be totally off the wall, but would you mind if we just took a look around?"

"A look around at what?"

"Oh, you know. Just snooping"

"Why on earth? Yes, I mind. We're leaving."

"It wouldn't take ten minutes."

"Yes, I mind."

"Do we need to get a search warrant?"

"Yes, no. If you could come back around six this evening, or in the morning, a look around would be just fine."

Honeycomb gave him a querulous look. A pout. "I meant now. Please?"

He climbed to his feet.

"I'm going to have to shoo you out now. Libby and I need to hit the road."

"Hit the road? That sounds like a major trip to me. Does that sound major to you, Agent Smothers?"

Agent Smothers nodded at Agent Honeycomb. "It sounds major."

Two against one. Definitely time to end it.

"Whatever. I'm asking you to leave now, so please: to the front door."

He spread his arms like one herding chickens.

"Thank you," he said at the door as they prepared to step out.

Without a backward look or another word, they moved

off. Then at the edge of the porch, Agent Smothers turned his black, island face, and said, simply, "We'll be back at six. With a search warrant. Be here, please. If not, we'll let ourselves in. And that's never pretty."

Ansel watched them climb into their car and pull slowly away.

He waved. He couldn't think what else he should do, so he waved.

"Who wash that?" asked Libby, making an appearance with silver tray, coffee carafe, and four cups.

"Business acquaintances."

"At the house? Why are they at our housh, Ansh?"

"Mistake. They couldn't stay for coffee. Big doings."

"What should I do with all this coffee? Pour it out?"

"Yes. Pour it out. We're leaving. Now."

Chapter 15

Twenty-five minutes later the cab buzzed. Ansel buzzed back and it materialized at their front drive. It was green with a green-yellow checkered stripe along the side.

With no time to waste Ansel loaded Libby's plaid bag and his overnight bag. Then he steadied Libby down the stairs and at the bottom she pushed him aside and caned herself to the cab. She leaned against the front door, pulled open the back door, and swung her left side onto the seat. She then reached with both hands to grasp her right leg and drag it inside. She pulled the door closed. Ansel watched all this labor and admired his wife. He then ran around and jumped in beside her.

"O'Hare," he told the cabby, who nodded but just barely. He was a dark, Middle Easterner, earphone plugged into his right ear, softly speaking into an invisible mike. Whether he had heard him, Ansel was unsure, so he repeated himself. "O'Hare, please." The driver caught Ansel's eyes in the rearview and gave an annoyed look. He had definitely heard and his attention was definitely else-where and Ansel was definitely, definitely interrupting his conversation. Well, excuse me, Ansel thought, and looked away.

Ansel clicked the handheld and triggered the front gate. It swung shut behind them, its electric eye watching their egress.

"I don't believe you've told me where we're off to," Libby announced while at the same time flipping lint from her navy slacks. She was wearing the slacks, starched white shirt, and houndstooth jacket, gray and white. Her ladies' London Fog with faux fur was buttoned at the waist. The day had developed into one with blowing snow like confetti with a promise of much more to come toward evening. Ansel thought they would want to be airborne long before because, while O'Hare was the world's greatest airport when it came to clearing wintry runways, other flights would cancel and theirs would then oversell. The threat of being bumped was unthinkable and he guided his restless mind toward happier thoughts. Such as David, seeing him, maybe even later that night. And having the talk he desperately needed to have as he retrieved the firm's money.

Libby nudged him with her elbow. "Did you hear me? Where are we going?"

"We're going to Mexico City."

She leaned forward and punched the driver.

"Excuse me," she said in her most strident Libby-voice, "take me back home, pleash. Thersh been a mistake."

The cabby's eyes found Ansel's eyes in the glass. As well as eyes could shrug, Ansel's did. The driver looked at him quizzically.

"No, please keep driving," he countermanded. "My wife is just upset."

She punched his shoulder again. "Do you want to be arreshted for kidnapping? I'm not fooling around here, mishter. Take me home immediately."

Predictably, the driver took his foot from the accelerator.

"I doan know," he turned and said to the twosome. "Who is boss here?"

"I'm definitely boss," Ansel said. "This woman is my wife and she's been ill. We're going for treatment now."

"Thash a lie straight out of the pit of hell!" Libby cried. "Now shtop before I jump out!"

He began pulling into the right lane. It was clear he intended to take the next right and come back around heading to the pickup point.

"Listen to me," Ansel told him. "Here's one thousand dollars for you to listen to me, not her."

He freed ten hundreds from inside his sweatshirt sleeve and tossed them up front.

"There's another thousand when you get us there."

"I am sorry, missus," the cabby said, and steered the cab back to the fast lane. Their speed picked up and they were doing ten over. Ansel congratulated himself on having instincts that were right on: a grand never looked so good to that guy as right then.

"Policesh will be called and heads will roll," Libby promised the man. He didn't react at all, didn't seem to have heard her. She shrugged and looked out her window. Ansel watched her jaw move as she talked to herself--a willing audience since the stroke. That's fine, let her talk it over with herself, he thought.

That was close.

His mind raced ahead, scouting out his moves. How did he plan to get her on the plane? How would he ever get her out of the cab and into the airport? A million ideas were served up and were rejected in his brain. She was too damn wily for most of his scenarios, too experienced, too accustomed to his machinations. He knew he was a known quantity to her, predictable and avoidable. Then it came to him: her mother. Old, poor and feeble. Living in a cubicle in Boca. A twelve-by-twelve with easy chair, blaring TV, two burners and mini-fridge, and bathroom you couldn't bend over and tie your shoes in. Like he said, poor. Broke.

"In law school, in contracts law, we studied contracts," he told her.

She continued staring out her window and moving her jaw.

"Contracts have beneficiaries. One type of beneficiary is called a third-party beneficiary."

No change. Window-jaw, it was all the same.

"Imagine this. A and B make a contract. As part of their deal, C benefits. C gets something because of B's promise to A. A gives something to C because of B's promise to A."

"See where I'm going with this?"

The cabby nodded in the mirror. He got it.

Ansel pushed ahead. "So let's say I'm Mr. A, you're Mrs. B, and your mother is C. You and I make an agreement and your mother benefits."

Her head turned and then she was looking at the road ahead.

"What would my mother get? What would I have to do?"

"Your mother gets--fifty thousand dollars."

"What?"

He had her full attention then.

"That's right. I pay your mother fifty thousand dollars if you will go to Mexico City with me."

"Show me the money."

"It's taped to my right leg."

"I don't care. I want it right now or I'm not going."

He unzipped and untaped. Fifty packages of one thousand each were eased out of his pants, still attached to a volume of clear tape. He passed it over.

"Deal?" He still clutched the package.

"Deal."

He relaxed his grip. She unzipped her carry-on and forced the package inside.

"Do I have to give it all to her?"

"She's the beneficiary, I would hope so."

"All right then."

"Done. No more arguments?"

"I'm in. I have no idea what you're up to thish time, but my mother can damn well ush the money."

"I know."

"Thanksh. She thanksh you."

"I know she does."

"Thish will supplement her Shocial Shecurity every month."

"Good."

"Maybe I'll dole it out sho she can't go nuts. Maybe five hundred a month."

"That's six thousand a year. It will last nine years and change."

"She's sheventy-eight. That should be long enough. Her mother died at sheventy-nine."

"Good. We might get a refund."

"The hell with you, Anshel. Thash terrible."

"Sorry. Can you step it up another ten?" he poked the cabby. "We're going to hit heavy westbound on the Kennedy."

The cab moved appreciably faster.

Money.

No wonder David made off with two hundred million of it.

You could rule the entire rush hour flow with enough hundreds.

Chapter 16

Ansel's Google search confirmed that Mexican travel visas were issued at the destination airport. So that worked; they would acquire them there when they touched down.

But first, United Airlines ran a passport check at its O'Hare terminal fourteen.

Ansel passed the agent their two passports. Libby stood beside him, cane firmly planted on the speckled tile, impatience written on her face. Stroke victims could be very impatient. Stroke victims, hell, so could Ansel, he thought, and there was no stroke in his history. At least none that he knew of.

His impatience with the lady at the counter mounted by the second.

She looked at his passport and compared the name to his driver's license. Same thing with Libby's. Then eyes: up-down, up-down a dozen times while she compared their likenesses to reality. Finally she closed both booklets and passed them back.

He gave her his what-the-hell look. She smiled United Airlines-ly and spread her hands.

"Sorry. No-fly list."

"What?"

"You're both on the no-fly list. As of 2:40 CST. I can't check you in."

"Who do we talk to?"

"The State Department."

"Washington DC?"

"Uh-huh. Now, will you let me help the next in line? Next?"

He felt pressure against his back. A young couple buckled up against them insistently. There was nothing they could do, Libby and Ansel, except stand aside and give them their place at the counter. Then they were in no-man's land, that spot at the counter where there was no terminal and no smiling face.

"Ansh, are you in trouble?"

"I can explain."

"Lesh go find a quiet corner. I might talk funny but the brainsh shtill operative. Yours--not so much."

Chapter 17

They sat and talked and finally decided to take the next indicated step: they fell in line at Avis. Driving to Mexico City sounded hot and long and interstellar in miles, but what was actually left to them? If you couldn't fly, drive; they decided.

Libby hobbled off in search of the restroom while Ansel parked himself in line behind three Midwesterners--bulky topcoats in the dull blacks, grays, and blues of Chicago. Behind him was a cluster of three Asians speaking what he assumed was Chinese, and they were turning a roadmap end-to-end, exclaiming loudly as they tried to finger-trace some route. Call me racist, he thought, but it was astonishing that Asians would be using a tool so ancient as a roadmap when they all had GPS on their phones, iPads, and the car they would rent. But they were animated and several hands grabbed the map at once. Ansel turned away and began tapping his foot as the terminal operator told her patron to initial the circles and sign at the bottom. And so the litany continued, "Will that be full-size, mid-size, or economy?"

His mind played with the agent's speech rhythm: Will that be brain-scan, therapy, or lobotomy? Full-size, mid-size, economy? It was all the same to him. Just please *hurry*.

Until someone poked him in the back. Half-expecting to see gold FBI badges, he turned around. An Asian face smiled up at him. He was probably mid-forties, squat but muscular, round face and brown eyes like chocolate almonds. "Can you help?" he said.

"I can try," Ansel replied. "What's up?"

"We want to go to Grand Canyon. Is it far?"

"About two thousand miles that-a-way," he said and pointed west.

"One day, two day?"

"A good two days. A comfortable three. Why are you in Chicago if you're going to the Grand Canyon?"

The man checked his smartphone. Ansel saw he was using a translation app.

"My wife has been to OB-GYN conference. We came from Hong Kong."

At which time Libby reappeared. She looked refreshed and relieved.

"Hi," she said, and extended a hand to the visitor. "I'm Libby. Do we know you?"

"My name Herman Wang. This Mira Wang, my wife."

A gracious looking woman, also fortyish, smiled sheepishly and dropped her eyes to the floor. Very unprofessional and un-doctorish, Ansel thought, but there you were, nothing like the boisterousness of American docs. Which made Ansel think of Dr. Starkey and wince. Brain-scan, side-pocket or lobotomy. He commanded his brain to back off. It was sounding singsongy, like the visitors from the Orient.

"You're the doctor?" he asked, bringing Libby up to speed.

"Yes," she replied and suddenly took Libby's hand and began pumping. "Hello, Libby. Are you driving west?"

"Yesh. We're off to Mexico Shitty."

"Is near Grand Canyon?"

"Not exactly," Libby said. Her speech was half-speed in appreciation of the language differences. "But we're going right by there."

"So nice," Dr. Wang said and nodded at her companions. They all joined her, nodding: it's nice they're going right by there.

"Sho--" Libby exhaled, "Maybe we could drop you there."

It never ceased to amaze him what the stroke had done to her logic faculty. What, they were offering a ride to three total strangers, from Chicago to the Grand Canyon? Didn't she remember they were actually in a hurry to get to Mexico City? Was being in a hurry nothing to her?

"I'm sure they'll want to stretch out in their own car," Ansel told Libby and took her by the elbow as if to turn her toward the Avis agent. But she pulled away.

"It would be <u>nicesh</u> to have female company," Libby said with All-American cheerleader spirit. "You should ride with us. We can shplit the cost."

A rapid-fire discussion overcame the trio. Finally the first man surfaced from the noisy confabulation.

"We go with you," he said with an eager smile. "You rent the car, I buy the gas."

"Fair enough," chirped Libby. "Off we go then. Here," she said, and moved them out of line like a mother hen managing her chicks. "Shtand over here while we get the car. We'll need something full-shize," she told Ansel. He started to object. They wanted to keep a low profile and take a circuitous route. Back roads, secondaries, streets the FBI wouldn't think to monitor. No, they definitely needed to be on their own.

"It is sweet of you to offer," he told Libby, "but your friends should keep their place in line." He herded them back in line, and explained. "We'll be going by a route you won't want to take as it will be very slow. I'm sure you're in a hurry."

"No hurry," Dr. Mira Wang piped up. "We would like see your route."

Great. A friendly sightseer. And a tenacious one, at that.

"We can make suggestions and help you map out a route, but we'll be traveling without you this time, I'm afraid."

"Ansh, I'm getting ready to return your money," Libby warned. She looked him off and he retreated a step. She folded her hands as if addressing a choir. "You can ignore Anshel right now. He's gassy and embarrassed."

"I am not gassy," he maintained, as Dr. Wang gave him a studied look. He believed that her face said she suspected he might be gassy; he believed that her look confirmed a working diagnosis.

"Fifty thousand, headed your way--" Libby said.

Ansel gave in. "But I'll tell you what. Since you're visiting from another country I'm going to rearrange my schedule. We'll trade off driving, Herman and I. That way we can drive straight through."

"No good, straight through," said their companion, a man who must have been someone's father. His speech was almost free of accent. "I live in Chicago. We should get two motel rooms tonight and leave first thing tomorrow. Night-time traffic is very dangerous."

"Not any more than daytime," Ansel replied. "Afraid I must disagree with you, friend."

"Okay, then, we drive straight through. I driver number three."

"Do you men have licenses?" it occurred to Ansel to ask.

"International licenses. Very good."

He could think of no other possible ways to sidetrack Libby's display of United Nations goodwill.

"Full-size it is," he said, and stepped up to the counter for his turn.

"Full-size, mid-size, or economy?" the featureless face inquired.

"Full size. Fullest size possible."

———

THEY MADE it as far as St. Louis by midnight, what with the traffic, stops and all. Libby said they should spend the night and Ansel pretended not to hear, taking the bypass around the city and increasing speed.

They traded places three times and used two different drivers, Herman and Ansel.

The women talked non-stop and decided to quit watching *Oprah* in favor of *Ellen*, stop looking for fulfillment through their children, and opt for the Fjords of Norway Holy Land is too damn dangerous, they agreed. In fact, it looked as if the fivesome might be making that particular excursion as a group, possibly with a group rate.

Herman and Ansel shared very little; the father (it turned out he was Herman's father) said even less. From what little Herman had to share about his father, the old man was a foot soldier who stood alongside Chiang Kai-Shek at the siege of Shanghai and won some kind of meritorious battle ribbon the family still treasured. When Chiang departed China in 1949 for Taiwan, the father remained behind on the mainland, where Herman was born in 1950. From St. Louis to Oklahoma City, Ansel learned about the renaissance of midwifery in Hong Kong from Mira Wang, and heard enough from Herman on plastics injection processes to start his own toy factory upon return to Chicago.

———

HERMAN TOOK the wheel in Elk City and Ansel struggled into the backseat, shut his eyes, and slept five hours. He took over at a rest stop between Amarillo and Albuquerque and Libby joined him in the front seat. They talked and drank coffee from a rest stop machine. Actually it wasn't bad and, with the hibernation in the back seat, he found himself now refreshed and alert.

His cell chimed west of Albuquerque just as they were leaving the mountains. The call was from Melinda. He could almost feel the anger even before he tapped to accept. But if he didn't let her through, it would only get worse.

So he accepted.

"I hate you," she said immediately. He could tell the words had been demanding to make their way to him.

"I'm sure you do. Uh--I'm with Libby and some friends on the highway just now. Can we talk later?"

"We could, but that never happens. Put Libby on, please."

"And I would do that why?"

"Because I want to tell her she's about to have a step-child. I'm pregnant."

"What!?"

"I told you we had to talk! You've got me pregnant and now you're fleeing the police? Cute, Ansel. Should I give them your cell number and let them geo-locate you?"

"Now hold on, Mel. We can handle this."

"Handle what?" Libby asked, a comma of coffee on her chin. "Handle what, Ansh?"

"Tell her I'm pregnant. Ask her what you should do."

"Now hold on, Mel."

"Will you stop with the 'hold on Mel'?"

"We can work this out. For the record, I want this to proceed."

"What to proceed?" asked Libby.

"What to proceed?" asked Melinda.

"You know--the situation."

He was getting daggers from Libby. She reached for the phone and he jerked it to the opposite ear, next to the window.

"What shituation, Ansh?"

"You mean you want my pregnancy to continue? Or you want us--as in you and me--to continue. Stop talking like a spy! Give it up with the code! Tell Libby I'm pregnant! She'll understand, poor thing. No, don't tell her. You've already put her through enough."

"I have? How do you figure that?"

"You don't think her stroke was your fault? Got news for you buddy. That woman would never have had a stroke if it weren't for your little go-around."

"You know," he said, "we can discuss this later." It was time to cover his tracks. Hide the ball, that was it. "So you tell Coates that I'm going to be back next week and we can talk then."

"Don't you do this, you dick!"

"I don't care what Mr. Coates says! Tell him I'll be in next week!"

"You dick--"

He clicked END CALL.

Libby sat with her arms crossed on her chest. She was looking out her window, looking into the sunrise in the rearview mirror.

"What have you done to that poor girl, Ansh? Next thing I know, you'll be telling me she's pregnant."

"It was about a client."

"Client-shmient. She's pregnant, am I right? Just yesh or no, Ansh. You owe me that much."

"It was office stuff. Who's getting hungry?"

He studied his passengers in the rearview. They all appeared asleep. All except for the father, whose faraway look reminded Ansel of the Chiang Kai-Shek connection.

"So you really knew Chiang Kai-Shek? Do you want to talk about the retreat to Taiwan?"

The old man's faraway look never changed. Libby's face in the rearview was near field. Amazing mirror, he thought. His mind had settled down with the long hours of driving and for that he was thankful.

He kicked it up to 85 MPH and rubbed his chin. He flipped the rearview mirror's high beams deflector as the sun was beaming directly into his eyes from back behind in the east.

It was going to be a long day.

They should hit the Mexican border around sundown.

Chapter 18

Mexican Magistrate Judge Cesar Elvis Valenzuela was the son of a Memphis long-shoreman and a first grade teacher named Claudia Esmeralda.

Judge Valenzuela was tall by Mexico standards, all of six-one. At forty-two, the judge reminded Thaddeus of a Mexican middleweight challenger at the MGM Grand. He was put together, graceful, confident and well-exercised. He also exercised his mind, reading four foreign language newspapers daily.

His face was angelic and he wore his hair short on the sides and long in the back--again, the middleweight fighter look. He was educated at the University of Sonora and possessed a law degree from Universidad de Guanajuato, a highly respected Mexican law school that gobbled up five years and an additional internship of two years. He was appointed to his post by the President of Mexico and ruled his court and his cases fairly. However, he also was willing to supplement his meager salary by the use of what he called "stipends" from prisoners. Which meant, basically, that for $5,000 Thaddeus could purchase an expedited bail hearing. He was quick to smile and, when he met Thaddeus that first night, shook his hand firmly and welcomed him to his court, a happy smile belying his dislike of American lawbreakers.

They met in the Judge's chambers behind the courtroom in Nogales. It was close to seven o'clock by the time the single guard arrived with Thaddeus and Burton in handcuffs and leg irons. Thaddeus' paralegal Christine Susmann had arrived from Flagstaff with the ten thousand dollars and was waiting outside the court, running the engine of her car, in hopes she would soon be able to transport Thaddeus back to the States. It was a hope based on very sketchy knowledge of Mexican law and legal process.

Upon her arrival, Christine had met with the Mexican District attorney in Nogales. She learned several things, the most alarming of which was that in Mexico the judges also serve as adjuncts to the District Attorney and help the District Attorney put together cases against criminal defendants. She was also astonished to learn that Mexican law provided a presumption of guilt rather than a presumption of innocence as in American law. Thaddeus had two strikes against him and was still swinging away in the warm-up circle.

"That's right," Daniel Ortega of the DA's staff told her. "Down here you are presumed guilty if you are arrested. Your friend Mr. Murfee has been arrested on extremely serious charges. Smuggling a gun and possession of a firearm in Mexico could get him a sentence of thirty years in jail. Worst of all, the judge is helping our office in bringing charges."

Her sharp intake of breath was telling. "Thirty years? For having a gun?"

Attorney Ortega smiled. "No, madam. Not just for having. For smuggling."

"But when I read about the cartels down here it sounds like everyone is armed to the teeth."

"The bad guys are. But they are a problem that takes care of itself."

"You mean they shoot each other so no law enforcement is necessary?"

"Exactly."

"How much bail is usually required in these cases?"

"Oh, it could be twenty-five or fifty thousand dollars, U.S."

"We can do that."

"But these cases can take up to a year before charges are even filed. They can take a year to investigate. If there is no bail, your Mr. Murfee could remain our guest for many, many months while we investigate what happened here."

"Good grief."

"I know. Not good. Our law is based on Roman law and it is very unforgiving. If you know anything about the Roman church you will know that certain laws cannot be broken without terrible consequences. Mr. Murfee is presumed guilty of such a violation as we sit here. It will be very difficult for him going forward. You could call gun smuggling a mortal sin."

"Thank you for your time."

She had then proceeded on to the jail. She gave Thaddeus the upshot of what she had learned, speaking to him on a five-minute visit through the bars of his cell. She delivered the $5,000 bribe to him, which he handed off to a jailer. No receipt, nothing in writing, just gone. The alarm in the face of his usually placid paralegal rubbed off on him. He wondered if the five thousand would be considered yet another crime in and of itself. "We can only try," she said before the jailers escorted her out. He was left gripping the bars of the cell, white knuckles glowing in the dim light. He clearly was in a bad place. The other prisoners smiled among themselves. It was only a matter of time.

Now Thaddeus found himself in the judge's chambers, sitting cuffed and wearing leg irons. Across sat Judge Valenzuela. Burton slouched to his right, similarly restrained. The judge was peering through the lower portion of his bifocals, head tilted up and back, and his lips were seen to move as he read the incident report. Like most students of the law his eyes were weak from reading hundreds of thousands of pages in his studies. His blink rate increased the further down he read and Thaddeus could only hope it was unrelated to the crime charged.

He finally finished and tapped the report against the glass-top desk. "Interesting, Mr. Murfee. We will have to look into these very serious charges, I'm afraid."

"Can you give me any help?"

The judge shot him a severe look. Thaddeus could only assume the money had found its way into the jurist's hands and would hold some sway over him. Still, the look was unforgiving.

"Let me tell you how this works, Mr. Murfee. We don't want any unmet expectations here."

"Please do."

"Well, I should begin by saying, I am not your friend. I am part of the team that will investigate these papers and determine whether charges should be carried forth. Suffice it to say I am very disturbed by what I'm reading here. Some of this is very criminal in nature, hiding a gun beneath the dashboard of your car. And then attempting to bribe the border guard with $100. Just like you have attempted to bribe me with five thousand dollars."

There it was. Hanging in the air between them. Spoken, the bribe acknowledged, the legal effect of which dimmed his hope. Thaddeus strained against the handcuffs and came fully upright. He could feel Burton beside him slide further down into his chair. Thaddeus had the feeling that Burton was becoming aware he had joined the wrong team. He was trying to make himself as small as possible. Maybe even leach into the wood he occupied.

"My hope was that the court would see I'm able to pay bail. That was the full intent of the money given over to my guard."

"Nonsense. It was a bribe. I have received the funds and deposited them in an evidence bag. It will go into your file and will form part of the case against you. My guess is, we'll find your fingerprints on some of those hundred dollar bills. Now. Why don't we discuss how to lessen the impact of your sins?"

"Please, let's do."

The judge waved the guard away, who left and closed the door behind.

"Five thousand dollars is nothing."

"It is?"

"You will need twenty-five thousand dollars for me to give this case the full attention it deserves. And another fifty thousand for bail."

"Seventy-five thousand. I can have it here tomorrow or the next day at the latest."

"Excellent. Now why is this other gentleman with you?"

Burton looked down at his manacled ankles. His face said anyplace was better than here.

"This is Burton, my cellmate. I was hoping to pay his

bail too, as I thought he could help me with my real purpose in coming to Mexico."

"Which is?"

"I'm looking for a man, to help him and his family move away from the border."

"This man is your friend?"

"No. He is my client."

"I understand you're an American lawyer. You practice in Flagstaff?"

"I do."

The judge nodded. "We would certainly know where to come get you if you jumped bail."

"Yes. But that won't be necessary. I will appear. And I will serve whatever sentence the court issues against me for the gun."

"Do you wish to plead guilty now? Is that what I'm hearing?"

"No, Your Honor. I should get a lawyer before getting into that."

"You are right. We will wait on a plea. If charges are even filed."

"So my bail is fifty thousand and the court fee is twenty-five thousand?"

"Yes. Cash only, no checks."

"Where do we pay it?"

"To me. Come into my office when you're ready. I will get the papers together tomorrow."

"Thank you, Judge."

"Thank you, Mr. Murfee. Now you have a good night in that cell of yours."

"Hopefully it will be the last one."

"Hopefully."

"And Mr. Burton?"

"Marijuana possession is it?"

"Yessir," Burton managed.

"Five thousand bail. No court access fee."

"Thank you, Your Honor," Thaddeus said. "We'll bring eighty thousand tomorrow or the next day, latest."

"Good night, gentlemen. Guard!"

They were back in their cell at 8:15. The imprisoned crowd had surged and now there was no room on either bench. Thaddeus and Burton took a seat on the floor, side by side, where they would try to catch a few winks overnight.

Christine was on her way to Tucson. She would process a withdrawal at a Bank of America first thing in the morning. Then the doors to the cell would magically part, once the bribe and bail were paid up.

Thaddeus was counting the minutes.

By midnight he dozed and awoke an hour later, cold and disoriented. A new prisoner was being introduced into the cell. It appeared to be another American. The newcomer's eyes had to adjust to the dark cell, so he stood at the door that closed behind him and blinked for several minutes, adjusting.

When he could make out the numerous occupants he recognized Thaddeus as a fellow traveler, an American. He sidled over and plopped down beside him.

"Who are you?" the man asked.

Thaddeus side-eyed him. He was an odd-looking man with a flinty profile, sharp nose, sharp chin. He bobbed his head in an odd way, as if keeping time to an eccentric internal meter.

"Name, please," the man followed up.

"Thaddeus Murfee."

"I'm Ansel Largent. Know any good lawyers?"

"American or Mexican?"

"Both."

"Well," Thaddeus whispered, "we should talk in the morning. We're getting some very nasty looks from our friends trying to doze."

"Excellent," said Ansel Largent. "Now I wonder where Libby has been taken."

Chapter 19

Under orders from the Tijuana Cartel's young boss, Enrico Rodriguez organized a corporation under Canadian laws. It was chartered with headquarters in the Canadian Province of British Columbia and its name was Eastern Star Lines, Ltd.

Over a four day period of time, Enrico received four text messages, each from a different mobile device. He was sure they were one-use phones and didn't bother taking note of their callback numbers for he was certain they would have already been discarded or destroyed or both.

When all four messages were received, he pieced them together until he was sure he had a bank routing number and a bank account number.

Then, two days later, he received a fifth and a sixth text message. They said, in total, Hung Kai Bank & Holding, Ltd.

Working with the worldwide banking data that went with his job, he read about the bank and studied its ownership. He satisfied himself that it was who it said it was and he prepared for the big day, the day he would transfer the $200 million to Hung Kai.

First, he went online to Dubai Apartments and found a short term listing. The price was steep: $10,260 per month, but he had enough money in savings and stock options that he was able to make first, last and security deposit. He still had enough left to buy airline tickets, coach class, for his wife and infant son, to Dubai, Abu Dhabi.

"You are going to have to trust me," he told his young wife one night. Her name was Aña Marie and she was the product of a modern upbringing in Mexico City. Travel and change came easily to her, especially when her husband told her the move underway was the result of a huge promotion he had received at his work. They were going to be wealthy beyond their wildest dreams, Enrico told her, and she became excited. "Above all," he whispered, "when you reach our new home, contact no one. Don't even call your mother and tell her where you are."

She followed his instructions, packing clothing and toiletries for one week and shipping personal items such as photo albums, precious items from their son's birth, and jewelry. The address she used was the apartment in Dubai. Management there had even offered to receive shipments and store them in the couple's apartment for their arrival.

He procured a passport for her under her mother's maiden name. It was a name that would be untraceable; no one would think to try and locate her using the new last name.

For himself he purchased a forged birth certificate and a forged passport. Now he was no longer Enrico Rodriguez, Jr. Now he was Ricky Wellman of Omaha, Nebraska. The passport was American. His plan after several years in Dubai was to move to the United States and retire there. He had seen pictures of Colorado and it had burned a longing deep into his soul, the Rocky Mountains and the remote lifestyle. And it would be a welcome change from the deserts of Dubai. Cool, green, wild and untamed, that was the Colorado he yearned for. Maybe it wouldn't take years to get there. Maybe a year. Maybe less.

That was in the background of his mind as arrangements were finalized, accounts opened, withdrawals made, traveler's checks purchased for Ricky Wellman, and important papers packaged and shipped overseas.

On January 21 it was all in place.

The $200 million had waited for him day after day, the black numbers staring back at him on his computer monitor when he visited them each day. Now the numbers felt like an old friend. It had even begun to feel like they belonged to him.

At nine o'clock that night, he went back into his office at the bank and logged in for the last time. He set up the wire transfer, input Hung Kai's routing number and account number, and clicked SEND.

Like a phantom he was gone from the office, gone from Mexico City, and gone from the Western Hemisphere. All pre-arranged, all assumed names, all as agreed with Juan Carlos.

He was sure the money had hit the Hong Kong bank and was now taking on a life of its own, traveling worldwide under the authority of Juan Carlos and his banking empire. When the wash job was done, the money would be returned to him--thirty-five percent of it--to a Dubai Bank, also pre-arranged and waiting to see its opening balance swell from $1000 USD to over $70 million USD.

In fact, the money beat him to Dubai and was waiting for him when his plane touched down.

The reunion with wife and son was joyful and tender. They talked the first hour, and he explained that she could contact no one from their old world for at least twenty-four months. She was shocked at this, and dismayed, but he explained it was being done for her safety and the safety of their son, as a protection against kidnappers, now that the family enjoyed great wealth. At last she said she understood and that she agreed. There would be no contact, not with any of them, not even a call to the mother she adored and to whom she was extremely close.

It was better that way. She said she understood.

But already she missed her mother. Twenty-four months seemed like a lifetime. She would do her best to obey her husband.

That was it. She would do her best.

Chapter 20

The next morning at 5:30 the cell erupted with activity when first one man then another relieved himself in the open trench along the back wall. The splatter and moans were punctuated with the flutters and whoops of gas passing. Soon the cell was stinking and noisy.

Ansel and Thaddeus sat against one wall, on the floor, their knees drawn up to their chests as they hid in the early morning shadows. Neither wanted a confrontation. Increasingly, they were the unwilling recipients of angry glares and curses. "*Pinche Gringos*," they heard several times.

"I think we're being discussed," Ansel whispered out the side of his mouth. His head was bobbing again, the metronomic beat having its way. Thaddeus thought him odd, but he was friendly enough.

"I think you're right," said Thaddeus. "Don't make eye contact, please."

"What are you here for?"

"Misunderstanding. You?"

"FBI had a hold on my passport."

"That sounds bad. What did you do?"

"That's just it. I didn't do anything. But my law firm is missing megabucks."

"What are you, the accountant?"

"Managing partner."

"You're a lawyer? Where you from?"

"Chicago. MacDevon Largent firm. I'm Largent."

"You're Ansel Largent. I've heard of you."

"You're from Chicago?"

"Not from, but I have a law office there."

Ansel clucked his tongue. "Small world. What area of law?"

"Mostly criminal anymore. Some medical malpractice, but mostly criminal."

"Got a card? Just joking. No, I'm not. Are you interested in taking on a new client?"

"You don't even know me."

"Are you A-V rated?"

He meant Martindale-Hubbell, a legal registry of attorneys, publishers of a journal used by lawyers to find other lawyers when needed. A-V was the highest possible rating.

"I am. Five years now."

"What's your name?"

"Thaddeus Murfee. Don't shake my hand."

"I know you! You sued the State of Illinois and hit the lottery."

"We did all right."

"Seriously, Mr. Murfee. I do need a lawyer. The FBI will come for me once they hear I've been picked up."

"Sorry, I'm in jail. Can't help."

"I can get you out."

"How could that be?"

Ansel smiled what Thaddeus could only conceive was a mysterious smile. Several head bobs and a dodge.

"Let me handle that. If I get you out will you represent me?"

"That sounds reasonable."

"All right then, done. When I get out, you get out. I've got fifty thousand dollars under this sweatshirt. Will that do for a retainer?"

"That's the amount of my bail. Plus I need twenty-five thousand for a judge's fee."

"Judge's fee? What in the world?"

"You know. Grease the palm. This is Mexico."

"Sure, sure. Well, I've got another twenty-five thousand on each thigh. Let's call it seventy-five thousand, then.

"Done."

Pulling deeper into the shadows, Ansel--before Thaddeus could stop him--had removed the slab taped to his chest and was passing it to Thaddeus. Thaddeus quickly unbuttoned and stuffed the bills inside his shirt.

"That was stupid," Thaddeus whispered angrily.

"Seals the deal. No *quid pro quo*, no deal. Now you're on the hook. You're my lawyer."

"Don't do anything like that again. Not in here."

"Won't need to. You're retained. Now, would you like to hear my story?"

"Sure," said Thaddeus, "let me buzz for some coffee. Oh, that's right, they don't have room service here. My bad."

"You're jaded, my friend."

"I've been here almost a day. You'll get jaded too if you're in here that long."

"My guess is, the FBI will be here before that happens."

"Wouldn't be the worst thing in the world."

"Remember, you're coming with me."

"Sure. You bet."

"I'm serious, Thaddeus."

"Well, I've been paid. So I'm in."

At which point Burton came awake with a gasp.

"Who are you?" he asked Ansel.

"I'm the dummy who got arrested last night."

"Sure," Burton said. He yawned at the man and nodded, then went back to sleep.

"Friend?"

"My guide."

"Okay."

"Long story."

"Okay. Now, whatever happens from here on, just try to keep up. Don't say much."

"Who would I be talking to?"

"FBI."

"Sure. My lips are sealed."

Ansel gave him an anxious look.

"Please," he said and shook his head.

Chapter 21

The two Special Agents crossed at Nogales where they were well known. They were officed out of Nogales and crossed the same border virtually every day in pursuit of bad guys who had thought Mexico offered respite from the long arm of American justice. How wrong they always were. In the Twenty-First Century the FBI pursued fugitives around the world. Foreign or domestic, it was all the same to the Fibbies. Even the No-Extradite countries were fair game. Won't extradite? Fine, we'll show up in the middle of the night and kidnap you. The new, improved FBI.

They had a recent photo of Ansel Largent from the Illinois State Bar Association. It was mounted on the dashboard of their 2014 Ford Bronco where they could compare the guy in the holding cell to the guy in the photo. They had been fooled too many times to make that kind of mistake again.

Their names were Cashman and Lockhart and they were both twenty year veterans of the Agency. Cashman was white and wore dreadlocks, which disguised his real identity when that was important. Lockhart was white and female. She had exceeded FBI weight limits for her height and she blamed that on the Ben and Jerry's Funky Monkey she couldn't leave alone. Every night, curled up in front of the wide screen watching *Homeland, Season 1*, it was the same for her: a pint of B and J, a glass of California Chardonnay, and a slow drift into the slumber where the FBI always got its man. Cashman was the exact opposite: rawboned and thin-faced, he spent his off-work hours playing driveway basketball with his twin teenage sons, both of whom wanted nothing to do with law enforcement. Cashman had no problems with any of this. He wouldn't force working for the FBI on his worst enemy, as he was totally disgusted with the Liberal leanings of the Bureau since the current administration began its run. He longed for a return to holy Right Wing esteem for professional law enforcers like him.

"Enough with the bleeding hearts," he told Lockhart as they pulled through the border station. It was the morning following Ansel's arrest. "The President is a sorry Socialist."

Lockhart, as usual, stared out the window, ignoring the diatribe and focusing on a mental image of ice cream in a bowl a-swarm with cashews. Anything but politics; it made her want to throw up. But she couldn't tell that to her partner, so she stared out the window and nodded automatically at each pause in her partner's rant.

"Uh-huh," she said.

"Our perp looks like a dweeb," Cashman said after several minutes.

Lockhart gazed over at the dash-mounted photo.

"He looks like your basic WASP lawyer. Two hundred million missing? We're going to be all over CNN with this."

"I'm a FOX man, myself."

"Whatever."

"I can do news. I'm thinking of writing a book next year when I retire. Did I tell you that?"

She nodded haplessly. "Yeah, you did mention something about a book."

"I'm all over it," he said. "Picked up a new Macbook and I'm already making notes. Once I have my chapters laid out, I'll start fleshing it out. Gonna be hot, Lucky Lock!"

"Please don't call me that, Cash Crash. I've asked you how many times?"

"I like Cash Crash. It works for a pen name."

"Jeez, I should have known."

They pulled up alongside the Mexican border station.

"We'll park around back. I'll be good guy."

"I dibs bad."

"You're on."

They parked the SUV and went inside, flashing badges, which were ignored. The Mexicans knew all about the Fibbies, knew the two agents like two of their own, and were under strict orders to make whatever accommodations the FBI requested.

"You've got an Ansel Largent in back. We need to talk to him."

The Mexican Sergeant behind the desk nodded at the duty jailer.

"Bring Largent," the Sergeant ordered. "Green room is empty. Go inside and we bring him to you."

"Coolio," said Lockhart.

The agents switched on the light in the green room and got comfortable. Cashman removed the plastic wrap from a cinnamon toothpick and inserted the wood between his lips. He liked the casual look, the street look, when interviewing suspects. As the good guy, the prop relaxed the perps right off the bat, took away some of the sting of FBI-ness.

The jailer knocked once.

"Coming in!" he called.

"Enter," said Cashman.

Ansel Largent stepped into the room, handcuffed and waist-chained as if escape attempts were likely. He looked around the room, bobbing his head as he took it in.

"Sit," said Lockhart. She leaned back in her chair and assumed the hateful look of Bad Cop. Nothing Largent said would please her or wipe the look of disdain from her face. That was the role of the Bad Cop. She slouched and drummed her fingers on the table as Ansel was pushed down on a chair. His face was white and he looked to be in agony.

"Who are you?" he asked.

Both agents produced badges, flopping them on the tabletop.

"We're your worst fears," said Lockhart. "FBI."

"Actually, what agent Lockhart means, is we're here to help you avoid some unpleasantness, Mr. Largent," said Cashman with a smile. "We're just here to talk, that's all."

"You think I did it, don't you." It wasn't a question. "But I didn't. I swear it."

"We don't know who did it," Cashman said. "That's why we're here. We're only gathering facts at this point. In fact, when we're finished here you'll probably never see either of us again."

"Seriously?"

The agents traded a look and nodded. All for his benefit.

"Seriously," they said in unison.

"Unless you want to do the right thing," said Lockhart.

Ansel's eyes narrowed. "Right thing, as in--"

"Tell us where the money went. Your login, your bad," Lockhart said, a scowl on her face.

"We believe someone might have stolen your login and moved law firm trust funds, is what Agent Lockhart means," said Cashman. Good Guy. "Can you give us any help with that line of thinking? Anyone have access to your login?"

"One person might have," said Ansel. "But I want Thaddeus Murfee in here before we talk about that."

"That would be who?"

"Thaddeus Murfee. He's from Chicago, like yours truly."

"He has what to do with the missing money?"

"He has fifty thousand dollars of the firm's money on him right now. I'm not at liberty to tell you how he got it. But I think he's who you're looking for."

"What?" Again, in unison.

"It's a long story. Look, search him and see if I'm telling you the truth. He's the guy you're actually looking for."

Lockhart stood and went out of the room.

"Wait one," said Cashman. "Let us bring Mr. Murfee in here and see what we can find out."

Minutes later, Thaddeus was led, restrained, into the room. The jailers had manacled his wrists and waist-chained him. He blinked hard under the bright lights and looked around.

"Have a seat," said Cashman.

"All right. What is this chamber of horrors about?" Thaddeus said.

"FBI. We have some questions."

Thaddeus nodded and considered the situation.

"I don't think you're here about one lousy smuggled gun."

"We've been told you have a large sum of money on your person."

"That would be true."

Cashman and Lockhart traded a look. It was Lockhart's turn.

"Look, you're an attorney and you already know you don't have to talk to us. We get that. But right now things will go much easier on you if you just give it all up."

"Give it all up as in what, exactly?" He looked from face to face, perplexed.

"Mr. Largent says you have $50,000 of his firm's money in your shirt."

"Maybe I do. And?"

"And how did you come by it? No, let me ask it this way. What is your connection to the law firm of MacDevon Largent?"

"No connection. Not that I'm aware of."

"But you have $50,000 of their money, correct?"

"If you say so. I have $50,000 of Mr. Largent's money. He hired me to defend him."

"Defend him on what charges?" Cashman asked. He shifted the toothpick right to left, left to right. He looked friendly enough, but Thaddeus immediately recognized the ploy. Good Cop/Bad Cop. All right, he thought, let's get through this.

"Can't say. I was told his firm was missing, as he put it, megabucks."

"Did he say anything about how that happened?"

Thaddeus smiled at the Good Cop. "Now you know I can't discuss my client's statements to counsel. Sorry."

"So he did say something?" Bad Cop, frown, fiery eyes, angry mouth.

"Look, I don't know what you all think is going on here

and I don't know what crime you're investigating. But this much I do know: as we sit here, you know more about his situation than I do."

"So tell us what you do know," Lockhart said.

He saw no harm in that, so he went ahead.

"He came into the cell last night, we couldn't talk, so we whispered, and he hired me. I've got his money here in my shirt, but I'm not even sure why I have that. Is that what you wanted to know?"

"He says you took the money from the firm," Lockhart all but hissed.

"That's not exactly what I said," Ansel quickly inter-jected. "I said he has firm money."

"That's just it, Mr. Largent, is it your money he has or firm money?"

"Firm money. My money from the firm."

"Did he get it from the firm or did he get it from you."

"I can't answer that without counsel here."

"He says he is your counsel. And he's here."

"He's not my counsel and I never told you he was."

Thaddeus rattled his chains. "Hold on! Now wait a damn minute. You hired me last night to defend you. Because there were megabucks missing from the firm. Are you now saying that didn't happen?"

Ansel avoided eye contact. He fixed his point of vision on the far wall and said, evenly, "That didn't happen. You have money that belongs to the firm and you know how you came by it. I can't say any more than that for fear it may be used against me. I want an attorney."

"You little--"

"Hold on, Mr. Murfee. Maybe you should talk to counsel before you say anymore here. We don't want you making any statements that get suppressed by some judge because you didn't have counsel."

"I just want to clarify what happened!" Thaddeus had lost it and he was struggling. He knew better than to carry on, but he was at wit's end--no sleep, no food, arrest and crooked judge and now he had been duped by some lawyer out of Chicago? He had lost it, which slowly became clear as he went back over last night's conversation with Ansel Largent. He wanted to pinch himself because he felt like he was dreaming. It felt like running underwater.

"Mr. Murfee--" Largent was talking now--"I would strongly caution you against saying any more--one lawyer to another."

He threw his head back and rolled his eyes.

He had been had. The manipulative little bastard had worked him.

"Look, why don't we do this," Cashman said. "Why don't you come with us back to Chicago when we take Mr. Largent? We can all have a sit-down, everyone can lawyer-up, and we can work through this."

"There's nothing to work through," Thaddeus said. "You can leave me off the Chicago list, if you don't mind."

Lockhart smiled. "Oh, but we do mind, Mr. Murfee. We are going to need more information from you. With counsel present, of course."

"This can't be happening."

"Mind if we pat you down?"

"What for, you thinking I'm armed?"

"I'm thinking you're hiding fifty grand in your shirt. That would be evidence of the crime we're investigating."

"Yes, I mind."

"Well, stand up and lean against the wall anyway. Cashman is going to pat you down."

Thaddeus did as instructed.

The fifty thousand was located on second pat. It was extricated from his shirt and the rest of his frame was examined by Cashman. When he was done, he placed his large hand on Thaddeus' head and steered him back to his seat.

"Now. Thank you for your cooperation. We'll be leaving now. And you'll both be coming with us."

"Mexico has a hold on me," Thaddeus said.

"No," Cashman said coolly, pursing his lips and extracting the toothpick. "No, Mexico has no hold on you. Not anymore."

"Great. Case closed, then."

"Not exactly. From where I'm sitting, Mr. Murfee, the case is only just now open. We're only getting started here."

"Gentlemen, on your feet, please," said Lockhart.

"No one to say goodbye to back in the cell?" Cashman laughed. "Good. Let's walk outside and load up. It's going to be a long day for you gentlemen."

Thaddeus gave Ansel an enraged look. Ansel looked away, obediently falling in behind Lockhart and shadowing her.

But at the door Ansel stopped. One head bob. Two.

"Work with me here," he whispered sharply, then ducked on through.

"But--" Thaddeus managed, but the odd man was gone.

He never looked back.

Not once.

Chapter 22

Ansel explained Libby's disability to the agents. The FBI Chicago Office said she could join them on the Learjet.

They took off from Nogales at 12:20 p.m.

En route, the Largents, with Cashman and Lockhart, occupied the first four seats in the small jet. Thaddeus sat at the rear, nursing a Starbucks they had allowed him to purchase at a drive-through. He flipped through *In Flight*, a slick publication featuring leopard print bedclothes and radio controlled barbecue grills.

Three hours after wheels up they arrived at Chicago's Midway Airport, followed by a twenty minute commute to the Loop.

They arrived without handcuffs or other restraints and were shown upstairs in the Dirksen Federal Building.

Agents Cashman and Lockhart seated them in a windowless reception area--government decor--on an upper floor of the building where access from the elevator was by passkey.

"Wait here," Cashman told the threesome. "And don't try to leave. Security checks everyone out and you don't have free access."

"Are we under arrest?" Thaddeus asked. "Because if I'm not under arrest I'm out of here."

"You are being held as part of an ongoing investigation."

"Is that a Yes?"

"That's a neither. Put it this way. Security won't let you leave. Not until we talk."

"Then I'm being forcibly detained."

"Look, would you rather I arrested you and cuffed you to the wall?"

"No."

"Then stay put. Please. It will be easier on all of you."

"Well, I'm going home," Libby said. She stood up. "I haven't done anything wrong. I don't even know why we're here."

"Please. Sit down. They won't allow you to exit."

"Oh. Then I'll wait."

"Thank you."

Cashman walked away, shaking his head as he slipped a passkey into a security lock and disappeared behind yet another door.

"What do you make of it?" Ansel asked Thaddeus.

"What do I make of it? Of false arrest? Gee, I don't know, Ansel. What do you make of it?"

"If we work together on this, we all win."

"Ansh, what did you get me into," Libby whispered. She clubbed him on the ankles with her cane. "Bashtard.'

"I can't tell you, Libby. I don't want to make you an accessory."

"That's nonsense, Libby," Thaddeus said angrily. "You

126

and I have both been victimized by your husband. You're right to be pissed."

"I'm not pished. I'm hurt. He alwaysh does thish kind of stuff to me."

"Look at it this way," Ansel said. "Thaddeus, I sprung you out of a Mexican jail where you were going to spend the next thirty years of your life. I'd say you owe me big time."

Thaddeus watched the man's head bob and weave and he was reminded of a lightweight boxer seeking to avoid counterpunches.

"I was making bail today," Thaddeus replied. He leaned back and worked on his fingers and hands to increase circulation. "Sitting too damn long," he muttered.

Whereupon Cashman returned, and curled a finger at them. "You two gentlemen," he said, "come along. Mrs. Largent, please wait here."

"I knew it," she said. "When is someone going to let me go home and change thesh stupid clothes I've been wearing for three days? This is horrible and I'm tired and I need my medicine."

"We'll have you out of here and home by five o'clock. I promise. In fact, I'll drive you home myself, Mrs. Largent," Cashman responded. "On behalf of your husband, I'm sorry for all this."

Libby tapped her cane on the floor. "Five o'clock. Okay, I can do five o'clock. Is there a restroom?"

"Right through that door to the left of reception. Help yourself."

"Thank you."

"All right. Gentlemen, shall we?"

He waved his hand at the door he had used earlier. The two lawyers followed him.

They assembled inside a rectangular conference room with gray walls and a blaze-orange racing stripe where the wainscoting would have gone. A picture of the President occupied the end wall, and above that hung a drop-down screen.

Agents Cashman and Lockhart took the far side of the table.

Ansel was ahead of Thaddeus, so Thaddeus took the end chair, two empty seats away from Ansel. The need to distance himself from his co-whatever couldn't have been clearer.

Eight frosty bottles of Aquafina occupied the center of the table. Thaddeus slid two of them his way and killed one without stopping.

"Thirsty," he muttered, and wiped his mouth with the back of his hand. He set about nursing the second water.

"Let me cut to the chase," said Cashman.

"Please do," said Thaddeus.

"Mr. Murfee, Mr. Largent is the managing partner at MacDevon Largent here in Chicago. The firm keeps a trust account, of course. Access to the trust account was rigidly controlled. As of last Friday the only firm members who had access were JM MacDevon and your client, Ansel Largent."

"Hold it. Stop right there. He's not my client."

"He says he is."

"Well I say he isn't."

"Mr. Largent?"

"You FBI people took the fifty thousand I paid him. He can't just abandon me now. Not today, not here. I'd have to report that to the Bar Association."

"You said you didn't give it to him," said Cashman.

"It gets confusing," Ansel answered. He looked at the table top.

Thaddeus slumped back. "Fine. For today, for right here, I'm your lawyer. But as soon as we leave here you need to find someone else. I'm out. Let's just get through this."

"Fair enough," sniffed Ansel. His head bobbed twice to the right and his lips moved but nothing further was said.

"Back to the chase," said Cashman. "Sometime between last Friday and Sunday night the sum of $200 million was transferred out of the account. We have the network administrators telling us the exact time was 4:20 Sunday afternoon, but we have Forensics working that up. Double check."

"Then there's also the matter of a deceased partner with a bullet hole in her head," said Lockhart. "That's a local matter, but two very pushy detectives from Chicago PD would love to get their hands on you."

"That I know nothing about!" Ansel cried.

"Of course you don't," said Cashman. "Definitely not your style. Your style is more white-collar crime. So we'll focus on that. For now."

Lockhart unscrewed an Aquafina and took a long draw.

"The money transfer went to Zurich then bounced around the Caribbean and Europe before finally landing at Banco Nacionale in Mexico City. Now, who do we know in Mexico City, Mr. Largent? Who else was in on this?"

"Let me explain what really happened," said Ansel. "Should I say, counsel?"

All eyes were on Thaddeus. He gave Ansel a long, thoughtful answer:

"Look, you're a lawyer. You've studied criminal law even though that's not your specialty. I wouldn't ordinarily say this, but given your professional licensure, I would suggest you try to clear this up, *if*--and that's a big if--you know what happened and you weren't involved. If there is complicity then we'll end this conversation right now without another word being said. If I have to call Judge Douglas at the District Court and file *habeas corpus*, I will, and I'll get us out of here. But if you're comfortable with telling what you know, then please do. You're up."

Ansel nodded.

"I have a son," he said slowly. "His name is David. He's a junior partner in my firm."

"Should I be recording this?" Lockhart broke in.

"If you do there won't be another word said," Thaddeus smiled at her.

"Anyway, he's a junior partner. Last week I gave him temporary access to the trust fund. My login. He used it to make payment on a garden variety personal injury case he had settled. That's what we do, we defend accident cases and we take insurance company funds that are lodged with us and we pay them out to settle cases. That's how we happened to have $200 million in trust. Hundreds of settlements were pending and we were holding the insurance companies' reserves. So there was a lot there."

"Makes sense," said Cashman. "So who did what?"

"My son transferred the $200 million out Sunday afternoon. He left me a note on my laptop. He said the money was for a charity. I think I know where it went and why. I can tell you that it's no longer at Banco Nacionale but it is in Mexico, if we're not too late. If you will give me a week and restore me to the fly-list with TSA, I'll go to Mexico City and return with the money. That way the FDIC doesn't have to pay out on the loss and the net effect will be no crime committed by my David. It's win-win."

"How do we know you'll come back if we allow that?"

"You'll have to trust me."

"No can do. We already don't trust you."

"Then send me down there with someone and let them ball-and-chain me while I do my thing."

"Mr. Murfee? Would you take responsibility for your client and accompany him to Mexico?"

"Me? Why me?"

"Why not you? He's your client."

"Why don't *you* send someone," Thaddeus asked. "You snatch people anywhere in the world anymore. What's Mexico City to the FBI?"

"Ask the President of Mexico. He will deny any agreement with the FBI if anything goes public."

"So he doesn't want you there."

"Worse, we have orders from the President to stay the hell out of his country."

"But you came and got us from Mexico. How did that work?"

"We're good along the borders. Our border agents and the Mexican border agents work hand-in-glove, trading detainees back and forth. You were easy."

"But if we were in Mexico City we would be outside your jurisdiction. So back to Mr. Largent's question. How do you get us back if we decide to stay there?"

"Someone will be sent for you. Someone with a gun. Trust me, you wouldn't want to hide."

"So you let us go down there, just like that."

"Just like that. The government is willing to risk it in order to avoid paying a loss of $200 million dollars. That would create quite a wrinkle in an election year."

"I see. Now we're getting down to the real deal."

"Don't quote me."

"Don't tempt me."

"When would we go?"

"You can fly out tonight."

"How about in the morning?" said Thaddeus. "I need a night in a shower and my own bed."

"That will work. I'll expect you out of the United States by noon tomorrow. I'll expect you back in one week. If you're not back, all bets are off and we'll come after both of you."

"I have no dog in this fight," said Thaddeus. "Thanks for everything, but I'm not going."

"That's fine. Then get ready for your trip back to a certain Mexican jail. Trust me. This time there won't be a friendly judge about to set bail for you. And we'll do everything we can to help convict you down there."

"We'll leave before noon tomorrow."

"You're a reasonable man, Mr. Murfee. Thank you."

"What about my wife?" Ansel wanted to know.

"I'll drop her by home. You and Mr. Murfee can catch a cab and find a hotel. Your luggage is out in reception. You're free to go."

"Yes, free," said Thaddeus with a long sigh. "Free indeed."

Chapter 23

No 24/7 care could be found for Libby, so she made the trip to Mexico with them.

The flight from O'Hare to Mexico City ate up four hours and thirty minutes. A Taxi-Mex ride to the Presidente Mexico City Intercontinental Hotel took forty-five minutes through smoggy traffic snarls and two fender-benders. By 6:30 p.m. they were checking in at the hotel.

"We need to talk," Ansel told Thaddeus at check-in.

"Definitely."

"Let's spruce up and then meet in Alfredo Di Roma, 7:30."

"Italian? You're on."

An hour later they were shown to a window table where Ansel ordered a martini, Libby a Diet Coke, and Thaddeus coffee with cream. Drinks were served and relaxation settled over the three travelers.

"Why are we here?" Thaddeus said as he slowly stirred his coffee.

"In this restaurant? This hotel?"

"This city. Let's get down to the real deal, Ansel. Why don't you come clean with me about the missing dollars?"

"You heard what I told the FBI. David made off with the money."

Libby's hand abruptly stopped lifting the drink to her lips. "David? Are we off on that again?"

Thaddeus leaned back. He rubbed his chin and was silent for several minutes. Then, "And you think the money is where?"

"I think David used the money to buy freedom for a certain orphanage."

"Please, Anshel, can't we be finished with the David did thish or that?"

"Freedom?"

"Freedom from cartel influence. The drug cartels prey on children down here. David found a way around that."

"In one case."

"In one very small, isolated case."

"How many children are we talking about?"

"I've done some research. Near as I can tell there are approximately a hundred kids."

"That breaks down to two million a kid. Why am I not buying this?"

Ansel toyed with his drink. He stirred the skewered olives through the liquid. Libby glumly shook her head. She looked around at their surroundings, evidently choosing not to be a part of the conversation and saying as much with her body language.

Ansel said, "You're not buying it because you are by nature a suspicious person."

"Gee, you think? Suspicious of you? How could that possibly have happened?"

"The name of the orphanage is *In Loco Parentis*."

"Latin. In the place of a parent."

"Exactly."

"So we go there and they open their books to us?"

"Like I said, they don't have the money. The money went to the cartel."

"What cartel?"

"Tijuana."

"Then why are we in Mexico City? Why aren't we in Tijuana asking for your money back? Imagine how that would go over?"

"Because there's a chance--a slight chance--the transfer hasn't been made yet. I was on my way down here when they nabbed me at the border. All this delay makes our chances very slim. But it's the only chance we have."

"Banco Nacionale? That's our destination."

"It is."

"Have you ever been treated for any kind of mental disorder?" Libby asked with a sweet smile.

Thaddeus looked at Ansel as if a light bulb had been turned on. He was waiting to hear the answer.

Ansel's head jerked up and he bobbled the martini. "No. Yes. No."

"Okay...which is it?" said Thaddeus.

Libby scoffed and looked off.

"Yes and no."

"That yes would have been when?"

"Recently."

"Great. You want to tell me about that?"

"I take Risperdal for bipolar."

"No, you don't. Risperdal is an anti-psychotic. I'm enough of a criminal lawyer to know a little about my anti-psychotic meds, Ansel."

"No. Depakote and Risperdal."

"Depakote I buy. Risperdal for bipolar? You've got some kind of psychosis going on, friend. So why don't you come clean with me. What really happened to your firm's money? Libby, feel free to jump in here at any time."

Libby said, "Do you want to tell him or do I have to?"

Ansel dabbed his chin with a linen napkin.

Whereupon the waiter came for their order. Ansel ordered a veal dish and Thaddeus asked for the Chicken Alfredo. Libby opted for lasagna, heavy on the cheese. The waiter said he would be back with coffee, water, and a red dinner wine.

Thaddeus looked at Ansel. Ansel fidgeted with his drink.

"Like I said, why don't you come clean with me?"

"Yesh, Anshel, how about that?"

"Because I can't. It's not that I don't want to. It's that I can't."

"You mean can't or won't?"

"I can't. I honestly don't know what happened to the money."

"Well, the part about David. David took the money, correct?"

"That's my thinking. There was a message on my laptop."

"Damn, Ansel, we've got a moving target here. You're making this very difficult."

"Let me talk to Libby. She can help with this."

"I can help with shome of it," Libby agreed.

"I don't get the impression that Libby has the first clue what's going on here."

"I do and I don't," Libby said. "He should tell you himshelf. But you're not going to like what he hash to shay."

"Well, why don't we skip the part where I don't like what you say? Why don't you just tell me what you know?"

Tears came into Ansel's eyes. Within a minute his cheeks were damp.

Thaddeus sipped his coffee and looked away. He was close. Very close.

"Tell me what you do know."

Libby slapped the table with an open hand. "David ish dead."

"What?"

"David died when he wash eleven. Except sometimes Anshel forgets that."

"What!"

Ansel nodded violently. "She keeps saying that."

"So--let me see if I'm following this. David didn't take the money?"

"No. David ish dead."

"Then who--"

Libby flung back in her seat, exasperated. "Who took the trust funds? Maybe he took them."

"What did you do with them?"

"Good luck with that," Libby said.

Ansel folded his hands and rubbed his thumbs together. "That is the two hundred million dollar question. I really don't know."

"This--this--" Thaddeus had no words. He was incredulous.

"I know. I know. It's not an easy case."

"Well--is there a chance you will remember?"

"He won't remember what he had for supper by bedtime," Libby said. She shook her head with no small disgust and yet you could see a light of pity in her eyes as well.

"No. I've tried to remember. If I don't know what happened right now, it won't suddenly clear up on down the road. It doesn't work like that."

"So you had a psychotic episode and did some things and now you don't know what you did. Is that about it?"

Ansel nodded. "Probably."

"Damn, Ansel."

"I know."

"How could the firm give you access to its trust account?"

"They don't know. They know I'm sick, but they think it's my heart. I've let them think that, to account for my hospitalizations. Pacemaker maintenance, I tell them."

"We have shkeletons in the Largent closhet. Thatsh ash good ash it gets."

"Damn, Ansel."

Ansel looked aggrieved by his lesser but larcenous self. "So you have me, a client who maybe took a whole bunch of money and now he doesn't know what he did with it. Am I guilty of a crime?"

"That's a damn good question. There's probably a mix of legal insanity and a dose of embezzlement. Some of both. I don't know without doing some reading. Honestly, I've never had this case before. Insanity, yes. Temporary insanity, yes. Larceny--theft, burglary, armed robbery, yes. But both at once? Not so good there. Unstudied."

"So what should I do?"

"Find the money and get it back to your partners. That's first."

"If we can find the money and return it, is it still a crime?"

"I'm hungry, ravenous," Libby said. Thaddeus saw how this kind of stuff was old hat to her. She only wanted food.

"If I return it does that make the whole thing go away?"

"Good question. It certainly would be arguable. I can't promise anything, but if the money's returned, it works a lot better for you. Maybe a year or two behind bars instead of the rest of your life. Maybe a state prosecution instead of a federal one. Federal sentencing guidelines make you a roommate candidate for Bernard Madoff. State sentencing and prosecution you're out in a year. Maybe no jail at all, given your mental incapacity."

"So help me. Help me find it."

"Yesh, help him find it sho I can go home to my own bed."

"Damn, Ansel," Thaddeus muttered. He shook his head. He sipped his coffee.

Ansel winced.

"Would you quit saying that?"

"I can't. I'm astonished. I don't have words. Just when I thought I'd heard it all, now this. I don't even know where to begin."

"Well, we begin in Zurich."

"Then why are we here?"

"I don't know. Because I didn't know what else to say to the Fibbies."

"So what else haven't you told me? Let's get all that minor kind of stuff out on the table right here, right now."

"Nothing. You have it all."

"David's dead, you're sure of that."

"David ish dead."

"Listen to her."

"And you took the money like you were in a blackout."

"That's an educated guess."

"Bear with me. I'm struggling here."

"Here it comesh!" cried Libby. "I love lashagna. I wouldn't eat veal on a dare. Too cruel."

"Yes," said Thaddeus, "we don't want cruel, do we?"

Ansel lifted his new red wine. "To Zurich," he said.

Chapter 24

They were 40,000 feet over the Atlantic when Ansel asked the woman sitting beside Thaddeus if she would trade with him. She was happy to oblige and when she had gathered up purse, pillow, and carry-on and moved up beside Libby, Ansel settled in beside Thaddeus. Libby turned to her and they struck up a conversation so everyone seemed happy.

At least for the moment.

"There's something else bothering me," Ansel told Thaddeus.

Thaddeus leaned back against the seat and shut his eyes.

"Suzanne Fairmont was a young, tough litigator in our office."

"Okay."

"She was six years out of Cornell Law, married, one small child, and a terror around the criminal courts. She had never lost a trial, not even a speeding ticket. As you can guess, her services were in great demand, especially around

Chicago, where the latest headline crime is as fresh as today's bagels."

"Okay."

Ansel lowered the tray on the seat back. He removed his gold watch and placed it on the tray and began rubbing his wrist.

"Okay. She had just announced her run for District Attorney. Seems she had been pursued by several civic organizations to come over to the light and start putting bad guys away instead of turning them loose."

"Okay."

"She was found dead in her office last week."

"At your law firm?"

"My law firm. Two doors down from mine. Dead, and they said the wound wasn't self-inflicted."

"And you're telling me this because?"

Ansel returned the watch to his wrist. 'I just thought you should know. You're my lawyer."

"Hold on. Wait a minute, Ansel. Are you telling me you had something to do with Ms. Fairmont's death?"

Ansel turned white. "That's just it. I don't know. Honestly I would deny it all day and all night. But my reality isn't always the reality everyone else operates in. You follow me?"

"I think so. Do you have any kind of clue you might be involved in that? Did you own a gun?"

"No guns. I'm an insurance lawyer. We won't insure Smith & Wesson, Glock, Colt, any of them. As an industry we hate guns. No, I didn't have a gun."

"And she died by gunshot?"

"What little I know--yes, she died from a gunshot to the head."

"Damn, Ansel."

"So what do we do?"

"For one thing, you don't talk to the cops. You haven't spoken to the police have you?"

"No, I cleared out of the office so that wouldn't happen."

"Were you afraid of what you might say?"

"I was afraid of what I don't know. It's hard being me, Thad. When I'm up on my meds, it's all good. But if I miss or if I get stressed out, I can miss things."

"That's a nice way of putting it. I would have said you have psychotic episodes and probably shouldn't be practicing law. We have a different slant on it, you and I."

"Maybe you're right."

"We can cross that bridge later. Do you have any kind of retirement funds?"

"Why?"

"Because you might find yourself suddenly retired, if you don't wind up in jail first."

"401k. Plus a disability policy."

"You? Some carrier was actually willing to insure you against disability? Did you lie on the application?"

"I'm in the industry. We take care of each other."

"Good grief. I was shot and now *I* can't even get disability insurance. You're a miracle."

"We try."

Chapter 25

When the Chicago Police Department assigned detectives to high profile murders, one team always at the top of the list was O'Connor and Wainwright.

Jake O'Connor was twelve months shy of retiring from Chicago PD, having worked his way up to Lieutenant of Detectives. On Gold Watch Day he would have made chief.

His partner, Lucinda Wainwright, was an Olympic weight lifter with 2016 Rio aspirations.

Jake was tall, lithe, and a graduate of the University of Illinois-Chicago with a master's in forensic science.

Lucinda--who preferred "Lucinda," never "Lucy"--Lucinda was a graduate of Eastern Illinois University just a few years behind her idol Tony Romo of the Dallas Cowboys. Like her superstar hero, Lucinda had found her calling her freshman year. Except hers wasn't football, it was weight-lifting, or lifting as it was known to its adherents. She was muscular, of course, with legs like oak trees, with greatly exaggerated quadriceps muscles, which gave her tremendous lifting power. When Lucinda wasn't working out she supported herself as a homicide detective with CPD. When Jake wasn't writing a scholarly article on homicide CSI techniques, he supported himself (and wife and four children) as a homicide detective with CPD. Jake had seniority over Lucinda, so he ran the show.

In a way, then, the detectives had something in common with the homicide victim named Suzanne Fairmont. All were especially accomplished at their professional calling.

Suzanne, however, was much younger than the two detectives that would investigate her death by gunshot, for she was only twenty-nine when she died.

Many of the old sages who wrote features for the *Tribune* and *Sun-Times* allowed as how Suzanne was too young for the job of DA. She needed another ten years in the ring, they opined over the months leading up to her death. She was too green, too ambitious. But beyond that, she was every precinct committee person's dream: youthful, vivacious, incredible pedigree, high profile accomplishments.

So when she turned up dead that snowy Chicago morning, the orbits of the three shining stars suddenly closed and coalesced.

Right away, Jake knew the case was going to be difficult. No murder weapon and no known enemies. In fact, the usual enemies of law enforcement were known to worship at her feet. After all, to a man--or woman--they all owed their freedom to the lawyering skills possessed by Suzanne. None of them would have a motive to harm her. In fact, their motives were the exact opposite: they would all have a motive to see her live a long and safe life. Especially so, since her clients weren't the type to shut it all down with the commission and narrow escape from just one crime. They were repeat offenders, each one of them. Recidivists, Jake's thick books called them, sociopaths who could be counted on for repeating legal fees generated by repeating crimes and arrests. The denizens every successful criminal lawyer cultivates.

But one thing different about Suzanne's criminal law practice was picked up on early in the investigation. Credit Lucinda with sniffing it out first: all of Suzanne's clients over the last twelve months were white collar. With her increased notoriety as the go-to criminal lawyer in Cook County had come a seismic shift in the type of crime she was increasingly called to defend: embezzlements, insider trading, income tax evasion, undisclosed offshore accounts, bribery, credit card fraud--all of the paper stuff, the stuff that didn't require a gun or a battered head or a stolen vehicle. Her clientele over the last year had decidedly shifted away from violence, theft, and mayhem, and more toward the behind-the-scenes stuff of white collar ignominy. The criminals over the first half of her career were found in the the ghettos and dark places. The criminals over the most recent half of her career were found at the county club.

Which gave the two detectives fits, when Lucinda brought it to Jake's attention.

"This chick," said Lucinda over coffee in the detectives' day room, "wasn't about the kind of bad guys we usually get."

"How so?"

"I've been over the thirty-six files she opened over the last fourteen months. There's not a murderer, wife-beater, child molester, rapist, or grand-theft-auto perp among them. They're all business people, executives, tax preparers, and accountants. None of whom, you wouldn't think, would resort to a gun to kill their lawyer. Your usual dickheads with guns and bludgeons weren't in her file drawers."

"So we're looking for someone who maybe wasn't a client?" said Jake. "Interesting."

"How about a family member?" asked Lucinda. "I'm thinking we start with the husband. Maybe look for rejected boyfriends."

"She was married to a linebacker on the Bears practice squad. Mr. Violence, his teammates call him. But I've been all over him. Airtight alibi: he was home with their kid Sunday night while Suzanne played catch-up at the office."

"Can he prove that?"

"It gets better. Suzanne's parents were there with him. They'd had dinner and watched movies until eleven o'clock. Suzanne was expected home at nine. But it wasn't unlike her to stay late. That's what her family thought, so the parents leave around eleven-thirty and hubby falls asleep on the couch, waiting for her. He comes to next morning and that's when he makes the call and our maintenance man opens her office door and finds her dead."

"Okay, so what about the maintenance guy?"

"Can you think of any motive he might have to shoot her dead?"

"Likely not," said Lucinda. She flexed her huge right forearm and admired the muscle that popped up. "So the husband is airtight, the janitor ain't got motive. That leaves--"

"That leaves the law partners."

"Just what I was about to say."

"Top or bottom?" Jake asked.

"How about you take top and I start at the bottom."

"Meet in the middle?"

"So be it."

"Or should we team up on them?" Jake had paused as

he was packing up his investigative file. Maybe tag-team would come off better.

"They're lawyers. Good guy-bad guy ain't gonna work with them."

"Agreed."

"Let's get started. Who's first up?" said Lucinda.

"Got the firm diagram right here. Top attorney is Ansel Largent, Managing Partner."

"He was the guy supposed to give us a statement the first morning."

"Who disappeared; and hasn't been found since."

"Red flag."

"Big red flag."

"So where is he, best guess?"

"I wouldn't think he would flee. That would be too obvious."

"I'll get on that," Lucinda said.

"One other thing you need to know."

"What's that?"

He tossed her two pages stapled together.

"These are the security log, bank building ins and outs, law firm ins and outs."

"What do they tell us?"

"That your new friend, Ansel Largent, entered the bank just after eight p.m. the night of the homicide. M.E. says she was shot between nine and eleven."

"Well, well. So now we know."

"We know something else, too," Jake said.

"What's that?"

He tossed her two more stapled sheets.

"Reproductions from the security cams for the visitor who showed up next."

"What's her name?"

"Well, she had a security key."

"Name?"

"Elizabeth Largent."

"Probably Ansel Largent's wife."

"The plot thickens."

"One of them shot Ms. Fairmont—that's my prediction."

"We know where I need to start."

"Maybe we should work these two separately? You take her, I take him?"

"On second thought, let's do that."

Chapter 26

There was a layover and change of planes in Frankfurt, where they traded the Boeing 747 for an Airbus A319. From there they were in the air less than an hour to Zurich.

The Zurich outside air was stuck at -15°C when the Lufthansa flight touched down. But a warming trend was expected.

By the next morning it was 5°C when Thaddeus went for his run.

The sky was slate gray and overcast, with no sign of the sun.

Thaddeus knew a little about Zurich and remembered that cold nights usually brought sunshiny days, which was exactly what they found after breakfast when Thaddeus and Ansel caught a cab to the first bank where the purloined funds had been wired. The sun was out, traffic was dense but polite in allowing cars to blink and change lanes, and flowed smoothly to the banking district.

They climbed out of the cab at Bank Royale & Co. on

passed a note of paper to the Interpol agent. He had written the note at the suggestion of the woman out front, while they were waiting. "Except I don't have the time of the transfer. Approximate only, sometime between noon and nine p.m."

The diminutive man had already turned to one of three computer screens that flanked him and was busily typing and clicking away.

Ansel looked at Thaddeus and winked.

Thaddeus simply stared at him. He wondered whether the FBI no-fly would still be in effect when they tried to fly to wherever this lead took them. Time would tell.

So far, they had been lucky. The no-fly had been removed before they left Chicago with the agency's blessing and flew to Mexico City. There had been no time limit stated and whether it remained lifted due to oversight or planning, Thaddeus wasn't sure. In fact, he wasn't sure of much of anything, and guessed that about half the time they moved about they were being followed by agents. Then again, he thought maybe he was just being paranoid. But knowing the FBI and its unlimited resources as he knew them, a tail was probably to be expected.

Finally the agent looked up. He removed his round spectacles and began to polish them with a pocket square. His lips moved as he held up the lenses and observed them in the window light. Then he resettled them on his nose, looped the curves behind his ears, and folded his hands.

"Well," he said. "I am printing out some information for you."

"Well, what about my money? Did you trace it?" Ansel said in a rush.

"I did."

"And?"

"Well, your money was wired out of Chicago. The records say the account was accessed and the money transfer made by the credentials of one Ansel Largent."

"That would be me."

"Are you telling me you didn't wire the money?"

Ansel gave Thaddeus a helpless look.

"My client," Thaddeus began slowly, "suffers from a thought disorder where sometimes--"

"Sometimes I don't remember things," Ansel said, to finish the sentence.

"So you don't remember making the transfer? Did someone else have access to your login and account credentials?"

"Yes. No."

"He originally thought it was his son."

"That would seem to make sense."

"Except his son is deceased."

"Well--"

"Sometimes I imagine him still alive. In my imagination he has aged and grown up. He has attended law school and now works with me in my law firm."

"Interesting. Well, if there's nothing more--"

Clearly the agent was uncomfortable with this and Thaddeus could see he suspected a ruse being tried.

"No," said Thaddeus. "The son is deceased and my client--imagines things."

"A mental case."

"Those are your words, Mr. Georg," said Thaddeus. "We have yet to speak to his doctors about all this. In fact, it's only just lately, in the last couple of days, come to light."

Without a word, the agent turned in his chair to the soundless laser jet at his elbow. He extracted a single sheet of paper, print on one side only.

"Here's your data. I wish you both the best."

Thaddeus scanned the printout.

"So, last stop Mexico City?"

"Yes. From there we lose it. The next transfer is fragmented into a thousand recipients. How that was done, I can only guess. Which of them is the correct one, I would have no way of knowing. It's a new technology that does that. To date our own systems administrators haven't come up with a way around it."

"You're telling us my money went to a thousand different recipients?"

"Please. Read what is said."

Thaddeus nodded. "It says the money was wired to a thousand different recipient banks. But you're telling us this was done to confuse, that actually only one of these banks received the funds."

"Exactly."

"And this name at the bottom. Enrico Rodriguez. Clarify, please."

"Mr. Rodriguez is a vice-president at Banco Nacionale. He authorized the wire fragment."

"He sent the wire that put my money in a thousand banks?"

"He sent the wire that makes it look like your money went to a thousand banks. Actually it went to only one of those."

"Can we contact them to find out which one is the real one?"

"We could. The problem is, your money will no longer be there and, worse, your money's packet data will have been washed. This is what it means to wash money by wire transfer. It means the packet data is removed so your money can no longer send us a message and tell us where it has gone."

"So, I'm just out."

"Probably."

"Unless we can get it out of this Enrico Rodriguez," said Thaddeus. "Am I right?"

"That would be correct. Even then, he might not have the answer himself. There was a party on the receiving end who received the funds. Mr. Rodriguez might not even know the identity of this person. He might have simply been told to make such and such a wire and that wire triggered the fragment. Either he's in on it or he's not. You will have to speak with him."

"At Banco Nacionale in Mexico City."

"Precisely. Assuming he's still there. And assuming that's still his name. Which assumes that was ever his name. Now, gentlemen, I must get on with my day. So, if you will excuse me?"

"Thank you," said Ansel, and stood up.

"Yes, many thanks," said Thaddeus.

Together they hurried out of the office, Thaddeus folding the printout and placing it in an inner pocket.

Outside, they set about flagging a cab.

"So, we came all the way here just to find out we were in the right place when we were back there."

"Looks that way," said Thaddeus back over his shoulder, as he waved at a passing cab.

"So, back to Mexico City."

"I'm afraid so."

The young lawyer knew the FBI wouldn't take its hands off either of them until it got the money back. He would be harassed and harried by them until then. They might even send him back to that stinking Mexican jail if he tried to bow out now. So--the deal was made with the devil. He would stay in, he would continue to help Ansel, until that was no longer possible. They couldn't force him to do the impossible if the trail ran out.

He finally got a cab to pull over.

That was as good as it was going to get that day, a win in the cab wars.

Ansel chatted about this and that all the way back to the hotel.

Thaddeus stared out the window. The sun had returned to Zurich and it had warmed up another twenty degrees.

It was going to be a great day for a nap until it was time to go to the airport. He would call Katy and check in, spend a moment listening to his two daughters' reports, and then sleep.

The sleep of the innocent.

The sleep of the foolhardy.

He kicked himself for the ten-thousandth time. Damn fool, smuggling a gun into Mexico in the first place. What had he been thinking?

What could go wrong? That's what he had been thinking.

Well, welcome to reality.

He was just about to find out how really bad it could get, and he knew this deep down. Two hundred million dollars floating around Mexico was not a good place to begin. There would be some very bad people involved in this next part.

Some very bad people.

Chapter 27

Paul Georg ate lunch solo. There were five star restaurants within walking distance of the bank in Zurich. When he desired company he would take his lunch with him to the bank and eat in the employees' lunch room. But the five stars—those were too wonderful to share.

The day of Thaddeus and Ansel's visit he had brought his lunch with him. But after they left his office he informed the operators that he would be out for lunch. Until two o'clock.

Three blocks away, on Bahnhofstrasse, was a French restaurant where he was led to a booth enclosed on three sides.

He dialed the mobile and waited. There was a nine hour time difference between Zurich and Tijuana, but Georg didn't concern himself with that. He knew the man on the other end of the call to that particular number would answer anytime, day or night.

Juan Carlos Hermeda Ordañez answered on the second ring.

"Juan Carlos, Paul Georg."

"Si."

"They were here."

"You sent them where?"

"Mexico City. In search of Enrico."

"Follow them. We will switch off in Mexico City."

"Consider it done."

"We have also sent the present to your account at Credit Suisse."

"I checked. Thank you."

"Ten percent."

"I checked. It is correct."

"Destroy your phone."

"It will be done."

"Until next time."

"Until then."

Before destroying the phone, however, he did place one more call.

They had to be followed.

With one call he made that happen.

Chapter 28

None of the partners were surprised when the Chicago PD detectives O'Connor and Wainwright showed up at the offices of MacDevon Largent with a search warrant for the law office of Ansel Largent.

Melinda thought it rude and a huge time sink, but even at that, she wasn't surprised by the search. After all, Ansel had virtually disappeared from the face of the earth. He hadn't called in, there was no one at his home, and his cell phone went unanswered.

Jake O'Connor worked his security resources at Midway and O'Hare airports and located the passenger manifest with Ansel and Libby included, destination Mexico City.

Naturally, then, Chicago PD concluded he must have had something to hide and that he was on the run. Of course the cops would want to take apart his office. Who could really blame them?

Rumors of Ansel's complicity in both the embezzlement and the Suzanne Fairmont shooting raged like wildfire. One enterprising rookie lawyer named Shel Agenstein even started a pool. Odds on Ansel's complicity in both the embezzlement and the shooting were running eight to one, while complicity in only one crime was running three to one. Even Melinda laid down a bet on the sheet that circulated inauspiciously around the firm. Trouble was, according to Agenstein, even some of the junior grade partners were wagering--probably ignoring the real threat of ejection from the firm if a senior partner learned of it. And so, the names of the players were removed from the sheet and numbers inserted in their place. Only Agenstein had the key connecting names to numbers and he was sworn to secrecy by his boss, a tax court litigator who kept three Shel Agenstein's hopping with work.

Introduction of the news of the search warrant into the flow of gossip surrounding the underground wagering scheme heated things up to boiling. Would the search turn up anything? New bets were laid down. Shel Agenstein took in $3500 in new money. He found himself overwhelmed with emails and calls--all from people in the firm.

The two plainclothes officers and three uniforms swept into Ansel's office at 8:32 a.m. and didn't leave until 2:25 that afternoon. They worked until eleven and they were extraordinarily close-mouthed about their progress in turning up any kind of evidence when Melinda took their lunch orders for Little Brown Bag, downstairs in the building.

Melinda heard bags rattle and cop talk through Ansel's intercom, which she had activated. More than anything else they were looking for a gun or evidence of a gun, even gun magazines or NRA newsletters--anything that might suggest Ansel possessed a firearm. When that turned up nothing by noon, they switched gears and a forensics expert in computers began disassembling the computer and removing the hard drive. Again, it was a complete fishing expedition but one that was expected by the firm's Curious George's, who repeatedly stopped by and asked Melinda, "Anything?"

Then she heard a cry both over the intercom and through the closed door.

"Got it! Bring an evidence bag!"

"Gun!" said a second voice.

"Someone call a grand jury," shouted a third.

"Settle down," said a command voice, and Melinda was sure it was Jake O'Connor speaking, for it was stern and tough, like Jake. "We got us a shooter, here, Wain-o," he said to Detective Wainwright. She said something in reply but it was indiscernible.

Soon a photographer entered the outer office and let herself into Ansel's inner sanctum. Orders were given and, Melinda presumed, pictures were snapped. Lots of pictures, because the door didn't open again for another thirty minutes. This time from the inside.

"Now," O'Connor said to Melinda, as he settled himself into a reception chair in the outer office, "I need you," pointing at her with two fingers, "to help me find your boss. Now I know you'd do anything in the world to protect the man. I get that, and I don't blame you. But this thing has taken on a new life. We found a gun in your boss's office, a revolver. We believe it's the same caliber gun as shot Suzanne Fairmont. I'll be very surprised if it's not the same gun. That will take us three days to determine. The crime lab is swamped, but this is a homicide investigation and they'll move it to the head of the line. Not to mention, but I've got some drag down there anyway."

"Oh."

"So I need you to think real hard. Do you know where he might be in Mexico City?"

"Don't you talk to the FBI?"

"Us? No, we don't. They're working on a theft case, anyway. We'd have no reason to speak to them."

"Well they told me they had sent Ansel--Mr. Largent--to Mexico City on business."

"Really? How did you find this out?"

"I called their office and asked them."

"Who did you talk to down there?"

"Special Agent Freyer Smothers."

"You're sure that's who?"

"Of course. I made him spell it and I wrote it all down."

"Let me see that, please."

Melinda handed the detective the spiral pad on which she had made the note. He nodded and handed it back.

"Roger that. You called them."

"Mr. Largent had court and hearings and depositions and meetings. I had to clear his calendar, but the judges always need a date certain to continue to. So I needed to know where he'd gone so I knew how long to continue."

"I could use a girl like you in my office."

"Woman, thank you. And I wouldn't leave here for anything. Besides, you couldn't afford me."

"You're probably right at that," the cop said with a smile. He laughed. Melinda didn't laugh with him. She knew it was all an act. An act to engender camaraderie. She wasn't about to fall for that. Besides, she was carrying Ansel's child. She needed him free.

"So you should be talking to Agent Smothers. He's the one with the inside track on this."

O'Connor nodded heavily. "I see that. Thank you, ma'am."

"I hope I was some help."

"You were, you were."

"Are you taking any of Ansel's stuff from his office? Just so I can tell him when he comes back?"

"He can obtain a return of the search warrant. That's official. But just between you and me we're only taking his gun and his hard drive."

"How do you know it's his gun?"

O'Connor touched the side of his head. "That's why they call us detectives."

With that he turned and departed, taking his entourage with him.

When the door had closed behind them, she removed her mobile from her purse and hit 4--the speed dial for Ansel's mobile.

"Melinda," he said. "This isn't a good time."

She was stubborn. "Then make it a good time. The police were here and they found a gun in your office."

"What?" he was standing at his hotel window, just about to climb into bed. The flight from Zurich had taken forever and his stomach was burning. Too much time in the air, lousy food, and now Libby was giving him the evil eye.

"What?" asked Libby. "Whoosh that?"

He held the cell against his bare leg. "Melinda. Business. I'll go in the bathroom so you can get to sleep."

He went into the bathroom and closed the door.

"Now start over. What's this about a gun?"

"They came here with a search warrant. I had to let them in."

"Sure, sure."

"They were in your office from eight-thirty until after two. They found a gun and took it with them. And your computer hard drive."

"Big whoopee on the hard drive. That monstrosity of a computer hasn't been turned on in two years. I use my laptop."

"I know. They didn't ask."

"And a gun? One thing's for sure, it won't have my fingerprints on it."

"You're sure?"

He realized the bathroom tiles were icy on his bare feet. Who would have thought Mexico City ever got cold? He pulled his legs up and crossed them. Leaning back against the toilet tank, he said, "Of course I'm sure. I don't know the first thing about guns."

"You're sure there's not some part of you that does?"

"Please, let's not go there."

"Well, I'm just saying. We all know how you are."

"And how's that?"

"The multiple personality thing."

"It's not MPD. It's psychosis and it's one hundred percent preventable with my meds. Which I take religiously."

"Sorry. That was mean of me."

"You're damn right it was. Imagine saying something like that to the man you supposedly are in love with."

"Tell me."

"Tell you I love you? You know I do."

A soft rap on the bathroom door.

"You love who, Ansh? Melinda? Tell her I love her too, pleash."

"Libby says to tell you she loves you too. Goodbye now."

"Bye, Anse."

He returned to the bedroom, unable to look his wife in the eye.

She fixed her gaze on him, however, and wouldn't quit

staring even after he'd turned off the lights and climbed into bed. Then she turned her back to him and he could feel the bed shake with her soft crying.

There must be some way out of here.

The words to an old Dylan song.

The writer had had great psychic powers to know how that would fit me like a glove one day, he thought as he drifted off.

There must be some way out of here.

Chapter 29

Ignacio Solon--a small man with a very small reputation--was the son of a Spanish racketeer. Ignacio immigrated to Mexico with his parents when he was six. He never felt at home in Mexico, why, he couldn't say. Maybe it was because of the language differences, Castilian Spanish and Mexican being uneven, much like UK English and American English. Or maybe it was a feeling imparted to him by his parents. But he was standoffish growing up and even more so as an adult. Which made his job as a gun-for-hire that much easier: feeling no empathy with the Mexicans against whom he waged war when paid by the Cartel to do so.

At any given moment he might be working on a murder contract on his own, one-on-one on the target, or he might be heading up a gang of as many as thirty men about to invade a local police station and kill off everything in uniform. The cartels paid him what he asked and he asked a lot. So he lived outside Mexico City on a *finca*, a horse ranch of one-hundred-and-fifty hectares, mostly grassland, scrub oak, and gun ranges. Double chain-link fencing surrounded the nearly 400 acres, and roving guards on horseback patrolled night and day.

The call to arms came from Juan Carlos Hermeda Ordañez just after midnight. A man and two companions were coming to the city. They were in search of something they had lost and wanted it back. Juan Carlos was going to make sure they didn't get it back. He needed Ignacio to guarantee it.

"Wait until the right moment, then go after the young man. His name is Thaddeus Murfee and he is the one to be reckoned with. The old man and his wife mean nothing. They are no threat. Leave them alone and they will wither and blow away, if you take out the young one."

"How much?"

"One hundred thousand. It has already been wired to your account."

"That works. Anything else?"

"He is looking for me. He doesn't know my name and must not find it out. If he does he will come after me. Your job is to make sure that does not happen."

"Disposal?"

"Doesn't matter. Leave him where you kill him. He's American so he'll be shipped back to the States anyway. Just be sure there's nothing on him that would lead anyone to me."

"Of course, JC."

"When will you have this done?"

"Give me the details about this man. He will be gone within hours."

"Excellent. Here's what we know about him."

The description and background and hotel reservations followed. By the time he ended the call, Ignacio Solon knew all he needed to know about the American. He was just another target.

He would be unarmed.

It would be an easy take-down.

———

IT WAS AN UNEASY FEELING, ambiguous and amorphous, but it had settled down around him as they were walking through the Mexico City airport. Something was not quite right. He went back over the past twenty-four hours. The only one they had informed of their quest was Georg at the bank. Would he have turned on them? Thaddeus wondered.

Maybe yes, maybe no.

But the whole point was, he couldn't be trusted.

Thaddeus shot a look behind as they pulled their suitcases through the crush of people. How would he know in such a crowded place? He shivered as he imagined the feel of a knife blade sliding between his ribs as he fell among the crowd. Would they part way and step around him? Would anyone stop to help? He almost stopped and turned around to go the other way and see if anyone turned with him.

But he knew there were just too many people to catch it all. His only hope was to escape through the crowd and get to the sidewalk outside where he could defend himself.

More than ever, he wished for a gun. He had been right to bring one in the car. But it was gone now and all he had were his hands. He knew very little about hand-to-hand fighting and would probably go down easily. He increased his walking speed and Ansel tugged at his elbow.

"Slow down, Thad. Libby can't keep up with this."

He looked around and smiled at Libby. Her look of

consternation pulled him up short and he slowed way down. He moved beside her. "Sorry," he shouted over the crowd, "I wasn't thinking."

"Ish okay. I'm good."

"All right, then."

They made it outside to the sidewalk and were greeted with a long line of waiting taxis. Quickly Thaddeus herded them into the closest yellow cab and they swerved away into airport traffic.

They headed downtown where the corporate office of BN was located.

Unnoticed was the leathered rider on the black BMW motorcycle that pulled in behind them. It had been waiting curbside for them to appear.

The bike swerved to the next lane when the rider saw the young lawyer turn his head and look out the rear window of the cab. The rider looked straight ahead through the gray faceplate and made himself seem anything but interested in the cab or its occupants. The young lawyer turned back around and the biker pulled up closer, at one point coming close enough to the cab that the rider could have reached across and touched it, had he wanted.

But he didn't. This was not the place for an attack. That opportunity would come soon, maybe in the next hour. He twisted the accelerator and backed off thirty meters. He moved another traffic lane further away. Now there were cars between him and the cab. He faded into the flow and the next time the lawyer turned around he noticed nothing unusual.

THADDEUS AND ANSEL bribed a junior vice-president at Banco Nacionale and discovered that the money had gone from Mexico City to Hung Kai Bank & Holding, Ltd in Hong Kong. They were told the bank was a dropping-off point for the Tijuana Cartel in its money-laundering activities. The Mexican authorities were all in the know about this and the Cartel's use of the bank was legendary, for the amounts they had run through there. Thaddeus thanked the VP and gave Ansel a hard look.

"What?" asked Ansel.

"This isn't making this any easier to get your money back."

"What do we do? Fly to Hong Kong and confront that bank?"

"No. We have to go to the movers and shakers, the cartel itself."

"That's a good way to get your head cut off, from all I read."

"True. But what if we had something of theirs of value? What if we had something they wanted back? We need to find Hermano Sanchez. We need to find out what he knows about the cartel. To do that, we're going to need Burton."

"And Burton is who?"

"A guy I met in jail."

"Not the teenager with acne and the wispy little beard?"

"That's our guy. His father crossed cattle out of Mexico and Burton knows his way around. Unless you've got a better idea."

"How about we go find a private investigator and buy some info."

"And risk tipping them off that someone's asking questions? I don't think so."

Outside the bank, in the parking lot, Libby was waiting in the back seat of the rental car.

"What took sho long?"

"We were talking to a man about a horse." Her husband looked dismayed and was taking it out on her.

"What?"

"We're headed back to the border holding jail. We need to find a guy, Libby," Thaddeus told her. "We're going to be in Nogales for a couple of days. If you want, we can drop you at the hotel and you can sunbathe by the pool and do some shopping."

"I want. Letsh go."

Chapter 30

They flew to Nogales and rented a car. Behind them in line stood Ignacio Solon. He was dressed in gray slacks, navy button-down shirt, and heavy black shoes. It was cold so a fringed leather coat completed the getup. He looked more like an itinerant salesman of case goods than a hit man, which was exactly how he wanted it.

He watched as Thaddeus signed the rental agreement, initialed in four places, and his credit card was processed.

When Thaddeus, Ansel and Libby headed for the parked rental units outside the lobby, he followed without bothering to make a rental for himself. As they found their new Chevrolet sedan and loaded inside, Ignacio took a black Ford Taurus two over, keys in the ignition. It was a simple matter, then, to follow the three Americans out of the garage.

At the blockade the man asked to see his rental agreement and Ignacio showed him his Glock 17 in reply. The guard nodded, activated the wooden arm, which raised and allowed the Spaniard to fall in behind Thaddeus' vehicle from a block back. No time was wasted and now he had a clear view and the exact distance the tail required.

The Americans registered at the Hotel Independencia. At the registration desk, Libby kept as much distance between herself and Ansel as possible. The air between the couple was electric, Thaddeus noticed. Something had obviously set her off, but Ansel wasn't talking. As they finished checking in and received their keys, Thaddeus watched Libby flounce off to her room without a word to Ansel. The look of dismay was still etched on Ansel's face.

"I really let her down," he said.

"She'll get over it. She loves you. You're damn lucky to have her and you could sure as hell be more considerate of her."

"You're right."

The look of dismay faded. He nodded as if rightly chastised. "I can do better by her," he agreed. "By damn, I'm going to turn over a new leaf with her."

"That's more like it."

"I'm giving up Melinda."

"Who?"

"Someone at work. She's been coming between me and Libby."

"Why didn't I already know it was something like that? It's been obvious, Ansel."

"It has?"

"Sure, you've been holding back with her. She deserves better. Look how she's standing by you now. Even in your crazies, she's still beside you."

"Wow. You put it that way."

"What other way is there? She obviously loves you."

"Let's go find Burton. Let's get that money back and let me take Libby back home where I can take care of her."

"That's the spirit."

"I'm serious, Thad. I've been a real ass."

The two men went to their rooms.

Ignacio approached the front desk and paid the clerk two hundred dollars. He received Thaddeus' room number. Nothing more was said as Ignacio entered the hotel lobby and took a seat.

Fifteen minutes later, Thaddeus stood at the far end of the lobby. He had come down the back stairs. He saw the man he was looking for and approached him.

The hotel concierge was an oily Latino who wore shiny black trousers, white shirt with black tie, and a maroon vest. In a glance, Thaddeus sized him up as the type who would have a line on anything a guest could ever request. A gun, he told the concierge, I need a gun.

What make and model?

Thaddeus tried his Spanish. "*Con un silenciador. Es muy importante, el silenciador.* Do you understand?"

"*Sí.*"

An hour later he was knocking on Thaddeus' hotel door. He presented a nine millimeter semi auto Beretta 92FS. The barrel was threaded and the silencer twisted on easily. Thaddeus removed the silencer. He expelled the magazine and worked the action. Locked back, he peered inside the barrel. It appeared to have been cared for. He released the slide. He remounted the silencer. The magazine was full up. He reinserted the magazine and worked the action to load a round in the chamber.

"*Cuánto cuesta?*"

"Eight hundred. American."

Thaddeus counted off the bills and handed them over, plus an extra one hundred.

"A thank you gift," he told the concierge.

"Gracias."

"Now tell me. Tell me about the man in your lobby."

"There is a man waiting there. Ever since you checked in. I do not know him but I have been watching. Shall I call someone?"

"No. Leave him alone, please."

The man bowed sharply and turned away.

He closed the door and tested the balance of the gun. That easy. Why hadn't he thought of this before he tried to smuggle a gun across the border? Well, that was over and done with.

He unlocked the door and went to the bathroom. He turned on the shower's cold water, shut the curtain, and stepped behind the open door. The gun felt familiar in his hand. "Welcome to my family," he whispered.

Now to wait.

Ten minutes dragged by. He checked his watch. Maybe he had misjudged. Maybe it was not about him.

And at that moment, as he finished the thought, he felt the door to his room open. Felt it, because he sensed the slight change in air pressure. He waited, the hairs along his neck prickling up. Then--there it was, the unmistakable click of the front door as it closed. Now he was sure. His trap had been sprung.

The man in the fringed jacket crept silently into the bathroom. He paused at the shower curtain, listening.

He watched as the man ever so carefully raised his left hand to the shower curtain. When he brought up his right hand, Thaddeus saw the gun. It looked huge and he had no doubt it was meant for him.

With an angry jerking motion the man pulled the shower curtain out of the wall and, in that instant, saw that shower was empty and began to turn to where he knew Thaddeus would be waiting.

Thaddeus' first round caught the man in the lower jaw, knocking him backwards to where he sat--plopped--down on the toilet ring, a slightly stupefied look on his face. He slumped back against the toilet tank and his head lowered with a sigh onto his chest. The useless gun dropped from his hand and a wet spot appeared on the zipper portion of his trousers where he had wet himself.

Thaddeus watched and counted to ten. When he was certain, he stepped forward, bent down, and retrieved the Glock. It was heavy and substantial in his hand.

Now he had two guns.

And one less gunner.

With no small effort he managed to roll the newly minted Ignacio Solon up and into the bathtub, where he crumpled face down, hunched up on his knees, in what could only have been an extremely uncomfortable position. To anyone except the killer. He was fine with it.

Thaddeus washed his hands in the sink and examined his eyes.

Nothing there. No fright, no relief, no determination.

Just nothing.

And for now, that was just fine.

He cupped cold water onto his face. He felt re-born, energized, ready to do what he had come to Mexico for.

Maria. The very thought of a young girl being sold to a Mexican whorehouse repulsed him.

He turned to the man and kicked his side. The dead killer slumped over against the wall.

"*Puta.*"

DO NOT DISTURB said the sign he left on his door.

———

THADDEUS STEERED across two lanes of traffic and pulled into the Visitors' Parking at the border station. He turned the key and looked at Ansel.

"Why don't you wait here? Let me go inside and see about getting Burton out of jail."

Springing Burton required payment of the $5,000 bail, as previously ordered. Then they brought him up front to the office.

"Damn! I thought you'd forgotten all about me!" the teen cried. He threw his arms around Thaddeus and gave him a huge hug.

"Damn, man," said Thaddeus. "You need a toothbrush."

"You're right about that. And a shower and shave."

"We'll take you back to the hotel, get you cleaned up and changed, and then I've got a job for you."

"You need me to find someone? I'm your man."

Two hours later they met in Burton's hotel room. Thaddeus had paid the room fee for three days and he now gave Burton the key. Ansel found the young man a change of clothes in the gift shop, consisting of sweat pants, a T-shirt that said "Nogales!" and a light sweater. All told he looked harmless and Thaddeus decided it was not a bad look. He just might be able to talk to his people without putting them off, dressed like that.

They settled around an octagonal table set beside the window of Burton's room on the sixth floor of the hotel. It overlooked a rear parking lot. Beyond the property line were small houses with clay shingles, stretching out for a good half mile. Thaddeus stared down at the parking lot, lost in thought. Ansel and Burton went off in search of ice and soft drinks. When they returned with their refreshments, Thaddeus was ready to talk.

"We're looking for a man named Hermano Sanchez," Thaddeus told the teen.

"Who is he to you?"

"Just a guy. A friend."

"If he's a friend, why don't you know where he is already?"

Thaddeus spread his hands. "I lost track. It happens."

"Okay. Let's start with what he looks like."

A half hour later they had decided three things: one, there were probably a hell of a lot of Sanchezes in any town in Mexico, and two, the description of five-ten with dark skin and black hair might just be a little too ambiguous in any town in Mexico, and, three, the little man's cross-eyed appearance was probably the most definitive whorl in the identity fingerprint. He would be pursued on that.

So they started with directory assistance on Carlos Slim's telephone monopoly.

Directory assistance had eleven customers named either Hermano Sanchez, H. Sanchez, or Herman Sanchez. "Which did they want?" the operator asked. Burton wrote down eleven numbers and began dialing.

Forty-five minutes later, they were still no nearer finding Hermano Sanchez with the cross-eyes and a daughter named Maria, than when they started. But Burton wasn't dismayed in the least.

"I hit the streets," he said. "You guys wait here. I'm going to need about a grand, U.S."

Thaddeus peeled off ten hundred dollar bills from his clip.

"Buying information?" he said.

"Whatever it takes. Down here money talks. Even more than in the States."

"We can do that," said Ansel. "There's more, too, if you need it."

"This is good. It's a start. I'll be back when I have him located. Don't wait up."

"We won't," Thaddeus said.

The three separated, the two lawyers heading for their rooms, and Burton heading for the down elevator. Thaddeus left the **DO NOT DISTURB** sign on the door to his room. For now, it was exactly what he needed. Peace and quiet.

And oh, yes, a dead guy in the tub.

He ordered room service, a club sandwich, bottled water, and a carafe of coffee.

"I'd ask you to join me," he called toward the bathroom. "But right now you're just too needy."

He plucked the sign from his door. Then he called Katy and chatted for five minutes before Sarai wrested control of the phone from her mom. Father and daughter then chatted and he heard all news. Barbie world was humming along without a hitch. Then Turquoise came on and they chatted about school and about her decision to go pre-veterinary in college. Thaddeus smiled and tears crept into his eyes as he heard her voice and realized she was recovering from earlier traumas in her life.

Katy said she would take the girls and return to the condo in Chicago, as Thaddeus said it was much safer there. It was only for a few days and Katy said they would have a film fest while the girls were pulled out of school.

When he hung up he called his security service.

"Double your guys until I get back. Your alert is on red."

———

BURTON DROVE to the south side of Nogales and looked for a cantina where he would start asking questions.

Quietly at first, paying American dollars for the information that would lead him to Sanchez. It might take a day or two, but find him he would.

He spent the rest of the day checking in and out of several local cantinas and restaurants, always asking the same questions about the man Hermano Sanchez. Yes, he was a friend. No, he wasn't in any kind of trouble. No, Burton wasn't policia. No, the man wasn't in trouble over drugs. Still, people were suspicious and quick to deny knowledge or evince even the slightest interest in Burton's quest. Many just turned him aside with blank looks as if they hadn't heard the questions. Others just shrugged and walked off. I'm too white, he thought, after several hours failing to connect. Maybe he would need local help in locating his client. Maybe a private investigator.

The investigator was on the case less than an hour later.

———

BURTON RETURNED at noon the following day and located the lawyers in the dining room with Libby. He pulled up a chair and joined them. The waiter took his order and brought a diet cola.

"Well?" said Thaddeus.

"He lives on Calle de Guvallo, behind a restaurant. He works there washing dishes."

"So you found him!" Ansel cried. "Incredible job!"

The teen sat up erect and proud. "I told you I know my way around down here. The fee for my services is three thousand dollars. Then I'll tell you the street address."

Thaddeus and Ansel traded a look of surprise. There hadn't been anything said about a fee. Nevertheless...Thaddeus dug thirty one-hundred dollar bills out of his pocket and Burton plucked them from his hand. "Paid in full."

"So where is he?"

"His name is Hermano Sanchez, the guy I found. And he's got a daughter, Maria."

"Did you shpeak with him?" Libby asked.

"Yes. I told him I was from Thaddeus Murfee's office and we wanted to help him move to Mexico City."

"What did he say?"

"He was stunned. He thought I was there to arrest him for jumping bail in Flagstaff."

"You? Dressed like that?"

"I don't know. I guess because I'm American."

"Good grief. So what else was said?"

"I asked about Maria and whether they were bothering her. He didn't want to talk about that, but you could tell it wasn't good."

"So when do I get to talk to him?" Thaddeus asked.

"Right now. He's out in the lobby."

"What? Why didn't you bring him in?"

"He doesn't want to be seen with Americans. He's afraid they might be watching him."

"Let me talk to him," said Thaddeus. "You come along, Burton. I need a translator for this."

"Cool. Can I have my burger first?"

"Sure enough. Five minutes."

Ten minutes later, Thaddeus led Burton into the hotel lobby. He spied Hermano sitting on a circular couch, from the center of which sprouted a desert palm. The Mexican was sitting cross-legged, the omnipresent straw cowboy hat cocked back on his head. At first he seemed not to recognize Thaddeus, then he did, and a smile spread across his face. He was glowing.

"¡*Senor* Murfee! ¡*Mi abogado*!"

"Hello, Hermano," said Thaddeus. "Thanks for coming."

Burton translated and the Mexican man listened.

"Sure, sure," he said through Burton. "I am glad to come talk. You remember I call you about Maria?"

"I'm here about Maria."

"Okay."

"I want to help you move her to a safe location."

"That would be wonderful, *Señor* Murfee."

"And I want to ask your help, too."

"I will do whatever I can to help you."

"Can you tell me who your contact is at the Cartel?"

The man look terrified. He shook his head and his eyes darted about.

"These are some very bad men. They are commanding me to take another suitcase of marijuana to Flagstaff."

"Incredible."

"Yes, or they will take Maria from me. They say I still owe them much money for the lost suitcase when I got arrested. I said I don't owe them nothing."

"Good. Now. When are they going to talk to you again?"

"Tonight, after work, they will come to my house."

"How many will come?"

"Two. A young one named Juan Carlos and some old one I don't know. I think the old man has a gun. Something pokes out of his hip and he keeps it covered with his shirt. But I think it's a gun."

"What about Juan Carlos?"

"His father is the godfather. Juan Carlos is the one they send to take away the children to the whore houses."

"Sick bastards."

"That's right, *señor*. Sick."

"So here's what I want to do."

"Yes?"

"I want to kidnap Juan Carlos."

"Aii-iii, *caramba*! That is not good. They will kill us all."

"No, they won't. Not as long as we have Juan Carlos to trade."

"But how will you do this?"

"Okay, listen up. Here's what I need you to do."

Chapter 31

Hermano Sanchez and his family lived in a ramshackle double-wide that Thaddeus guessed was at least fifty years old. If they even made double-wides that long ago. It was mint green, very faded, and had a flat roof. with a vertical overhang that was covered in tar patches. The screen door was missing its top half and the place was bookended by two junk cars up on blocks. Both hoods were open and Thaddeus imagined they had been parted-out and then just abandoned where they sat. He looked the place over, made a decision, and dropped Hermano off. He drove back to the hotel to wait.

AT EIGHT-THIRTY HE parked along Calle de Guvallo in front of a Farmacias Guadalajara with a vertical block-letter sign saying **FARM**. Lights were on inside the pharmacy.

The restaurant next door, where Hermano would be inside washing dishes, seemed to be a jumping place with several couples coming and going in just the few minutes that Thaddeus surveilled the place.

At last he was certain he wasn't being watched and he quickly exited his car and hurried down the long driveway leading to Hermano's double-wide. The moon hadn't yet risen and it was dark as pitch, so he was careful where he stepped.

He angled off to the right/north end of the double-wide and cracked the rear door on the abandoned car. That afternoon, he had noted it was a Nissan, maybe mid-eighties. He climbed inside. The rear seat smelled dusty and oily and, as he sat down, he heard scurrying. Rats! He had sat down beside a rat nest, judging from the noise. They scattered to the front and to freedom out the open passenger door. Thaddeus willed his pounding pulse to back off and return to normal. Finally he was able to take a deep breath. Then he waited.

Bright headlights bumped up from the street and approached on the long driveway. He slouched and kept his profile below the window line. He held his breath as he waited for doors to slam. One--then he waited for a second. Nothing came. He could feel the air go out of his lungs with relief. It would be only one person--at least on the porch.

Then he heard the person knock on the front door, through the square where the screen would have gone.

He heard the door open and looked to see.

A tall man, wearing blue jeans and black tee-shirt, was framed in the open door. He said something to the woman who answered and then he pulled the screen open and stepped inside.

Several minutes passed.

Then he heard shouting--loud and angry. First a female voice and then a male. Then he heard crying and he pushed open the door to the junker. He withdrew the gun from his waistband and rushed to the end of the trailer nearest the door. At long last the yelling abated, but not the crying. It was a young voice, a sound of suffering that pierced his soul. He knew what was coming.

The tall man pushed her out the door, his hand gripping her upper arm. She was still crying and he roughly forced her down the three outside steps. His back was to Thaddeus when Thaddeus glided up behind him and put the muzzle of the gun against his left ear.

"Surprise, Juan Carlos. Don't move."

Juan Carlos froze.

"I have someone with me."

"No, you're alone. I already checked."

"What do you want? You know how bad this will be for you?"

"I do know. But that doesn't matter. What matters is the young lady you're kidnapping. Release her arm."

Juan Carlos did as he was told. When he let her go, the girl turned and flew up the steps and clambered inside her home. Thaddeus heard the door open and slam shut behind him, cutting off the interior light. Then it was dark with just the hint of a rising moon.

"Walk straight ahead, up the driveway," Thaddeus commanded.

"No. Shoot me here or turn me loose."

"As you wish."

Thaddeus dropped the muzzle of the gun to the man's calf and pulled the trigger. In the dark in the quiet yard the snap and Pffft! of the hollow point found the meat of the man's calf and exploded through his flesh. He cried out and bent double, grabbing at the wound.

"You *cabron*! You have shot Juan Carlos Ordañez! You

will die and your family will die and the family of your family will die!"

"Maybe so. Maybe not. But I am going to tell you again. Walk up the driveway or I shoot the other leg and carry you. It doesn't matter to me."

Bent double and dragging his useless leg, the man lurched up the driveway. At the sidewalk, Thaddeus headed him toward the rental car and opened the trunk.

"Inside."

Juan Carlos fell inside the trunk, where he lay on his back, his useless leg bent and pulled to his chest. In the light of the trunk Thaddeus could see that the wound was oozing a small amount of blood. Just as he had predicted.

"If you make any noise. Any. I will shoot you and feed you to the coyotes in the desert."

He pressed the muzzle of the gun against the man's forehead.

"Understand me?"

The man clenched his eyes shut and moaned. But he nodded.

"I need a doctor," he whispered.

"I know. Maybe you will get one, maybe you won't. That depends on your father. Now we are going for a drive. Remember, silence."

Thaddeus slammed the trunk lid, climbed inside the car, and headed south on Federal 15, Heroica de Nogales.

Just beyond the airport he took a gravel road to the west.

Two miles later they were in wide open desert, the sky was filled with stars, and the moon had risen.

He turned off the headlights and sat, waiting. No one came from behind and he was glad. As he had predicted, the young whoremonger had come alone.

He climbed out and popped the trunk.

"My guest seems to be in pain," he said to the man bathed in trunk light. "Maybe you would like to call for help, yes?"

Juan Carlos nodded. His look was pain crossed with anger. His feeling state flipped between the two, as he was angry but hurting too deeply to dwell there.

"What will you do with me?"

"If you're lucky, you will live. If you are unlucky, you will die with a bullet in the back of your head as I give you a head start running."

"I can't run, *puta*."

"Oh, that's right. Then the chase won't take so long. It will be unfair. Like you with nine-year-old girls."

"Is that why you shot me?"

"No, I shot you because I loathe you. If I shot you because of the children, it would be in your scrotum. Then I would work my way up, a bullet here, a bullet there. Then I would leave you for the coyotes. Who knows? All of this may happen yet. You should pray, Juan Carlos."

"*Puta!*"

"Now, take my cell phone and call your father."

He handed the phone to his prisoner. The man punched a long stream of numbers into the phone. Waited, waited, then he spoke.

"Papa? *Un momento, por favor.*"

He handed the phone back to Thaddeus.

"Juan Carlos Ordañez? Senior? I have junior with me."

A long epithet of curse words streamed out.

He spoke again. "Juan Carlos Ordañez, you probably love this piece of shit. That's your problem. Now you write down these numbers."

He slowly spoke the MacDevon Largent Attorney trust

account numbers, both routing and account, into the phone.

"Get that?"

"*Sí*."

"*Bien*. Now. You will wire two hundred million U.S. into that account in the next two hours. If you do this successfully, I will give you back this piece of shit. If you refuse, you will never see him again."

He ended the call and tossed the cell onto the passenger's seat. Then he went back to the trunk, slammed the lid down, ignoring the protestations of the junior Juan Carlos, and took his seat behind the wheel. On the radio he found Sirius and spun the dial until he found a talk show. Howard Stern. The topic seemed to be about the mutilation of women in the Arab countries. It was a good topic, for it kept him in the anger zone. He was going to need that zone, that hatred, before midnight.

He sat back, shut his eyes, and listened.

As he sat there, he began to get in touch with how easy the shooting had become. No more did he wring his hands in despair at hurting another human. No more did he sit up in the night gasping as the faces of the dead strolled past. None of it touched him, at last, and he realized he was removed beyond the feelings normal people would have. It had taken time, and it had taken hundreds of hours of soul-searching since his first shooting in Orbit, Illinois, but he was satisfied. Not happy about his emotional life, not sad about it, just satisfied. It could no longer restrain his finger on the trigger, it could no longer cause pause in his plans. He was free.

At eleven p.m. he called Ansel. He told him to login to the trust account. There was a long pause, followed by a cry of joy.

"How much?" he said when Ansel breathlessly picked up the phone and jammed it to his ear.

"All of it."

"Two hundred million?"

"Yes."

"Can you change the login?"

"I already did."

"Good. I will see you in about one hour."

"I don't know how to thank you, Thaddeus. My eyes are filling up."

"I'll tell you how to thank me. Sit down beside Libby on the bed. Give her a sweet back rub. Whisper in her ear how much you love her. And mean it. More than anything you have meant, you must mean it with her. She's precious, man. Treat her that way."

"I will. I promise."

Thaddeus ended the call.

He returned to the trunk and inserted the key.

Juan Carlos Ordañez the junior sat up.

"This is it, am I right?"

"It is," said Thaddeus.

"You are going to kill me, am I right?"

"No."

"I promise I won't hurt them no more."

"I know."

"Believe me."

"I believe you. It always comes to this."

"But you will shoot me anyway."

"No. I am going to leave you here, in the desert, wounded, without water, without food. It's the same thing you've been doing to the children: leaving them wounded, without necessities, without love, and helpless. That is your fate now."

"My father will kill you. And your family."

"He will try. But he will fail."

"At least leave me water."

"You didn't think to bring water? Did you leave water for the children? Did you?"

———

WITH THE MONEY safely back in the trust account, it was time for Ansel and Libby to go home. Thaddeus accepted the task of representing Ansel through the investigation and any indictment and Ansel told him he would send over a check as soon as he got back to the office.

"What do I tell the partners about the trust funds?" he wanted to know.

Thaddeus shook his head. "I would tell them nothing. Just say something like there was a problem with the account and the bank falsely reported a wire transfer. Tell them the transfer was actually someone else's account. Or some such song and dance. Hell, man, you're a lawyer-- make something up!"

"Can do."

Libby looked at her husband with new eyes. She leaned against him for support even when she didn't need to. She took his hand and held it several times while they made their plans with Thaddeus. It was charming to see, and Thaddeus was happy for them. Evidently his instructions to Ansel had hit home and the man had come clean with his wife and re-committed to her. All was well and Thaddeus was glad for them.

They flew out of Tucson that next afternoon and were home in Chicago by nightfall.

Chapter 32

Tony Blake took the call from Thaddeus. Tony had been with Thaddeus eighteen months. He was a BAG agent--Beta Armed Guards--and carried a concealed weapon. Along with the eight other agents placed around Thaddeus' condo in Chicago, they were all out of LA.

Guard duty was 24/7 and they worked twelve hour shifts, most of the time sitting and waiting for something to happen. They played cards, drank coffee by the gallon, and made Netflix rich, both on and off duty. The five acres where Thaddeus' house sat was double chain-link fenced and patrolled by armed guards driving ATV's. The perimeter guards were from Black Cloud Security out of San Francisco. All communications, BAG and Black Cloud, went through a custom communications console and Thaddeus received an RSS feed of all conversations, alerts, and reports.

Tony was Thaddeus' personal bodyguard. He was angry that Thaddeus hadn't taken him along when he went to

Mexico. Normally, if Thaddeus was in the vicinity, Tony Blake was nearby as well. Never a public figure, which is exactly how Tony liked it and played it. Thaddeus called Tony and alerted him to the new threat.

"Tijuana Cartel. I left the godfather's son in the desert. Without water."

"You didn't."

"He was a very bad man."

Tony, at the communications console in Flagstaff, massaged the spot between his eyes where the headaches lurked.

"So who can we expect to come here? "

"Unknown. But when it rains it pours. I took out a family member. They'll want ten family members for payback."

"Sure they will. Do I move Katy and Sarai out of town?"

"Yes, I have told them to fly to Chicago. The condo."

Thaddeus kept a second home, this one in Chicago on the Gold Coast. The Gold Coast was a historic district in Chicago. It was part of Chicago's Near North Side community, and was roughly bounded by North Avenue, Lake Shore Drive, Oak Street, and Clark Street. It has long been among the most affluent neighborhoods in the United States, probably on the same economic plane as Manhattan's Upper East Side. Thaddeus and Katy kept an apartment in a high rise, bounded by other high rises, row houses, and sundry mansions. Just south, the home office of his law firm was located on the Chicago Loop. Thaddeus preferred the Chicago home for his family during times of high stress, mainly because the environment was more easily controlled than the wide open spaces of Flagstaff and its environs.

"She's going to be a very angry lady that you made her leave the clinic. She's an important doctor there."

"I've called her and smoothed it over. She'll take a hiatus from her job."

"Indian Health Services? They're going to hate you, my friend."

"Sure they are. Which is fine. Call Albert, have him bring the jet. You and Ross help them load up. Try to do it in the middle of the night when you can have eyes-on. After Albert has them safely in Chicago, tell him to bring the jet to Mexico City."

"Mexico City International Airport?"

"Yes. Tell him to sleep on the plane until I get there. General aviation. He knows what to do. But I don't want him leaving the plane. Not for anything."

"You're thinking they might track the plane to Mexico?"

"I'm thinking they won't stop at anything to get back at me. The plane is vulnerable. It's a moving piece that is hard to defend."

"Got it."

"And Tony."

"Yep?"

"They could be there at any moment. Time is of the essence."

"Sure. I already know that. Do I go with them or am I with you?"

"You go with them until they get situated and locked down. Then come back out here."

"So I'll see you in about four days, I'm guessing."

"No. I'm on my way to Mexico City and I won't be back for several days. My family is in your care. It is up to you now."

"Done."

"Take care."

"You too, Tony. You know what to do."

"I do. *Adios*."

"Yes, goodbye."

———

HE BOUGHT a second identity in Hermosillo at a cost of $5500. It included a U.S. passport, California address and driver's license, American Express Platinum card, Social Security Card, and two club membership tags for his keychain. He returned to Nogales and rented a motorhome, using the new ID.

When it was gassed and ready, he helped Hermano Sanchez load his family of six and their belongings. The motorhome was crowded but there was bunk room for everyone, including Thaddeus.

Then he set off for Mexico City.

When they reached Parque Estatal Canon de Fernandez they stopped for the night.

Thaddeus found a rental pad for the motorhome and did a transfusion of fresh water and black water.

The family lodgings offered bathing accommodations and a friendly restaurant serving American food. Everyone was starved and ate with very little conversation. Afterward the older kids set off exploring while the younger ones tried out the jungle gym, merry-go-round, and swing set. Hermana, Mathilde, and Thaddeus pulled out lawn chairs and watched the little guys running and playing. They all turned in before ten o'clock. Thaddeus planned to make Mexico City by tomorrow night and wanted to get a good early start.

The next night was spent at a KOA campground on the

north side of Mexico City. A three bedroom apartment, furnished, was located before the next day and Thaddeus paid cash for a full six months in advance on the rent. He took the rental in his own--assumed--name and purchased five thousand dollars in travelers' checks for Hermano's signature. "For you, for Mathilde, and for Maria and the kids to get your start in your new home."

"*Gracias, Señor* Thaddeus, *gracias*!"

"This is as far as I can go with you. Now it's up to you."

The little man nodded. His eyes crossed and uncrossed in a blink. "I know, I know. Mathilde will clean at the hotels and I will wash dishes."

"That works."

"And the kids can go to Catholic school. There is one two blocks away."

"Well the name of Sanchez covers more than sixteen pages in the telephone directory, so you should be anonymous down here."

"You already told me, no land line."

"Right. Buy the prepaid cells and throw them away every week. But it's me they'll be coming after. I expect no problems for you."

"*Gracis, Señor* Thaddeus. *Vaya con Dios.*"

"Same to you," said Thaddeus. He spread his arms wide.

Warm hugs followed, some tears, and exclamations of gratitude from the Sanchez clan all around. He was embarrassed by the outpouring and quickly left with the motorhome. There was a check-in facility just outside the airport and an open van shuttled him from there to the General Aviation terminal.

He wasn't in the General Aviation terminal pilots' room long before Chicago law partner Albert Hightower walked in. Albert was the senior partner in Chicago and loved flying the firm jet more than he loved eating. He spent weekends around the plane, examining it, caring for it, upgrading avionics packages--the pursuit of perfect was never-ending.

They traded a man-hug and headed for the dining room.

As they chomped burgers and sipped their bottled Cokes, Albert brought Thaddeus up to speed on Katy and Sarai and Turquoise in Chicago. All was well there, security was in place, and Katy was actually enjoying her time away from work at the clinic.

"Looks like a win-win for you, my friend," said Albert.

"We're just getting started, Al. These guys want my head to play soccer with."

"Tony filled me in."

"He stay in Chicago?"

"Yes, until I get back. Then he'll fly commercial back to Flag."

"Perfect."

"And where are you headed?"

"Chicago. We have a new client there. Name of Ansel Largent."

"Not of MacDevon Largent law firm?"

Thaddeus nodded. "The same."

"What's his problem?"

"Murder."

"Who did he supposedly kill?"

"The next District Attorney of Cook County."

"Damn, you're going to be very unpopular around town."

"Really? When was I ever popular there? Tell me that, *Señor* Hightower."

"You're right."

Thaddeus napped all the way to Chicago. The motorhome excursion from Nogales to Mexico City had been a nerve-wracking one and he was exhausted. Exhausted but happy for Hermano Sanchez and Maria. He had done what he went to Mexico to do--and much more.

But the girl was safe. Maria of Sonora was in her new home, new bed, fifteen hundred miles away from the border.

His head rested on a soft pillow and he was scrunched beneath a light blanket from the Gulfstream's overhead compartment.

He dreamed of Maria and he dreamed of his own Sarai and Turquoise. It was a dream where he was walking through a battlefield filled with smoke and dying and injured soldiers. Up ahead a group of men and women wearing surgical gowns and masks motioned him to join them. He watched as they inserted an instrument into the eye of their patient.

"These hurt people are light gropers. Your job is to open their eyes to the light."

Next thing he knew, he was gowned and opening eyes himself.

When they flew into U.S. airspace the luxurious aircraft broadcast its ID to Albuquerque Center Air Route Traffic Control.

"Welcome home," the center operator said. "Welcome home."

Chapter 33

William Eckles fancied himself a born politician. His father was a ward committeeman in Chicago's largest precinct, his grandfather (still living) had served four terms as Cook County Sheriff and still knew everyone in the county.

Eckles himself had grown up with a keen ear for party politics, the topic at the dinner table every night except Sundays, which had been reserved for "good deeds of the spirit" reports from Eckles and his four sisters.

At the age of thirty-two he tossed his hat in the primary election ring for District Attorney. It was thought by the pundits that Eckles was a shoo-in for the office and that Chicago organized crime and street gangs would soon be reeling under his administration as he set about creating his legacy from Lake Michigan out west to the horse farms, from Evanston to the South Side. His area of influence included five million souls, which balanced out at over forty percent of the population of Illinois. That was enough votes to carry the enterprising politician to even greater political heights, maybe governor, maybe United States senator. The next step was yet to be revealed.

Eckles was a modest man in dress and looks, but flamboyant in speech. He was average height and carried an extra twenty pounds around the waist. He was dark complexioned with a round face and protruding ears but a winning smile and firm handshake for everyone who crossed his path. He had swum to the surface in the District Attorney's office where he was the Administrative Assistant. That title placed him but one rung below the retiring District Attorney, whose heir, hopefully, was William Eckles.

Except there was one fly in the ointment, and her name was Suzanne Fairmont. Suzanne's star was on the ascendancy as the chair of the criminal law section of the State Bar, and as the chair of the criminal law section at MacDevon Largent, the firm founded by Ansel Largent and James MacDevon. Then she announced for the primary and set herself against ADA Eckles.

Suzanne was great press; Chicago had never had a female District Attorney. The *Tribune* and *Sun-Times* could be counted on to run front page stories on young miss Fairmont any time the firm requested press coverage of this or that event in their candidate's career.

In short, she was an extremely attractive candidate and was smart enough to position herself as a fresh face and the choice of voters fed up with Cook County politics-as-usual.

Women knew her face and knew that she stood for tough gun laws, a clamp-down on schoolyard bullying, equal rights for women, and that she had a strong aversion to machine politics. There was a ten point gap, however, and the old-timers were sure she'd never close it by Primary Election Day. So she appeared everyday on some local TV talk show, enlisting the female voting bloc to ring doorbells and make calls. The gap closed by one point, then closed again. In the polls she lagged but four percentage points behind Bill Eckles. Then just two. It was predicted she would peak and overtake him forty-eight hours before the votes were cast.

Two days before the election Suzanne was found shot to death in her law office. The entire city was stunned. The craftiest pols laid the deed at the feet of Bill Eckles, or perhaps someone senior in his genealogy.

Voters across the enormous county were outraged. The District Attorney and Chicago Police Department held a joint news conference in which swift justice was promised, a massive dedication of man- and woman-power was described, and prayers and condolences communicated to the bereaved family.

Two days later, came new news guaranteed to boost the ratings of the story times ten. This was news that was leaked as was the habit with any Chicago criminal investigation, and it had to do with the seizure of a gun from the law office of the managing partner at MacDevon Largent. The leak even went so far as to confirm that the gun was the same one used to end Suzanne's life.

The police and the prosecutor, in combination, were the source of the leak, of course.

The purpose was to predispose anyone who might be called upon to serve either as grand juror or trial juror. There was nothing like good press to help convict, and prosecutors everywhere used the tactic, although, if accused of an ethical violation in leaking information, prosecutors knew to point the finger of blame at the cops. The cops had broad shoulders and didn't report to any State Bar committee on ethics. And the cops were only too glad to take credit for great, community-pleasing, results.

It worked, because the Cook County Grand Jury took less than three minutes in their deliberation, to return an indictment. Of none other than Ansel Largent.

The detectives who testified at the grand jury were Jake O'Connor and Lucinda Wainwright. Neither was asked by the District Attorney about fingerprints on the gun. So, the indictment sailed through. It was filed with the Cook County Circuit Court and a warrant issued for the arrest of Ansel Largent.

Word arrived that Ansel had returned aboard the Gulfstream jet of his lawyer.

Chapter 34

The homicide investigation took a sudden detour.

Which made Detective Jake O'Connor furious.

He headed up the team that recovered the gun from Ansel Largent's office, and he had every right to his anger.

He was on the horn with the CPD crime lab.

The gun, it turned out, was impossible to link to Ansel Largent either through fingerprints or DNA. But--and this was huge--forensic testing proved that the gun had been used three years earlier in a South Side shootout that left a number of gangbangers dead and two innocent people seriously wounded. The South Side shooting was the work of one Ruben Washington. He was, as O'Connor could already hear Largent's defense attorney proclaiming, the last known person in possession of the firearm. And now he was a convicted felon. Worse, Illinois DOC had already paroled him back onto the streets prior to Suzanne's murder.

Which raised a reasonable doubt.

Enough of a reasonable doubt to set Largent free.

Enough reasonable doubt for the defense to argue that Ruben Washington had in fact been the shootist and that after the murder, he had planted the gun on Ansel Largent.

But what about motive? Why would some South Side gangbanger murder Suzanne Fairmont? There was a glimmer of hope for O'Connor. That connection made no sense.

His hope was only temporary. It dissipated with the news that Ansel Largent himself had recovered the law firm's missing trust funds and the firm had been made whole.

O'Connor called the FBI to confirm this. He normally hated the FBI and wouldn't call them for anything, but this time he was in a serious corner. After all, return of the money was death to any embezzlement case because the crime required proving, beyond a reasonable doubt, an intention to permanently deprive the rightful owner of his property. With the money coming back home where it belonged, the key element of embezzlement had sprouted wings and fluttered right out the window.

That was depressing. O'Connor planned to use the embezzlement to illustrate that Largent was someone predisposed to committing crimes and someone who, in helping himself to two hundred million dollars that didn't belong to him, would think nothing of putting a bullet in the brain of someone innocently at the office that night when the theft took place.

These threads were all woven together to present a complete, logical picture. O'Connor had found that tapestry cases were the easiest cases to make.

Why? Because juries were, for the most part, not very bright. At least not in Jake O'Connor's worldview. How could they be? They were comprised of voters, who insisted on re-electing the same con artists who had screwed them last term. That, O'Connor knew, was your average juror. Not very bright but inclined to vote. The failure of the embezzlement case threatened to totally unravel the murder case.

But the mandatory leaks had been made and the indictment announced, so a patrol officer and her sergeant were dispatched to arrest Ansel Largent and lock him up.

They arrived at Ansel's house at five o'clock in the morning. He was still in bed and only as the result of some furious shouting and threats over the intercom system were the police officers allowed onto the premises and inside the home. The officers accompanied him upstairs for pants, shoes, and shirt. Then he was handcuffed and taken back downstairs and out to the waiting patrol car. It was freezing in January, so he was returned inside and a wool topcoat from the hall closet draped over his shoulders.

In the back of the patrol car he spoke for the first time. "Wait! I haven't had my meds!"

"Relax," said the sergeant, "the jail doctor will make sure you get what you need."

"Yes but I really need my meds first. I'm at a huge mental disadvantage without them."

The two police officers traded a look and burst into laughter.

"Brother, you're at a huge mental disadvantage even with them!"

"Please," he pleaded.

At that point the sergeant merely waved his hand at the prisoner and turned back around to stare out the windshield as the other officer drove.

"Relax. We're coming into some heavy traffic."

Ansel was taken to the Cook County Jail and booked.

He was then incarcerated in a day room where a TV blared and inmates wandered around, bumming cigarettes and giving off threatening looks. Medication-deprived, Ansel's mental acuity went from ten to about a three over the next several hours. Then he went into a slump and a fog. He was depressed and seriously losing touch with reality as the lack of the antipsychotic in his system began to manifest. He imagined he was at a carnival and couldn't find his way off the midway. He imagined that he was aboard a cruise ship and the passengers had been quarantined due to the Ebola virus. Then his reality began shifting in and out as imaginings took flight to greater heights and greater loss of control set in. At two o'clock he wet himself. He had thought he was at the urinal when in reality he was facing into a corner and had relieved himself there. A guard was called and not much made of the incident. The guard returned to the windowed outer station and made a brief entry in the day sheet that one of the inmates had wet himself. He didn't give the name, just the date and time. At four o'clock a deputy came for him, cuffed him, and led him away.

"Where are you taking me?" Ansel asked.

"The Chief of Detectives wants to talk."

"Thank goodness," Ansel said. "Maybe he'll see how preposterous this whole thing is."

He was shown into a nine-by-twelve windowless room with indoor-outdoor carpet from the 1970's. A worn wooden table and four conference chairs came with. Jake O'Connor greeted him and shook his hand. He was smiling and immediately apologized to Ansel for the arrest. The jailer rolled his eyes and closed the door behind him.

"Maybe we can clear this up here and now," said the detective.

It had been over twenty-four hours since Ansel had ingested his medications. As sometimes occurred when facing great stress, the part of Ansel's brain that sorely missed the medicine, took over. He imagined the police officer a potential client. He relaxed and prepared to listen to yet another hurting heart.

"There's something I've been wanting to ask you," the detective said to Ansel.

Whereupon Ansel heard, from the potential client, "I want to ask you to help me with a problem."

Not quite the same thing, but fairly close.

The detective drew a silver revolver from an inner pocket. He laid it between him and Ansel.

"Ever see this before?"

Ansel stared at the gun. Evidently he was being asked to defend an insurance case where firearms were involved. So...he picked up the gun and looked it over.

"Nice," he said, and balanced the gun in his right hand. "Just the right heft."

"Exactly," said the detective, who was astonished at his good luck. The guy had actually touched--no, make that "tried-on"--the murder weapon. Joyous day!

Ansel then replaced the gun on the table.

"What kind of injury did the plaintiff suffer?" Ansel asked, inquiring about the state of health of the adverse party in the insurance case.

"Not bad," said the detective. He took out a handkerchief and plopped it over the gun. Ever so carefully he then lifted the gun, taking great care not to touch it with his skin. He enfolded the hankie like a diaper around the firearm, and replaced it in his inner pocket. Just that easy. It had been just that easy.

"Okay, Ansel," said the detective. "Thanks for coming in

today."

Ansel waved aside the thank you. "Not a problem. Feel free to call me anytime. My secretary will give you my card on the way out."

"Perfect," said the detective. "I'll put it in a safe place."

The detective rapped on the door and the jailer returned inside.

"Thanks again," said Ansel. He stood and allowed himself to be steered away by the jailer.

Whereupon Jake O'Connor personally delivered the murder weapon to the Chicago Police Department's new forensics lab.

"Prints and DNA," he told the receiving clerk. "I need a report by tomorrow morning."

The gun was bagged and personally hand-carried by the clerk to the nearest laboratory technician.

"Put whatever you're doing aside," the clerk told the lab tech. "This just came in from the Chief of Detectives himself. Prints and DNA. Stat!"

The clerk confirmed that she would personally see to it that the lab report was emailed to Jake O'Connor's departmental email first thing in the morning.

O'Connor left to find Wainwright. It was time for a celebratory drink. Maybe two.

And it was time to bury the first lab report on the gun. The one that reported no prints, no DNA.

Two phone calls were all that took. The report was wiped from all hard drives.

Just two calls.

He met Wainwright on Michigan Avenue at a bar called Fleet's. It was a nondescript place that couldn't make up its mind whether it was football themed or baseball themed, with a crashing confluence of past stars from both sports intermixed on the walls. O'Connor loved the place because nobody with a brain ever went there, making it a safe hangout. Wainwright turned up just after nine o'clock. She had been taking witness statements from the lawyers and clerical staff office on the same floor as Suzanne Fairmont. It was boring, repetitive, and she was exhausted.

"Never have so many known so little," she complained to her partner. "How these people remember to get home is beyond me."

"The affluent don't need to know how to get home. Their Porsches and Jaguars all have GPS that remembers the way. Bread crumbs."

"I'm beat. What are you drinking?"

"Tap. Tastes like Bud. Maybe Miller's."

"Give me what he's having," she tossed off to the bartender. When her mug arrived they found a booth and settled in. Peanuts in a basket looked enticing and the rules required shells to the floor, so both officers of the law helped themselves.

After several mouthfuls and a second mug of beer for his partner, O'Connor couldn't keep it to himself any longer.

"Guess who I did?"

"You mean guess what you did?"

"I mean guess who."

"It's late, Jake. At least give me a clue."

"Ansel Largent."

"That's a clue? That's the end of the game. Unless you have more to tell me."

"He's a strange cat. A good half bubble off level."

"I picked up on something like that just talking to him. We're all here because we're not all there, kind of guy."

"Exactly."

"So you arrested him. I saw the sheet."

"Not only arrested, I went to see him."

"How'd that go? Probably not well, since he's a lawyer and knows better than to talk to the police."

"You would think that, but you'd be wrong, Lucinda. Let me back up. They bring him in the room and I'm all chummy and handshakes. You know."

"Good cop."

"Exactly. So we shoot the breeze for a minute and then I take out the gun we retrieved from his office. Just take it out and put it on the table between us."

"You took it out of evidence lockup?"

O'Connor winked at her. "Friends in high places. So I show him the gun."

"Of course he'd never seen it before."

"Didn't get to that. Next thing I know, he picks it up. Picks it up and squints down the barrel and makes the bullet sound. Bam!"

"You're giving me goose bumps. He actually touched the murder weapon? Do I know where this is going?"

"You sure do. He puts it back down and I pick it up with my handkerchief and take it to the crime lab."

"Beautiful. So now we have two lab reports on the same gun. In the first report, there's no evidence linking him. No prints, no DNA. And now, in the second report, we have prints and DNA. All over the murder weapon. So now we've got two conflicting reports. How's this help with anything? I mean, you're all bubbly and all, but I'm not getting it."

"You're not getting it because I haven't told you what comes next."

"Which is?"

"I call the system administrator and have him wipe the first report."

"No effing way!"

"Yep. We're down to one report. And it puts the murder weapon in the hand of the guy whose office the gun came from. Smooth, eh?"

"Like silk."

She caught the bartender's eye and had two more sent over.

"We're not going down that road, are we?" she said after the refills had arrived.

"Honey, we're so far down that road we need GPS just to get back out."

"I don't like it."

"What's not to like. We know the guy's a thief--he made off with two hundred million. That tells me he's a guy with a criminal mind. Shooting Suzanne Fairmont was just more of the same to him."

"What about motive?"

"I've got that covered. She was shot the same night as he makes the money disappear. Obviously she knew something was up. Maybe she confronted him and he followed her back to her office. I don't know. We'll make that up as we go."

"Maybe they were lovers and had a fight."

"Autopsy produced no sperm, can't go there. Now. Are you with me on this? Or do I need to find a new partner?"

"I'm with you. I think you've got the right guy. He steals two hundred mil, he'll just as easily shoot someone. Evidently he knew enough to get his prints and DNA off the gun before he squirreled it away. So that tells us he was trying to hide his complicity."

"Now you're talking."

"So why does he touch it this time around?"

O'Connor touched the side of his head. He raised an eyebrow. He nodded.

"Nutzoid."

"Bingo."

"I think it just might fly."

O'Connor's face fell. "Just might? Hello, Luce, we've got a guilty waiting in the wings right now. All we need to do is take it to the DA."

"How do we explain our new evidence to the DA?"

"Simple. Reports got flummoxed between two cases. The first report went with a different shooting. We discovered the mixup and saved the day. You can take credit for that."

"I need something with the DA. They look down at me over there. I hate to claim the female glass ceiling thing, but I think that's it. This could make me look like a very competent dick."

"I know that. That's why I'm handing it off to you."

"My stomach's full. I hate beer. Let's try some whiskey."

"I'm buying. Bartender!"

Five minutes later, Lucinda Wainwright relaxed her back against the booth and sipped her Jack. The guy was guilty, she had been certain of it all along. It was just like the old traffic cop days. You made up a little stuff for court, something to prove probable cause, and before you know it the defendant was weaving in his own lane. Maybe crossing the centerline. She'd done it hundreds of times before she got her detective shield. What was one more little adjustment this time around? The guy was a lawyer and he was stupid enough to pick up the gun? He definitely had it coming, anyone that stupid.

"He definitely has it coming," she said through her amber haze.

O'Connor tipped his highball glass to her.

"You're got that right."

———

AT MIDNIGHT that first night the jail physician interviewed Ansel, as was standard procedure for new prisoners.

Libby had called four times and left four messages for the doctor about Ansel's need for his meds. The doctor confirmed the drug regimen with both the wife and the prisoner, and wrote out a prescription to the jail pharmacist.

Ansel received his usual medications the next morning following his arrest and incarceration, forty-eight hours since his last dose.

Over the next six hours the world began to come into focus for him. He dimly realized where he was and what had happened, and he placed a call to Thaddeus. As did Libby.

Less than an hour later Thaddeus was there, admonishing him not to speak with the police.

Would Thaddeus defend him, he was asked.

Of course.

Terms were set and Thaddeus returned to the family condo on the Gold Coast that night. Katy and the girls were back in Chicago where they would be better guarded, following the threats against Thaddeus' family. He talked late that night with Katy and brought her up to date on what all had transpired that day.

Chapter 35

District Attorney James Stephenson was a 2002 graduate of the University of Illinois School of Law, top third of his class, and anxious for a chance to snag the gold ring. This time around, it looked like it just might be his turn.

Detectives O'Connor and Wainwright had just finished telling him about the administrative screwup over lab reports at CPD Crime Lab, none of which surprised him. The crime lab had only been around since 2011. Before that, all guns and prints went through the Illinois State Police Crime Lab in Chicago, but those fools were twelve months behind in everything. So the addition of the CPD crime lab, while removing a huge roadblock in the speedy trial requirement of all criminal cases, still had a wrinkle here and there.

For one, reports got mixed up between cases. Check.

For another, DNA testing, while essential to the successful prosecution of all non-eye-witness cases, sometimes was compromised because of marginal crime lab practices. Check.

Finally, the crime lab was understaffed. There simply weren't enough techs on-board to handle the caseloads that were exponentially expanding with every new report. Check.

It was not unusual for a tech to report to a courtroom at eight o'clock in the morning, sit around while the court did arraignments, and not shake loose until noon or later. For one measly case, out of the thousands pending. There were only twenty-seven techs in the entire lab, so things were slowing day-by-day, and wait times were growing longer. Which made DA Stephenson a little less suspicious of this report mixup he was hearing about on the Suzanne Fairmont case. Things were known to get badly shuffled over there. Evidently this murder case, even though high-profile, had not been immune. Still, the DA had his suspicions, because if it was a mixup, it was almost too good to be true. In short, it resurrected the Suzanne Fairmont murder case.

"How did you get this report located?" he asked O'Connor. "I can't get anyone over there to give me the time of day, and I have seniority in this office."

"Actually, it was misfiled. It happens."

Stephenson nodded noncommittally. He wasn't quite buying O'Connor's story of a misfiling, but he was also seasoned enough to know when to push and when to back off. This was a time for backing off, so he let it slide.

"Well, the DNA and prints make the case. You deserve a medal for breaking this one open, Detective."

O'Connor's ears actually reddened. "I try, sir."

"Don't be fooled," said Wainwright, who was still nursing a hangover though it was almost noon. "He's the most professional detective we have. And the most thorough. Jake doesn't miss a hair or a fiber."

Jake blushed. "That's heavy praise coming from this lady. She's been around the block and knows whereof she speaks."

"All right," said Stephenson, "when we're through blowing smoke up each other's ass, let's get down to the nitty gritty."

Both detectives nodded. Yes, they agreed, it was time to get hard-nosed about the prosecution. Time for someone to get carted off to prison.

"For openers, you two need to leak this report to the press. I like Melinda Tichenor over at *News Five*, so give her a call. We owe her an exclusive on this."

"Got it," said Jake. "I know the Tichenor woman. She's good people."

"We've got an arraignment on Largent this afternoon. I'd like to turn the report over to defense counsel at that time. No sandbagging on this one."

"You're going to *Brady* him already?"

He was making reference to the *Brady* case, a legal requirement to turn over all exculpatory evidence to defense counsel.

"This isn't *Brady* stuff because it doesn't exculpate. This convicts."

"That's what I meant," said O'Connor, "of course it's not *Brady*."

"No, this is called 'Impress the Judge'. I want to impress the judge with how forthcoming we have been from the gate. It will speak volumes in defeating the usual encyclopedia of defense motions. By the way, who's the lucky defense hack?"

"My little bird tells me he was visited this morning by

Thaddeus Murfee. He's a guy who's more often screwing off in Flagstaff than working Chicago cases."

Stephenson knew immediately who he would be facing.

"Not entirely true. He got a defense verdict in the Erme-line Ransom case downstate. Then hit the State of Illinois for a bundle."

"That's the guy? I thought the name sounded familiar."

"He's very thorough. Well, so are we. This is one case his guy's not going to walk away from. We've got the gun in the guy's office. We've got his prints. We've got his DNA. We have no other suspects."

"We don't have motive," said Wainwright, "unless we say Suzanne Fairmont walked in on Largent while he was stealing the firm's trust account."

"Something like that," said Stephenson. "Let me roll that around for a day or two. I'll get back to you."

"I like her walking in," Wainwright said. "It makes sense."

"We'll work on it," Stephenson told her.

She tried to think of something else to bring to the conversation.

"But I'm liking your idea too," Stephenson added.

Chapter 36

Circuit Court Judge Lawrence X. Zang was perplexed. He had just been handed "Defendant's Motion for Psychiatric Examination."

The attorney-proponent of the motion, was Thaddeus Murfee. Which wasn't what perplexed the judge.

What perplexed him was how Ansel Largent, the founding partner of one of Chicago's largest and best-heeled law firms, was going to explain to his busload of insurance company clients that he was mentally incompetent and probably had been for five years now. At least that's what his motion was claiming. Would that mean all the insurance settlements that Largent had wrangled were in fact flawed? Had the insurance companies been overpaying, thanks to the ill-formed judgments of an attorney who was incompetent? Worse still was how the carriers would explain to stockholders that one billion dollars in settlements might have been unnecessarily paid at all.

But then the judge relaxed. That incompetency-how-do-we-tell-the-clients issue wasn't his problem.

"Let me read," he told the lawyers before him. "New matter." He studied the motion.

Judge Zang was only thirty-eight, the survivor of divorce wars in family court, and new to the criminal bench in Cook County. Every day he woke up and gave thanks that his turn in the barrel had finally ended. He was no longer dreading another day of he-said/she-said in family court. Now he was in the Big Leagues, the criminal calendar, Major Felony Division, Cook County Circuit Court. It was as if he had finally walked through the right door.

As they waited on the judge, DA Stephenson politely approached Thaddeus and his client and placed a one-inch sheaf of papers on the table. "Discovery," he whispered to Thaddeus. "Round one."

Thaddeus nodded and began absently flipping through the turnover. He expected to find the usual incident reports from the uniforms, and there they were. The usual case workups from the detectives, and there they were. And then the lab report. This he read word-for-word. While the uniforms and the dicks just made it all up as they went along, lab reports were supposed to be scientific, truthful, complete, and accurate. Reading along, he came to this sentence: "Latent prints: right thumb, right index, right ring, full palm. Matched to booking prints of Ansel Largent, defendant." Which stopped him cold. He backed up and re-read the sentence. It hadn't changed.

He slid the report in front of Ansel. He drew an underline with his finger, pointing out the fingerprint findings. As Ansel read, Thaddeus skimmed further on. It got even worse. Preliminary DNA found on the pistol grips matched that of defendant Ansel Largent. The percentage of probability that it wasn't his DNA fell a billion times short of reasonable doubt.

Thaddeus felt his stomach clench. This wasn't supposed to be.

Ansel had promised he had no connection to the gun seized from his office. He had promised there would be no fingerprints left there by him. He had promised, most steadfastly, there would be no DNA--at least not belonging to him. Now all of that was contradicted by some lab rat named Justin Simone, B.S., who had signed off. A wave of nausea all but overwhelmed Thaddeus. This wasn't supposed to be happening. He knew his client very well and he would have bet the ranch that Ansel Largent had nothing to do with the tragedy two doors down from his own office.

He saw that Ansel's hand had begun to shake.

"You've got to get me out of here, Thaddeus," he said hoarsely. "I need my meds."

Thaddeus whispered. "He has the motion to set reasonable conditions of release. We'll get to that before we're done here."

"Oh my God. I have no idea how they got my prints on that gun. No idea."

"Straight up, have you ever handled that gun?" Thaddeus whispered.

"Never. Wait. Last night. That detective did show me a gun."

"What?"

"Yes, he came and spoke to me."

"And he showed you the gun?"

"Yes. I'm certain of it now."

"Did he have you handle it?"

"I thought he was an insurance client. I thought he was there about an insurance case that had to do with a faulty firearm. I thought it was a products liability case."

"So that's a yes, you did handle the gun?"

"I suppose so. Yes, I'm sure I did."

"Then they ran it over to the crime lab and now we're stuck with this lab report."

Thaddeus flipped to the report's front page.

"Here it is. Date-stamped yesterday. Signed off by Justin Simone yesterday."

"Tell me something, Ansel. Why would a smart man like you handle a gun from a detective? I'm not seeing it."

"They arrested me before I took my meds yesterday. I'm telling you I thought he was an insurance client."

"You had a psychotic episode."

Ansel whitened. "It's been known to happen."

"Is that how the money got loose from the trust fund and went to Zurich and skipped around the world?"

"I suppose so. I've asked myself the same question at least ten thousand times. My meds must need adjusting. Sometimes it's up on the Risperidone, sometimes it's down. Just depends on whether I'm imagining things or not. I vacillate between two milligrams and four milligrams."

Ansel tapped the side of his head. "It gets very busy up in here."

"I'm sorry that's happened to you. But right now I don't have time to sympathize, I've got to get you out of this mess."

The scheme came into focus for Thaddeus. His guy had been set up. Which would be impossible to prove. The cops would deny last night's visit involved the gun. There would be a record of a visit by the detective with Ansel, wouldn't there be? Still, that didn't prove he had brought along the gun. Only Ansel could testify to that and he had been reeling inside a psychotic episode at the time. He was liable to say anything. A million things. All different. A world of possibilities darted through Thaddeus' mind. The wave of nausea returned and burned his throat.

He poured out a paper cup of water from the pitcher on counsel table.

Instant relief. The scratchy feeling in his throat subsided. The nausea seemed to recede. But this report was going to make getting bail all but impossible. The law said, where the proof was evident and the presumption great, bail would not be required. This was true for capital cases and cases for which a sentence of life imprisonment might be imposed. Which was Ansel Largent's predicament exactly. He was looking at life imprisonment and, under the felony-murder rule, definitely would be looking at life. Illinois had abolished the death penalty, thank God for that. Unless the feds somehow became involved, but so far there wasn't even a hint of that.

The District Attorney wouldn't allow this plum to be turned over to the feds. This case involved Suzanne Fairmont, the candidate for the most important job in Cook County. This case was a career-maker.

Thaddeus looked across at DA Stephenson, who seemed to be examining the hairs on the back of his hand. He knew, brother, he knew what he had. His ticket to the throne room, election to a statewide office of some kind, if he got this conviction. While he appeared to be all nonchalant, Thaddeus knew that beneath that remote exterior there was a raging furnace. He had no doubt his time had come around at last.

Finally Judge Zang pushed his reading glasses up on his forehead and addressed the attorneys.

"The court is going to appoint its own psychiatrist to examine the defendant. Defendant's own physician will likewise be granted access to the defendant for counsel's purposes of pre-trial psychiatric examination as well as for treatment of any potential mental disorders, as set out in the motion."

"Your Honor, the state likewise needs access to the defendant for its own psychiatric workup."

"A three-way? Very well, counsel. Equal access to both the state and the defense will be ordered. Mr. Largent, I expect you to cooperate with the physicians selected to study you, is that clear?"

"Yes," Ansel said weakly.

"Now, let's take up the matter of bail. Mr. Murfee, it's your motion. You may be heard."

Thaddeus scraped back his chair. He stood fully upright, dressed in his brown pinstripes with tan vest. His round eyeglasses lent him a rather owlish look, but a look that Katy said was very attractive. He wasn't "sexy," she said, but he looked clean-cut and accomplished. Which he took to mean he was passable but wasn't going to cause any ladies to swoon. Fair enough, he was all right with that.

"May it please the court," he began.

The judge leaned forward. Thaddeus made eye contact and launched into it.

"Your Honor, my client Ansel Largent is a fifty-year-old lawyer, admitted some twenty-five years ago to the practice of law in this very court, a card-carrying member of the State Bar of Illinois, chair of the Defective Products Committee of the Defense Research Institute, a major in the Army Reserve, and a very active member of the Evanston community where he's been a homeowner for twenty years. He's married, has one son, away at school in California, and has a ton of connections to his community."

Thaddeus paused and sipped from the paper cup. Then he continued.

"His office has delivered to me his passport, which he is willing to surrender, and glad to do, because he has no plans to run or try to get away. Reason? He hasn't done anything wrong and demands a jury trial to prove it. We would ask that bail be set in a reasonable amount and that he be freed on his recognizance bond. That would be unusual and counsel for the state will object, but in a case like this it's certainly warranted. Bottom line, he's a member of the bar. He's not going to run. Thank you."

Whereupon DA Stephenson was immediately on his feet and gesturing wildly as he said, "Ridiculous! To even suggest a recognizance bond to this court is an insult! Here's a man facing life in prison, against whom the proof is evident and the presumption great that he in fact committed the crime he's been indicted for. Your Honor, I have just this morning provided defense counsel with a laboratory report from the Chicago Police Department's Crime Lab."

"And?" said the judge without indication of which way he was leaning.

"The crime lab report recites finding defendant's fingerprints all over the murder weapon. That's one. Number two is that the gun has been tested and shown to be the gun that murdered Suzanne Fairmont. Number three, the defendant's own DNA is smeared all over the gun. For him to come in here and deny that the proof is evident and the presumption great is to laugh in the face of the very science upon which we in the legal system of this great state rely to guide us each and every day. The state would submit that no bail should be set. Passport or no passport, if Mr. Largent decides to leave the country I daresay that as a lawyer he knows how to buy a new ID for a couple of thousand bucks and leave. So that means nothing. Regarding his ties to the community, people tied to the community commit crimes every day. That fact alone doesn't make him any less likely to commit another crime or to flee this court. And his admission to the practice of law in this court is nothing more than a red herring. Lawyers commit crimes every day, bar admission or not. Just read the *Bar Journal* for the disciplinary cases our ARDC brings against lawyers in this state, some of whom, I daresay, have stood in this very court and addressed this very judge! No bail should be allowed, Your Honor. Thank you."

With that, a very flabbergasted District Attorney took his seat, doing his best to demonstrate how insulted the court should be that the defense would request bail at all. At least that's what his face and body language said. Deep down--again, in that inner place where lawyers hide their true feelings--he knew the court was very likely going to allow bail and that there was a slight chance the defendant would get out on a signature bond. His own recognizance. Stephenson caught his breath and tapped his fingers against the tabletop, his Morse code to the judge that the court shouldn't take but a moment or two before dismissing the defense motion and sending this criminal back to the jail where he so obviously belonged. His tapping turned to drumming turned to demanding.

The judge looked up and looked at Stephenson's hand and said, simply, "Please. I'm thinking."

"Sorry, Your Honor," said Stephenson. "I'm just anxious to protect the people against this man."

"Hold on," cried Thaddeus, "there's no evidence showing my client is a danger. None at all!"

"What about him shooting Suzanne Fairmont? Isn't that a pretty damn good indicator of his character?"

"In your dreams," said Thaddeus. "He's not only not a

threat, I'm going to prove to you he didn't commit this crime, fingerprints and DNA be damned!"

"Gentlemen," said the judge. "Please. Oral argument is over."

"Thank you, Judge," said Thaddeus, as is the wont of lawyers whether they get their way or not.

"Thank you, Your Honor," chimed in Stephenson.

To the casual onlooker it would have been impossible at that moment to tell the winner from the loser--both attorneys thanking the judge and both attorneys wearing the look of success.

But, that was court and that was the public affect all lawyers wore.

What happened next was totally unpredicted by either attorney.

"Gentlemen," the judge began, "Let me begin by saying that I personally know Ansel Largent. In fact, for a period while in law school, I clerked for him. I know Ansel Largent to be diligent, community-minded, and forthright in his dealings with authority. Mr. Largent, will you come to court if I let you out on your own recognizance?"

"Yes, Judge."

"Well, that's fine, because I'm not going to do that. And here's why. The court owes a duty to the citizens of this state to protect them. And it owes a concomitant duty to act in good faith and, perhaps as important, to maintain the appearance of good faith. If I let a man indicted for murder loose on just his signature, imagine what kind of message that would send to the people of Chicago. On the other hand, if I set an exorbitant bail, that wouldn't be fair to the defendant who does, in fact, have commendable ties to the community and has a top notch reputation with the judges of this circuit. So I'm going to demonstrate how Solomon was a piker."

The lawyers looked at each other. That didn't ring a bell with either of them.

"What I'm saying is, in my Solomonic wisdom, I am going to order bail on signature release, but only if and when the defendant proves by the testimony of the court's very own psychiatric witness that he's neither a flight risk nor a danger to others. That's my order. Paper to follow. We're adjourned."

With that the judge was up and retreating to his office.

First words out of Ansel's mouth, "What the hell did he just do?"

"Cut the baby in half without actually cutting it in half," Thaddeus said with a wry grin.

"You mean he let me out but not yet."

"Exactly. He wants to see what goes on in that noodle of yours. Does he know about your mental problems?"

"Well, I believe--yes I'm sure--he was working for me the day I forgot to pull up my pants coming out of the men's room back at the office."

"What? Repeat that?"

"It happened right about the same time I saw my first shrink. I walked down the hall with my pants down around my ankles."

"And the judge was there."

"He wasn't a judge then. He was a law student."

"But he did see."

"Actually he gave me a ride to the doctor's office. That's how he knows so much about me. I was crying on the way and I guess he hasn't forgotten."

"Damnation, Ansel. This case gets wackier about every

ten minutes. No, I'm sorry I said that. Let me take that back."

"You don't have to worry. I do have my issues. Luckily most of them are controlled with medication."

"Damn, I'm sorry. It must be really hard."

The deputy waiting patiently at Ansel's elbow reached and touched the prisoner's upper arm.

"We about ready?" the deputy asked.

"Sure. Ansel, I'll report in to Libby. Make sure she's getting the care she needs."

"I know. Thanks for that."

"And I'll be over this afternoon. We'll lay some plans for the doctors."

"Good. We need to do that. You need to tell me how to act."

"Ansel, that's just it. It ain't an act, my friend. Which might just be enough to spring you."

The DA ignored them as he blew by, Detective Jake O'Connor bringing up the rear.

"Hello, Ansel," said the detective to Ansel. A small smile played at this mouth.

"Go to hell," said Ansel.

"That's no way to talk to an old friend."

"You haven't heard anything yet," said Ansel.

"That's enough," Thaddeus said.

Ansel stood and crossed his wrists behind his back to be cuffed. He nodded and eyed the back of the detective as he went out the door.

"Boys, old Ansel is just getting started."

Chapter 37

In 2011, late August, Libby and youngest son Winston drove from Chicago to Berkeley, California. Winston had been admitted to the University of California at Berkeley and a dorm room was waiting for him. All that was needed were clothes, computer, study lamp, and books. Libby and Winston drove Winston's five-year-old Highlander and pulled a small U-Haul, loaded with Winston's golf clubs, electric cello, stereo equipment, computer, two seasons of clothes, and all the rest of the mishmash that goes into existing as an eighteen-year-old young man away from home for the first time.

They stopped three nights along the way, watched movies until eleven, laughed and ate pizza, and enjoyed their last outing as mother and son. They both knew it was coming, the nest-leaving, so the trip and the feelings were bittersweet. Winston, of course, was glad to be moving out from under his parents' thumb; Libby was having nothing less than mood-swings that ranged from excited anticipation at having total freedom in her life to downright depression at the idea of being childless in the connected-at-the-hip sense.

Things happened fast once they reached Berkeley--almost too fast for Libby's comfort zone. First was the matter of the new roommate. It turned out that Winston's new roomie was a young man from Peoria, Illinois, which meant Winston and Charlie immediately had a world in common and instantly became best of friends.

Right away, Libby started getting hints from Winston that if she didn't stay over the full three days he wouldn't be disappointed.

She began feeling like a fifth wheel, and that first night found herself alone, in a Ramada Inn, crying for no reason she could think of. Except she did think of it, when she finally felt her true feelings, and she admitted that her little boy had just walked out of her life and that he wasn't coming back. At least not as the Winston she had known.

The next time they would see each other--Christmas--she knew their entire relationship would be different than ever before. He would be a young man with experiences she hadn't shared with him, and she would have moved on too, in her own way, and, no matter how much she hated to admit it, she knew that she would really be enjoying her freedom by then. And might even feel the tiniest bit restricted by having him around even for just a week at Christmas. When she admitted these things her tears immediately dried up, she swallowed hard, and made her plans.

She decided she would leave the next day instead of waiting until the fourth day, as planned. After all, he needed his space and he was okay and on his way; she didn't like the fifth-wheel feeling and just the idea of taking on the role of over-protective mom, or mom-who-can't-say-goodbye, or doting mom--it was just unacceptable. She was too much her own person for that.

So...she changed her airline reservations and flew back to Chicago that same day, arriving two days early.

As it turned out, Ansel of course wasn't expecting her back. Not two days early.

She arrived at 1:07 p.m. at O'Hare and took a cab all the way to Evanston. At the gate she used her clicker and was driven to the front door.

She found herself standing inside the foyer, and she guessed Ansel was downtown at the office. Her first thought was how much she wanted to take a bath in her own tub, light some candles, and have the last cry she would allow herself to have, over Winston's moving out, and then she would climb out, dry off, and begin her new life. Thoughts of being wined and dined by Ansel as they got to know each other again, in intimacy, danced through her head and she found herself doubting if she was actually even going to need that last cry.

She lugged her suitcase upstairs and swung into the bedroom.

Only to find Ansel and Suzanne Fairmont lightly sleeping, clearly exhausted by a recent round of lovemaking, as both were nude, and arms and torsos and legs were entwined as only intimate sex partners will entwine.

At first she was speechless. She knew Ansel had had his dalliances and over the years she had turned her head, as they were historically brief little flings and flirtations, occasionally an afternoon hotel here and there, but had amounted to nothing. She had found that acceptable and even had admitted she found several men over the years interesting to her, but never enough so that she acted out her own fantasies. Ansel had been the actor; she, merely the dreamer.

But this was over the line. Screwing in her own house? She guessed not.

She threw her suitcase at them, swung it in a huge arc and flung it. It landed with a *thud*! And the lovers were instantly awake and grappling for sheets and blankets.

"I can explain this," said Ansel. "It's not what it--"

"What are you, reading lines out of some script?" Libby said, her voice firm and even. "You can't explain jack!"

She folded her arms across her chest and watched Suzanne bolt up and pull the sheet fully around her body, as her lips began trembling.

"I--I--"

"Busted," said Libby. "No, I--I--I nothing, lady. I've got eyes and I don't give one hoot in hell about you--you--you. Now you get your panties cinched up and Ansel will call you a cab. Won't you, dear?"

"I know what you're thinking," said Ansel, "but I can--"

"Please spare me. Two lawyers and so far not a credible sentence. Why am I not surprised?"

But something inside Libby snapped.

The last thing she remembered was a red blanket rolling across her brain and dimming her vision.

She awoke four hours later in the Evanston Medical Center, and was told by the ICU nurse that she'd had a stroke.

She tried speaking. But nothing came out.

Ansel was beside her, holding her hand, and she knew, dimly, that she wanted him gone. That was it: gone.

"Leave me alone," she tried to say. But it came out, "Wee n--" and then stopped. Dimly she recognized that she had lost the ability to speak. And that her entire right side was numb. Including her beautiful face. She remembered seeing clips of stroke victims on TV and she knew instantly how she must have looked. She closed her eyes and tears came.

Two months later she would speak her first sentence.

"My hushban ish a ashhole."

"Excellent," said the speech therapist. "You've come so far."

And the feelings were there.

She loathed Suzanne Fairmont with every fiber of her being. She had stolen her husband and she had stolen Libby's health. Libby was certain that without the adulterous scene she experienced that afternoon, none of the rest of it would have happened. There would have been no stroke. There would have been no hatred of her husband. Her life would be moving on in a much different direction than now.

She hated Suzanne.

And wished her dead.

Chapter 38

El Capitan worked the slide on his Glock and aimed the pistol at the back of the man's head.

The man, in this case, was an Australian who had been stealing off the top. The oldest trick in the drug wholesaler's book: receive forty kilos of coke, sell twenty of them at street prices and twenty at street plus ten percent. Pocket the difference. Two or three times and a guy could retire. Even an Australian guy who loved his women, white beaches, and Mexican cocaine--there was enough in his pocket to hang it all up and snooze.

But El Capitan knew everything. He owned Southern California, where the coke had been marketed. If street was one hundred an ounce, he knew it. If street was one hundred and one an ounce, he knew that, too. In fact, he kept a spreadsheet on all the counties in all the states above the border. So when the Aussie sold at one-ten and reported back one hundred, El Capitan knew he had a cheat with his foot caught in the trap.

"Do you have any last words?" El Capitan asked the Aussie.

The man opened his mouth to beg for his life.

But before the man could get a word out, the drug king had squeezed the trigger.

The man slumped face-down on the patio.

"Get rid of this piece of shit. And hose this place off. The dogs lick this blood up. Makes me sick."

Two bodyguards jumped to it. Two others followed the chief back inside the hacienda.

Four American college girls greeted him, all in varying stages of undress.

"So what do I get for my ten thousand dollars, ladies?"

The blond from Berkeley smiled and removed her tee-shirt. She was totally naked.

"Whatever you want," she said.

"We've only got 'til tomorrow night then you have to be back in school. So let's get this party started. When I count three, I want to see everyone naked. One, two--"

"El Capitan," said a bodyguard whose mobile phone just chimed. "It's Juan Carlos Ordañez."

"Jus' when I was going to have my fun," said El Capitan with a flashy grin at the ladies. He accepted the cell phone from his underling.

"JC," he said, "what's up, dog?"

The voice on the other end sounded distant, if cell phones could sound distant. The connection was very iffy, as El Capitan was in Mexico City and Juan Carlos Ordañez in Tijuana. Not all the bugs were worked out of Carlos Slim's cell towers, but it was getting better. "We jus' got ripped two hundred million," said Juan Carlos Ordañez.

"What the hell? You better splain to me how that happens!"

"This gringo took my son and he was going to kill him. Unless I wired the two hundred mil we got from Banco Nacionale."

"I'm listening. I'm listening, but I'm not liking."

"It's true."

"*Cabron*, you listen to me. I want that money back. Is the boy safe?"

"He is. We got him back two days ago."

"Why did you wait so long to call me then?"

"I tried to handle it on my own," Juan Carlos Ordañez lied. The truth was, he was too frightened to call his boss and tell what had happened. He felt like a dupe. Maybe he even felt like a dead dupe.

"I told you already. You call me first thing about this kind of shit. Don't you know I mean that?"

"I do. I'm sorry."

"So where is my money now?"

"It went back to Chicago."

"Chicago? Like Chicago, Illinois?"

"*Si.*"

"Aii, *caramba!* We got to do something. Do you know this man that took your son?"

"I do. He was staying in a hotel and used his real name."

"Who is this man?"

"Thaddeus Murfee. *Un pinche abogado.*"

"This man has huge *cojones*, like boulders, JC. I don't like him already."

"Me too. I hate him."

"You jump on the next plane out. Come to my place and we'll make a plan."

"What will we do?"

"We? First I have to choose do I kill you or not. Then

we'll see. Oh, you're leaving already? That makes me feel much better, then. *Cabron*."

He threw the cell phone against the wall.

By the next afternoon, before two, Juan Carlos Ordañez was sitting poolside at El Capitan's *finca*. He was drinking a single malt scotch and toying with the sweat from the glass, watching it run down and spatter on his white duck slacks. He was wearing yellow Jimmy Choo patent loafers, the white slacks, and a white silk shirt unbuttoned down the front. A straw Panama completed the look of the man of great wealth taking his ease. Which he was and he was. A Cuban cigar blossomed smoke around his head as he leaned back in the recliner and waited for El Capitan to join him.

He was making himself look as relaxed and calm as possible, though he knew his unpredictable, impulsive superior might just as soon walk out and shoot him between the eyes as walk out and join him for a drink and make a plan about the money.

But Juan Carlos was nobody's fool. He had a plan to make El Capitan take him back under his wing and give him the space and time to take back the two hundred million and that's all he asked. The rest of it he would make happen.

The rear sliders were thrown open and El Capitan came striding around the pool. The first thing Juan Carlos noticed was that he wasn't packing heat, but that didn't mean his bodyguard couldn't supply him in a whisper. Still, he was able to relax and draw a deep breath when it first appeared he was in the clear.

El Capitan smiled and began rubbing his hands together. He slapped Juan Carlos across the shoe and plopped down beside him in a pool chair.

"So. When do I get my money back?"

"By Friday. I have it all worked out."

"You do? Without me you have made a plan?"

"I thought you--"

"Just kidding, *cabron*! I like your plan already because it gets my money back. Now give me the details."

"The money was wired out of Hong Kong to Chicago."

"And who did that?"

"I did, El Capitan."

El Capitan waggled a finger under Juan Carlos' nose. "Bad, bad boy. You shouldn't take my money without asking first."

"They had my boy. He said he would kill him."

"I know all that already. So. My money goes from bank to bank. What happened next?"

"It went into a law firm in Chicago. That much I know."

"Law firm? You mean some *putos abogados* got my money?"

"That's right. Only it was their money first."

"Ah, but fair is fair. We stole it fair and square."

"That's true. We stole it fair and square. Now they got it back."

"Okay, so what's our plan? I hope it's a good one and I don't have to shoot you today. It's too hot to shoot someone. *Caramba*!"

"The same man who took it from the law firm one time will take it again."

"And why would he do this?"

"Because he has a son. Away at college."

"A college stud? Really? Where?"

"At Berkeley. And this *puto abogado* worships this kid. He will get your money."

"Seems like a lot of trouble for us."

"It's a lot of money, El Capitan."
"Now tell me some shit I don't know, homeboy. Eh?"

Chapter 39

Ruben Washington was a Manual Arts High School dropout, ninth grade. Rootless and hating the world, he had pulled twenty-four months in Juvie for shooting up a convenience store when a gunfight erupted down the canned goods aisle. When it was all over and the smoke had cleared, Ruben lay under the Folger's Coffee display, bleeding profusely from a neck wound, while two Crips one aisle over lay crumpled and dead. It had been a two-on-one and the odds had been against him. But he was faster with his silver Sanchi .38 revolver than they were with their .22 Berettas and their wounds were mortal while his was only life-threatening. Before he could bleed out, the EMT's had him transfused and racing for the ER two blocks away where a trauma surgeon laced him back together and staunched the flow of blood. Forty-eight hours later he woke up handcuffed to a hospital bed and spent the next two years in the juvenile court system, bouncing between being tried as a minor and tried as an adult.

As he quickly learned, the Cook County judicial system

was mean and heartless. It held no love for a gang-banger with two kills to his credit.

He turned eighteen behind barred windows.

When he was released, he possessed no marketable skills, his educational record made him unemployable because it didn't exist, but none of that mattered, because the heavily redesigned Ruben Washington proudly displayed the SS13 tattoo on his neck and the initials of two dead Crips on his right shoulder. Which meant he owned street cred. Enough to get him laid, made, and paid. Magnetic, it all flowed to him easily and endlessly, drugs, dollars, and drive-bys.

On his twentieth birthday he was running the whole show and celebrated with a gift to his mother of $100,000 cash. Not having yet digested mom's cake, Ruben and two funny boys shredded four Crips in a drive-by just-for-fun. That's what you did on your twentieth birthday when you were SS13 and scrambling on the South Side.

The gun that saved his life in the convenience store was the same gun that killed Suzanne Fairmont. It had been stored in the CPD evidence warehouse, awaiting use at trial. Then the trial went away, and a green van that said Metal Fabricators down the side made a haul of weapons from closed cases. These artifacts were trucked away to melt-down. Ruben's gun was saved by a larcenous sergeant who just couldn't resist the weapon's pearl-handled grips. It would have been melted down that afternoon if he hadn't plucked it off the van. The sergeant took the gun home and put it in his gun safe and immediately forgot all about it.

It remained in the safe for two years, until his sixteen year old swiped the key and had a look inside.

Maybe not all genetic, the pearl handles swept him away just like they had his old man. The kid lifted the gun, felt the heft, and claimed it for his own. That afternoon he purchased two boxes of full metal jacket target loads and headed for the hills behind Barrington. He fired two rounds and hit a Coke can with the second blast. He was about to drill it again when the hammer met the firing pin and flame shot backwards out of the cylinder, searing the kid's sighting eye and blinding him.

The gun was a Sanchi MJ7, an Italian make that had been imported and distributed by All American Arms of Newport, New Jersey.

Having introduced the gun into the stream of commerce, All American was named in the lawsuit filed by the sergeant on behalf of his one-eyed son, who now entertained a view of the world in something less than 3D.

Discovery motions were filed, the errant firearm was produced, and the gun wound up in the hands of the defense counsel hired by the insurance company that insured All American Arms.

That defense counsel happened to be Ansel Largent, who kept the gun in a clear plastic box on his desk, awaiting shipment by Melinda to the non-destructive testing engineers selected by Ansel as his client's expert witnesses. Three virgin full metal jacketed shells accompanied the gun and remained yet loaded in the cylinder as the day the plaintiff failed to heed every mother's advice that "you'll put your eye out!"

It was this gun that ended the life of Suzanne Fairmont when bullet number four entered the back of her head and stirred the contents of her skull like a high speed food processor.

She was dead before she could turn to see why her office visitor had come close.

Chapter 40

Psychiatric protocols had the psychiatrists triplicating the inquiry into Ansel Largent's mental state as of the night Suzanne Fairmont died.

In Illinois law, the issues of mental state at the time of the shooting and the competency to stand trial are two totally different animals. The question of Ansel's fitness to stand trial looked at whether, because of the defendant's mental condition, he was unable to understand the nature and purpose of the proceedings against him or to assist in his own defense. Because the issue of competency to stand trial had been raised by Thaddeus prior to trial for the underlying charge of first degree murder, Ansel was entitled to have this issue decided by a jury. Which is what Thaddeus told the court he wanted for his client.

As Thaddeus expected, after a trial by jury, the verdict by a preponderance of the evidence was that Ansel was found fit to stand trial. Over a four day period, the jury listened to the opinions of one psychiatrist and two psychologists regarding the ability of Ansel to assist in his defense.

It was an easy and quick decision for the jurors. After all, here was a man who had been running a law practice and carrying a full case load in a firm that employed over eight hundred lawyers. If he managed all that successfully--which he did--then surely he was able to help Thaddeus Murfee with the defense of his case. The jury deliberated less than one hour before returning with its verdict.

While the verdict wasn't unexpected by Thaddeus, what he had done in even raising the issue was to create possible error for appellate counsel if the case went south and an appeal was required on down the road. It was simply a matter of planning ahead and Thaddeus, in order to fully protect his client, was pulling all the strings he could to try to create appealable error that might be grounds for a new trial or even reversal of a verdict if it came to that.

Thaddeus met with Ansel at the jail the night before the jury's finding.

"What have they done?" Thaddeus asked, inquiring about the steps taken by the doctors.

"Lots of written testing. I've had two MMPI's, a physical exam, and a ton of other things. The shrink left this list of what they would be doing."

He pushed a written sheet across the metal table. The list said:

To determine a diagnosis and check for any related complications, you may have:

A physical exam. Your doctor will try to rule out physical problems that could cause your symptoms.

Lab tests. These may include a check of your thyroid function or a screening for alcohol and drugs, for example.

A psychological evaluation. A doctor or mental health provider talks to you about your symptoms, thoughts, feelings and behavior patterns. You may be asked to fill out a questionnaire to help answer these questions.

Determining which mental illness you have. Sometimes it's difficult to find out which mental illness may be causing your symptoms. But taking the time and effort to get an accurate diagnosis will help determine the appropriate treatment.

The defining symptoms for each mental illness are detailed in the Diagnostic and Statistical Manual of Mental Disorders (DSM-5), published by the American Psychiatric Association. This manual is used by mental health providers to diagnose mental conditions and by insurance companies to reimburse for treatment.

Classes of mental illness. The main classes of mental illness are:

Neurodevelopmental disorders. This class covers a wide range of problems that usually begin in infancy, childhood or the teenage years. Examples include autism spectrum disorder, attention-deficit/hyperactivity disorder (ADHD) and learning disorders.

Schizophrenia spectrum and other psychotic disorders. Psychotic disorders cause detachment from reality (delusions, paranoia and hallucinations). The most notable example is schizophrenia, although other classes of disorders can be associated with detachment from reality at times.

Bipolar and related disorders. This class includes disorders with alternating episodes of mania -- periods of excessive activity, energy and excitement -- and depression.

Depressive disorders. These include disorders that affect how you feel emotionally, such as the level of sadness and happiness. Examples include major depressive disorder and premenstrual dysphoric disorder.

Anxiety disorders. Anxiety is an emotion characterized by the anticipation of future danger or misfortune, accompanied by feeling ill at ease. This class includes generalized anxiety disorder, panic disorder and phobias.

Obsessive-compulsive and related disorders. These disorders involve preoccupations or obsessions and repetitive thoughts and actions. Examples include obsessive-compulsive disorder, hoarding and hair-pulling disorder (trichotillomania).

Trauma- and stressor-related disorders. These are adjustment disorders in which a person has trouble coping during or after a stressful life event. Examples include post-traumatic stress disorder (PTSD) and acute stress disorder.

Dissociative disorders. These are disorders in which your sense of self is disrupted, such as with dissociative identity disorder and dissociative amnesia.

Somatic symptom and related disorders. A person with one of these disorders may have physical symptoms with no clear medical cause, but the disorders are associated with significant distress and impairment. The disorders include somatic symptom disorder (previously known as hypochondriasis) and factitious disorder.

Feeding and eating disorders. These disorders include disturbances related to eating, such as anorexia nervosa and binge-eating disorder.

Elimination disorders. These disorders relate to the inappropriate elimination of urine or stool by accident or on purpose. Bedwetting (enuresis) is an example.

Sleep-wake disorders. These are disorders of sleep

severe enough to require clinical attention, such as insomnia, sleep apnea and restless legs syndrome.

Sexual dysfunctions. These include disorders of sexual response, such as premature ejaculation and female orgasmic disorder.

Gender dysphoria. This refers to the distress that accompanies a person's stated desire to be another gender.

Disruptive, impulse-control and conduct disorders. These disorders include problems with emotional and behavioral self-control, such as kleptomania or intermittent explosive disorder.

Substance-related and addictive disorders. These include problems associated with the use of alcohol, caffeine, tobacco and drugs. This class also includes gambling disorder.

Neurocognitive disorders. Neurocognitive disorders affect your ability to think and reason. This class includes delirium, as well as neurocognitive disorders due to conditions or diseases such as traumatic brain injury or Alzheimer's disease.

Personality disorders. A personality disorder involves a lasting pattern of emotional instability and unhealthy behavior that causes problems in your life and relationships. Examples include borderline personality disorder and antisocial personality disorder.

Paraphilic disorders. These disorders include sexual interest that causes personal distress or impairment or causes potential or actual harm to another person. Examples are sexual sadism, voyeuristic disorder and pedophilic disorder.

Other mental disorders. This class includes mental disorders that are due to other medical conditions or that don't meet the full criteria for one of the above disorders.

Thaddeus slid the list and its enumerations back across the table. Ansel carefully inserted it back inside his jailhouse folder.

"Impressive," said Thaddeus. "No damn wonder it's taken a month."

"I know. If there's anything else to know about me, I don't know what it would be."

"Well I've read the reports, which I'll leave with you. Just faxed over to me this afternoon."

"Just give me a quick summary."

"Besides being a weird duck, you're a pretty ordinary duck. However, you are bipolar and do need the Risperidone med. Antipsychotic. But we already knew that."

"That's followed me around probably since college days. I just thought everybody saw strangers lurking in bushes."

"Thankfully no. People like you and me, maybe."

"Why? You're not bipolar, are you?"

"Let's just say I've had my share of bad guys after me in my young age. Sometimes they were in fact waiting in the weeds."

"That's different. I see things in bushes--or parked cars. Then I walk over to investigate and guess what? No one there."

"So that's how you thought David had taken the trust account money?"

"I can only guess. To me, it was as real as this hand," he said, holding up a very white hand. An untanned hand that made Thaddeus realize how much Ansel was probably missing daylight.

"From what the doctors are saying in the reports, long story short, you have a moderate dissociation disorder as well. They say it operates along a spectrum from zero to a hundred. Some days you're all there, maybe a twenty. Some days you're not hitting on all cylinders, maybe an eighty. Some days you're at a hundred and should have stayed in bed."

"That's in addition to the bipolar?"

"Exactly."

Well, now we won't be shocked tomorrow when they find you fit to stand trial. Don't be surprised when I tear into the Court's doctor and the DA's doctor tomorrow. I'll only be doing it to make a record."

"For appeal. Of course. I would expect no less."

Thaddeus smiled. "So, prepare for the worst and hope for the best."

"Let's get to it then."

"Will Libby be there tomorrow?"

"I don't know. Why?"

"How's the new treatment with her been going?"

"We're good. We had our problems in the past. I did, actually."

"What happened?"

"I got caught in bed with another woman. Suzanne Fairmont."

"What! The victim?" Thaddeus was incredulous. "Why haven't you told me this before now?"

"I wanted to. But it hurts Libby so damn much still. I just didn't think it needed to come out at trial. Not while she's there."

Thaddeus narrowed his eyes. "So, let me get this straight. You were in love with Suzanne?"

"Maybe, probably. I don't know."

"Did you shoot her--no, don't answer that. It doesn't help me to know if my clients did it or not. Besides, I know you didn't."

"Of course I didn't shoot her. I had broken it off with

her. Probably forty-eight hours after Libby's stroke. Thad, I felt so guilty. I felt horrible. I know Libby would never have had that stroke if she hadn't found me with Suzanne."

"You don't know that. There was probably a predisposition. A weak artery somewhere."

"I don't think so. I think it was my colossal screwup that pushed her over the edge. I'll never forgive myself."

"Hey, that's up to you. What I need to know is, how was Libby toward Suzanne after you broke it off? She ever talk about her with you?"

"Sure, there was counseling. Plus church. That helped lots."

"So you learned your lesson and you've been a good boy ever since."

"Not exactly."

"Jeez. What else, Ansel?"

"Melinda, my secretary. We have this flaming thing going on. It's been limited to office encounters only. Well, maybe two-three times in a hotel. But we've never done the run-off-to-the-islands thing."

"Well thank goodness for that. Ansel, do you mind if I tell you something?"

"Does it matter?"

"You need to learn to keep your dick in your pants. The little head is getting the big head in trouble."

Ansel spread his hands. "Don't I know it. But there's more. Melinda's pregnant."

"Married?"

"Yes."

"Good. Have her blame it on him. He'll never be the wiser, he'll love the kid and father it, and you won't need to break up a marriage. Do what works, Ansel."

"She's in love with me."

"Man, I don't give a damn. You back out of there, excuse yourself, and leave the strange alone. You've got enough to do, between the law firm, your practice, and taking care of Libby."

"That's what I want to do. Clean slate."

"I suggest you write Melinda a long letter ending it. Mail it to the office. She'll have two options. She can accept that's it over and go live her own life, or she can get angry and show it to Libby. But the risk of that is that she knows Libby might get angry and show it to Melinda's husband. Then she's screwed. My guess is she won't like it, she'll quit her job and leave you in the lurch, but it'll be over."

"You're right. I'll write her."

"Good enough. Now I'm out of here."

"Tomorrow. And thanks, Thad."

"Welcome."

———

THE NEXT DAY, Ansel met Thaddeus in the courtroom and handed Thaddeus a sealed envelope. Thaddeus saw "Melinda" written across the front, and nodded. "I'll see it gets to her. At the office." Ansel nodded solemnly. Thaddeus believed Ansel was ready to get right and that made him dig in that much harder for his client. More than ever, he wanted to deliver the guy from the funhouse that his craziness had built.

Then the jury went out for an hour, found him fit to stand trial, after which, Thaddeus immediately renewed his motion to modify conditions of release. In short, he meant to spring Ansel from custody. The fitness jury had filed out of the courtroom and been dismissed when Thaddeus requested the court's attention.

"Your Honor," he began, "now that my client has been found fit to stand trial, I would renew his request that he be admitted to the terms and conditions of bail on his own recognizance. The court previously stated that once the defendant proved that he is neither a flight risk nor danger to others, you were going to order release on his signature. Well, my client has been found fit to stand trial, he has fully cooperated with the examining physicians, and he is not a flight risk in that, prior to the charges being filed in the case but after the death of Suzanne Fairmont, the defendant accompanied me to Zurich and Mexico and at no time indicated any reluctance to return to the U.S. Had he in fact been guilty of this crime it wouldn't have made any sense for him to come back. But come back, he did. Which should be the best possible indicator on which the court can hang its hat and release this man on his signature. Thank you for listening."

DA Stephenson was quickly on his feet, arguing, "But judge, there has been no showing that he's not a danger to others. The state would again remind the court that fitness to stand trial and psychotic or sociopathic tendencies toward others are two separate concepts both medically and under the law. Just because he understands the charges against him and can help his counsel prepare his defense does not mean that the streets will be just as safe if he's walking them. The defendant has failed to show he's not a danger to others and for that reason alone should not be released, either with a cash bond or on his signature. The proof is evident and the presumption is great that this man is a killer."

"Counsel," said the judge, looking directly at Thaddeus, "I am inclined to agree with defense counsel at this time. While there is very strong proof before the court that the defendant was connected to the gun by virtue of it being in his office and by virtue of it bearing his fingerprints and DNA, still that's not the standard for setting bail in these cases. Bond will be set as a 'D' bond in the amount of three million dollars. Mr. Largent, you must post ten percent to be released. Other conditions of release will be set out in my written order. Are we finished?"

"Yes, Your Honor," said both attorneys.

———

THE DAY FOLLOWING HIS RELEASE, Ansel appeared at his law firm. Melinda had resigned.

He called a directors' meeting and discussed his ongoing role with the managing directors. It was decided that he would continue in his role as managing partner. He also explained how he had intervened with the hackers who had managed to divert the firm's trust account and how he got the money back. He said there had been some strong-arm tactics employed by the FBI and that indictments were being drawn up for presentation to the grand jury. He assured them that an FBI report was being prepared that would fully explain what had happened and who the guilty parties were. There were going to be prosecutions and the board was relieved to hear that. They were equally adamant that no punishment was too severe for the hackers who had made off with their trust funds.

They discussed the death of Suzanne Fairmont and the gun that had been found in his office. Reassurances were made regarding lack of proof and Thaddeus was called into the room to make a brief presentation of the defense case. A vote was taken and it was decided four-to-three that Ansel would continue in his role as managing partner even during the pendency of the prosecution.

At present his case load was taken over by two junior partners and their associates and that would continue. Four out of thirty-seven insurance companies had pulled their accounts out of the law firm when they had learned of the indictment. The remaining thirty-three had decided that it would be too expensive and too damaging to their insureds to switch horses in midstream. Ongoing cases would have required twice the attorney's fees to make a switch. However they had also requested that other partners handle their work while the indictment was pending.

With the exception of his discontinuing the day-to-day practice of law, and Melinda's abrupt resignation, it was as if that Black Monday had never happened.

As always, he continued to have access to the firm's trust account.

———

WHILE THE PSYCHIATRIC inquiry had proceeded, the murder case itself also had gone ahead.

Under Illinois law the question of fitness to stand trial does not delay preparation and advancement of the case in chief so, while he was working up the psychological issues, Thaddeus was also investigating the evidence collected by the police.

Among those artifacts were, of course, extensive photographs of the crime scene.

Hundreds of frames were shot and blown up to 8x10 and turned over to Thaddeus by the DA.

There were pictures of the head wound, close-up and wide angle. There were pictures of the victim at rest in her chair, her head slumped away from the force of the muzzle blast. There were pictures of powder burns and stippling on the skin and hair at the site of entry of the bullet into the head. There were pictures of the hardwood floor around the victim's office chair where she had been sitting. There were pictures of her desk, her body, her clothing, the file spread open on her desk, the murder weapon seized from Ansel's office, hundreds and hundreds of pictures. But one photograph stood out.

From among 368 photographs, one in particular grabbed Thaddeus' attention.

The office itself wasn't large by firm partnership standards: 15x17. As you came into the room you were greeted by a hexagonal table with slate top, four chairs equidistant around the table, and Suzanne's desk and chairs off to your right. She would have been facing her assailant when he first came into her office and, it had to be assumed, she would have known him, because her body was still seated in her chair--there evidently had been no effort on her part to stand and try to move away before being shot.

But there was blood--lots and lots of blood. Head wounds bleed profusely and hers was no different, for the bullet had entered and exited her head. The entry wound was not prodigious, maybe the size of a small marble. But the exit wound, entering on her right and exiting on her left, was huge, and had sprayed and leaked blood not only on her clothing, chair and desk, but also onto the floor.

And it was one picture of the floor that stopped Thaddeus cold.

The floor itself was unremarkable. It was a hardwood that was lighter in color than the blood which had sprayed it. Nothing remarkable there.

But what was remarkable was the patterning in and around the pool of blood on the hardwood. The blood itself, darker than the wood of the floor, looked as if it had been tattooed with some kind of object that left small tread marks. The tread marks were parallel, maybe two inches long, with four distinct treads per circle.

It stumped him.

And it didn't.

He had his ideas, but there was further inquiry to be made.

He already knew what he was looking for. Now to lay hands on it.

Chapter 41

It was cold that Monday in the third week of April.

Unusually frigid temperatures clung to the midwest and kept the thaw at bay. Ice slick sidewalks had been salted but the melted water quickly re-froze and people slipped and slopped as they navigated the Chicago court district.

At the street corners it was abnormally congested, with block-long plumes of smoke issuing from the traffic crawl. And everywhere were the jaywalkers, some successfully darting across, others getting halfway and slipping to the frozen surface, and on it went. The careful driver had one foot near the brake and one hand near the horn at all times.

Thaddeus hop-scotched the ice patches and clipped along two blocks from his LaSalle Street office.

He swung into the building and joined a frantic herd on the elevator for the monumentally slow ride upstairs. All eyes were glued to the passing numbers on the floor indicator. Occasional embarrassed conversations flitted between passengers who knew each other, or at least recognized each other and thought they might like to know each other better.

On the assigned courtroom floor, he found a crowd of reporters and cameras. It was as expected, because of the notoriety of Suzanne Fairmont, the only real challenger for the office of District Attorney. It was the headline of the day, the News at Five lead story, and Thaddeus had assiduously avoided calls from the press for comments and the occasional TV crew drop-in at the office. While he was friendly and affable, he really believed that trying cases in the press was verboten and to be avoided like the plague. Woe to the attorney who said one thing to the press that turned out to be other than what he had predicted once trial got underway. It was the same thing with opening statements to the jury: very little detail, hit the dynamics, avoid the specifics, somber tone, mildly ingratiating but not smarmy, sit the hell down.

He had made his way down front through the crowd. TV crews were set up outside the courtroom and reporters jabbed mikes at him as he shot past, mouth-clenched, his body language clearly indicating no comments would be made.

He had told Ansel to arrive at least an hour early in order to avoid the throngs outside, and the bailiff, by special decree, had unlocked the main doors momentarily and allowed Ansel to come inside, re-locking behind him until nine o'clock.

Both attorney and client were dressed in navy blue with pinstripes, both wore heavily starched white shirts, both wore regimental ties of some indiscernible regiment or other--all by design. Thaddeus had wanted them to look as lawyerly common as all other barristers looked that day, as they did every day in Midwestern winter. No need to stand out right or left or up or down. Vanilla, just plain vanilla. And if you really didn't want to insult anyone you even left the regimental stripes at home and opted for plain red, yellow, or blue. Those neckties always made it beyond all tests by the psychologists specially retained to sway jurors.

Thaddeus looked back over his shoulder. Prospective jurors and press and court-addicts jostled elbows and vied for seats. A huge swell of anticipation roiled the crowd at 9:00 a.m. Silence followed.

At 9:03, Judge Lawrence X. Zang was ready to address the packed court room.

"The defendant has been charged with first degree murder in the death of Suzanne Fairmont and he is facing life imprisonment for his natural lifetime in the Illinois State Penitentiary," Judge Zang announced. "Among the jurors in the courtroom right now, are there any among you who believe you should be excused from jury service here today based on what I have just said about the nature of this case?"

He gave it almost a full minute.

"Or about the identity of the victim, Suzanne Fairmont?"

Again, almost a full minute ticked by while everyone stared straight ahead.

Finally a wizened little man wearing a blue cardigan and an ancient necktie featuring a red bull, stood and said, "Did Suzanne live on my block?"

"What block would that be, sir, without giving your full address?"

"Thirty-seven-hundred North Sheridan, Room 400, Chicago, Illinois."

"That's a little more information than I needed, but thank you. And what is your name, sir?"

"Do I have to say it?"

"Please."

"Charlie Winters. Charles Nightingale Winters. Now you got me."

Smiles played across the mass of faces following the exchange.

"Let me ask counsel. Do either of you have any information regarding the victim's address? Whether she would have been a neighbor of Mr. Winters?"

Simultaneously both clusters of lawyers, cops, and investigators at counsel tables flashed on the fact that no one among them had any idea of Suzanne's address.

The judge finally lost patience with the buzz along counsel tables as everyone fumbled for some kind of knowledgeable response.

Then Mr. Winters continued on. "It probably don't matter. The Suzanne I know about has been gone fifteen years now."

Whereupon the judge's head snapped up. "Oh, all right, then, Mr. Winters. We wouldn't be talking about the same Suzanne Fairmont, then, as the victim in this case is alleged to have died more recently."

"Can't be her," said Mr. Winters. He sank back into his chair and absently rolled his necktie up and down, up and down.

"All right is there--"

"I'll just volunteer," said Mr. Winters. "First sergeant always said never volunteer. But that was beer call. Combat, you better be first with your hand up."

"Thank you, Mr. Winters, counsel will note that. The clerk will now draw names from a basket. If your name is called, please come forward and the clerk will seat you in

261

the jury box. The court will then ask you questions, as will the two lawyers."

The clerk called names until the box was filled. They were an amalgam of Chicago voters from all walks of life. Young, old, black, white, Asian, Latino--every species of American was represented. Overall there were six more women than men, which happened time and again in Thaddeus' trials, and always made him wonder why more women made it onto juries than men.

Questioning of the jurors went on for several hours. Finally it was time for peremptory challenges. Thaddeus and Ansel put their heads together and struck jurors from the list—those they believed wouldn't serve them well. The state did likewise, until a jury panel was selected. While neither side was totally satisfied with the final makeup of the jury, what they were actually left with were the mildest of the worst. As was always true. Because if one juror was especially liked by the state, Thaddeus would strike that juror. And if Thaddeus wanted someone, the state would always strike them.

The jurors were welcomed by the court and sworn. Preliminary jury instructions were given, just general guidelines for the role of juror, what could be expected, length of trial, hours of court, hours of lunch, morning and noon breaks, and how to get a message to the judge if a problem came up during the week.

The attorneys were then asked to give their opening statements. The state went first. For the trial portion of the case, the DA's office had sent to the fray William Eckles himself. It was high profile and Eckles needed votes; what better place than the highest-profile case of the year, to garner votes and love.

William Eckles scraped back, climbed to his feet, and

took to the podium. Eckles was understated in looks: plain grey suit and yellow tie and socks, a military grade flattop hairstyle, black-frame eyewear and a confident look. He launched right into his speech, which Thaddeus immediately knew he had practiced several times in front of his mirror, for it was articulate and persuasive, bordering on argument but avoiding that precise terrain, as argument wasn't allowed, just a recitation of what he expected the facts and evidence to be. He smiled a very bright and winning smile several times at the jury as he went along, and Thaddeus was pained to see that at least four jurors were making copious notes as his adversary spoke.

Then came Thaddeus' turn.

"What you have just heard isn't evidence," he began. "Instead, it's a mere recitation of what Mr. Eckles expects the evidence to be. In all fairness, now that he has shown his hand, so to speak, I would respectfully request that you require him to prove to you each and every fact he has just told you about, beyond a reasonable doubt. And if he doesn't prove one or more of those facts, I would ask that you find my client not guilty as the state hasn't met its required degree of proof. Now here's what I think the evidence is going to show."

Thaddeus recounted the night in question, that, as Eckles had just said, Ansel was in fact at the office the night Suzanne Fairmont was murdered, but that he had heard no gunshot and, if he had pulled the trigger himself, as the state was claiming, you would expect him to flee from the scene, which he hadn't done at all. Instead, the parking garage attendant would testify that when Ansel checked out at his station that night, he didn't seem to be hurried or flustered, and there was nothing about him that was other than his ordinary demeanor. Phone records would be introduced that would show Ansel had been working up one of his cases that night, and that he had called his client and two witnesses from the office, and spent all told about two hours preparing their testimony for upcoming depositions and listening to their concerns. Those three witnesses would testify that Ansel was all business that night, that he wasn't hurried or bothered, and that he had worked with them on their case like he always did. He was thorough, polite, and perspicuous and they saw nothing extraordinary in his approach, his tone, or his telephone demeanor. He was, in their words, the same old Ansel as always.

Then Thaddeus went over what DA Eckles had had to stay about the gun recovered from Ansel's office. Without delving into particulars and giving away his game plan, he simply reminded the jury that they should jump to no conclusions about the gun, the fingerprints, the DNA, and that it was seized from Ansel's office until they had heard Ansel's side of what actually happened. He assured them that when they heard the truth about this they would be outraged and that this particular evidence alone would be enough for them to return a verdict of not guilty.

After the lay witnesses, the defense would call at least one forensics expert, maybe more, but Thaddeus kept this vague on purpose in order to disallow the state full preparation for his expert or experts.

Finally, Thaddeus said that he would put Ansel's wife on the stand to talk about his demeanor that night, what time he had left home, what time he had returned, whether he had any signs of blood or other unusual signs on his clothes. She would testify that she had personally washed the jeans and sweater shirt he was wearing that freezing night, and that she had noticed nothing unusual about the clothes such as blood spots or any other indication of his having been involved in a close-up shooting. She would also testify that Ansel hated guns, that he cried out against the NRA whenever it was mentioned on CNN, and that he regularly supported financially the James Brady lobby and movement to make the acquisition of firearms much more difficult in the U.S. Ansel had signed the petition at bradycampaign.org, urging Congress to require stringent background checks on all gun sales. The actual inclusion of his name among those who had signed the petition would be proved, along with a facsimile of the petition itself. This would, Thaddeus promised, go to his state of mind and his complete abhorrence of guns and possession of firearms without stringent checks. For him to have a gun in his own office, Thaddeus summed up, was preposterous. It just didn't fit the puzzle that was the overall case.

Thaddeus sat down, the judge took a fifteen minute break, and the jury went back to the jury room and restrooms. Presentation of the state's case would begin when they resumed.

The first witness after the break was Chief of Detectives Jake O'Connor. He first recited his training and his long career with the Chicago Police Department. He had received three Commissioner's Commendations for meritorious service, and FOP Outstanding Citizen awards in 1992 and 2001. He testified that he commanded a group of Army Reserve MPs and held the rank of Lieutenant Colonel, that he held a master's degree in forensics from the University of Illinois at Chicago and professional training and experience.

Jake was tall, lithe, and moved easily about the courtroom, coming down from the witness stand several times to explain photographs and drawings with a pointer, and to demonstrate how the gun seized from Ansel's office worked and describing the bullets that had been found in its cylinder as target loads.

He was conservative and didn't smile easily, but when he did smile--twice in four hours, Thaddeus was counting--his manner was winning and immediately caused all jurors to smile right back at him.

In great detail he testified how he had found Suzanne slumped in her office chair that night and that the gun that killed her had been seized from Ansel's office two doors down the hallway.

Several dozen photographs were marked and intro-duced and explained, including two of the wood floor around Suzanne's desk.

Then came Thaddeus' turn to cross-examine.

He stood and began, "Mr. O'Connor--"

"Lieutenant O'Connor, sir."

"Lieutenant? Your first name is lieutenant? So should I call you lieutenant lieutenant?"

"Objection! Harassing."

"Please move on, Mr. Murfee. Lieutenant O'Connor, you may answer to mister or to lieutenant, but you will need to answer."

"Mr. O'Connor, isn't it true you visited Ansel Largent at the jail late in the afternoon following his early morning arrest?"

"Yes. I was there very briefly."

"Describe your purpose in going there."

"I wanted to get his statement. I wanted to discuss Ms. Fairmont's murder with him, since we found the gun in his office."

"So you took the gun with you to meet with him?"

"I did not."

"And isn't it true the gun had no fingerprints and no DNA when you seized it from his office?"

The police officer broke off eye contact. He looked at D.A. Eckles. No help there. Slowly, he formulated his answer. "Prints and DNA were in fact found on the gun."

"But not until you had my client handle the gun at the jail, correct?"

"He didn't handle the gun at the jail."

"What if he testifies and tells the jury you brought the gun to your meeting with him at the jail?"

"He'd be mistaken. Or he'd be lying. I don't know him well enough to say which."

"Isn't there another possibility?"

"Not that I'm aware of."

"Isn't it possible that because the police and the sheriff's office deprived him of some very key medications that he was mentally imbalanced at the time you spoke with him?"

"I'm not a doctor. I know nothing about his mental balance. Or lack of."

"Well, I am going to call as a witness Ansel Largent's psychiatrist. Her name is Abigail Wurster, M.D."

"If you say so."

"And she is going to testify that your police department refused my client's request to take his medications the morning of his arrest. Would you have any reason to disagree with that testimony?"

"I can't really say. I wasn't there."

"You weren't there at the arrest?"

"Correct."

"But you've seen the arrest report? Here, this has been marked as Defense Exhibit 22. I'll hand it to you and ask you, have you seen this before?"

Thaddeus handed the exhibit to the officer, who spent several minutes reading through it.

"Okay, I've read it."

"Third paragraph from the bottom. What's that say?"

"'We were preparing to leave the home of Ansel Largent when he requested that he be allowed to take his morning medications. Subject was advised we had no authority to allow someone in our custody to ingest medications, so his request was refused. He stated that he would "go off the deep end" without those meds. Is that far enough?"

"That's it, thank you. Did you find, when you met with my client that afternoon at the jail, that he had in fact gone off the deep end?"

"I don't know what that means. I'm not a doctor."

"Are you saying he seemed normal to you?"

"Yes."

"How many times had you seen him before that afternoon?"

"Ansel Largent? Never."

"So you wouldn't know his normal affect from an abnormal affect, would you?"

"No, I wouldn't."

"So he could be off the deep end when you saw him and you wouldn't even know that, correct?"

"Correct."

"So let me ask you again. My client's psychiatrist is going to testify that your police department refused my client's request to take his medications the morning of his arrest. Would you have any reason to disagree with that testimony?"

"No, not now. I don't know if I would call it refusal, they just didn't have authority."

"Whatever you decide to call it, the police officers

prevented him from taking his meds after he asked, correct?"

"Correct."

"So when the psychiatrist says your police officers refused to allow him access to his meds, you wouldn't disagree with that, would you?"

"No."

"Now, do you know what antipsychotic medications are?"

Thaddeus had no doubt this would go nowhere, but he wanted to get the questions in front of the jury.

"More or less. They stop psychosis."

"Excellent. You agree that antipsychotic medications are used to treat psychosis?"

"I guess. I'm not a doctor."

"Have you ever seen someone having a psychotic episode?"

"Yes. I've seen people who didn't know what was going on. I've seen people who didn't know where they were. I've seen people who didn't know what they were doing. But your client knew all those things the afternoon I saw him. He knew what was going on, he knew where he was, and he knew what he was doing."

"And you're sure of this because?"

"Because he wasn't acting crazy."

"Exactly. In your experience, as you've told us, people going through psychotic episodes act a certain way, correct?"

"Correct."

"And because Ansel wasn't acting in any of those ways, you assumed he was okay and knew where he was, what he was doing, and what was going on, as you put it, correct?"

"I think he did. Yes."

"But again, you're not a doctor."

"Obviously I'm not."

"So he could have been entirely off the deep end in a psychosis and you wouldn't know it, correct?"

"I think that's right. I'm not trained to know all of it."

"With this in mind, did he handle the murder weapon at the jail?"

"He did not."

"You're sure you didn't have it with you?"

"I'm positive. I didn't have it with me."

"But you did handle it that day, correct?"

"Negative. I did not handle it that day."

"So if he testifies you had him hold the gun at the jail, you would disagree?"

"Yes. It didn't happen like that."

"What witnesses were with you in the room where you saw him?"

"Just me and him."

"Aren't you police supposed to act in pairs?"

"Yes."

"Especially for taking statements, interviews, to make sure there's a second witness to what's going on?"

"Yes, that's the idea."

"But in this case it's just your word against his word about the gun, correct?"

"Correct."

"Sounds about like fifty-fifty?"

"Yes."

"Which isn't beyond a reasonable doubt, is it?"

"I didn't mean that it wasn't beyond a reasonable doubt. What was beyond a reasonable doubt? Me having the gun with me?"

"You cannot prove beyond a reasonable doubt you didn't have it, can you?"

"Just my word."

"Well, let's try this."

Thaddeus walked back to counsel table and picked up another document with an evidence sticker already affixed.

"Let me hand you what's been marked Defendant's Exhibit forty-four. Look it over, please."

The detective read it over as asked.

"Okay."

"What is that?"

He spoke softly. "Evidence room receipt."

"Louder, so the jury can hear you."

"It's an evidence room receipt."

"Does it bear your signature?"

"Yes."

"And it says you checked out the murder weapon from the evidence room, correct?"

"Yes."

"And that would have the same date on it as the date you visited Ansel, the date of his arrest, correct?"

"Yes."

"So again. Isn't it possible you had the murder weapon with you when you visited Ansel Largent?"

There was a pause while the lieutenant read the exhibit once again. It was obvious that he was formulating an answer.

"I checked out the gun to--to"

"Yes?"

"I don't remember why. Probably to test-fire it or something. That was probably it."

"Were you at the police range that day?"

"I don't remember."

"Would the range check-in sheet have a better memory of that than you?"

"Yes."

He didn't hesitate this time. Thaddeus could see the certainty come into his eyes that Thaddeus had been prescient, that he had the police shooting range log over on his table. He took great care to say again, "Yes, the range record would be correct about that."

Then Thaddeus surprised him. He didn't produce the range record at all. At least not at that time.

"So when you just told us you didn't handle the weapon that day, that would be false, wouldn't it?"

"Objection! Mistake, maybe, but not a lie."

"Who called it a lie, Your Honor?"

"Please answer."

The officer shuffled his feet. "Yes, that would be false."

"You did handle the gun that day."

"I did, yes."

"But you want the jury to believe you didn't have it with you at the jail, correct?"

"That would be correct."

"Now, according to the lab report, the weapon was received from you the same day you checked it out of evidence, correct?"

"I wouldn't know."

Thaddeus headed back to the table. "Maybe this will help."

He handed the officer another set of papers clipped together.

"Can you identify this?"

"Exhibit fifty-five. It's a lab report, CPD crime lab."

"Please look at the date the crime lab received the gun."

"Okay, I see it."

"Anything about that date just jump off the page at you?"

The officer put on his reading glasses and read it again.

"Well, it's the same date as I checked it out of evidence, if that's what you mean."

The officer's hand shook as he held the paper. The jury looked at the shaking hand. Several made their notes.

"So let me summarize. On the date you saw my client at the jail, you also checked the gun out of evidence that day and you took it to the crime lab that day. At the crime lab, according to the report you're holding, they found Ansel Largent's prints and DNA on the gun. And you still say he didn't handle it at the jail?"

"I didn't have it with me at the jail."

"So you checked it out, left it somewhere, visited the jail, then picked it up and took it to the crime lab? Is that what you're asking the jury to believe?"

"Yes."

"That is all, Your Honor."

"Re-direct?"

D. A. Eckles tried to rehabilitate the witness, but the fact remained, he had checked out the gun from the evidence room the day he visited Ansel Largent. There was no getting around it. Then he had taken the gun to the crime lab. There was no getting around that. The rest was pure argument. And Thaddeus was ready for that, at the correct time and place, which would be during closing arguments. He would go back over this whopper at that time.

Chapter 42

The Mexican National knew where Ansel Largent lived in Evanston.

He knew the location of his law office in Chicago.

He knew the route he took back and forth, knew his dry cleaners, knew they actually ate the stuff Taco Bell served-- or at least ordered from there and took it home--and he knew where Ansel gassed up the Buick he drove.

The target spent from six a.m. to eight a.m. at the office most days, then went to court and attended his trial. He seldom went out to lunch and never wore the same suit twice in the same week, not while he was being observed.

Ansel's garbage revealed he read both the *Chicago Tribune* and the *Sun-Times*, cut out the top one-half of an ad for Phone-Jack from the discarded *People* magazine, and shredded and discarded a bushel of paper every other day. The shreds were thought to be mostly mail, and most of that was thought to be junk mail.

They slept upstairs. Two different windows, either end of the second floor.

The front gate was successfully opened and the front door to the house and security system were also opened and disarmed with the same four-digit code. The code had been coaxed from a woman named Elvira Hernandez, who cleaned three days a week and drove an ancient Jeep with a garbage bag taped where the right passenger window had once been located.

Mrs. Hernandez had been terrified by Juan Carlos, who pulled her over two blocks south of the Largent property when she was making her way home one stormy April evening. It was four p.m. and almost dark; vehicles were finding their way with headlights, and a light snow was blowing sideways. The Glock, poked against the side of her face, immediately achieved its purpose and Juan Carlos let himself in the house that night while the couple slept upstairs. He disarmed the security system using the same four numbers and quietly began creeping upstairs.

At the second door in the hallway, off to the right, he heard the snoring of a male. He could tell it was male from the snorts and coughs intermittently interrupting the snores perhaps every three or four minutes. After twenty minutes of listening to the ruckus, he entered the room and sat down on the side of the sleeping man's bed. He laid the barrel of the pistol against the man's cheek. A wary eye opened.

"Huh?"

"Sssh, don't be afraid. I'm not here to hurt you."

Ansel's eyes grew wide with terror.

"What the hell?" He struggled upright in the bed.

"Easy. Sit back. Good boy."

"What is it? Is Libby okay?"

"Libby is fine. I want to talk to you, not Libby."

"What do you want?"

Juan Carlos crossed one leg over the other.

"I want my money back."

"What money would that be?"

"That would be the two hundred million dollars you took from me."

"That was never your money. That belongs to my law firm."

"Oh no," said Juan Carlos. He poked the muzzle of the gun against Ansel's chest. "No, no, no. You mustn't think that. Once the money came to me, it was mine. That's how my world works."

"Just shoot me. I'm not giving it back."

"Does the same go for Libby? Shoot her too?"

"No."

"Or what about Winston. My soldiers know where he lives in Berkeley. They're outside his apartment right this minute, I can call them up and give them the word and your second son dies. Should I do that?"

He pulled his cell phone from his pocket and tapped its face. A blue light spread over the bed as the cell phone activated.

"No."

"When can I expect my money back?"

"I don't know."

"This is Wednesday. Let's say by Friday noon. I am leaving you with this envelope. It contains information for the Dubai bank where you will wire my money. Two hundred million dollars, American. Noon Friday. Or I will mail you Winston's head in a box. Do you understand?"

"Yes."

"Will it be done?"

"Yes."

"Now go back to sleep."

Ansel grabbed the man's arm.

"What if I want to make an adjustment?"

Juan Carlos looked puzzled.

"What kind of adjustment."

"Suppose I make a counter-offer. That's what we do in America. Someone makes an offer, someone else makes a counter-offer, then a deal gets made. Are you open to a counter-offer then?"

"Depends."

"All right. Here it is."

"I'm listening."

Eleven minutes later Juan Carlos walked out the front door of the house and calmly walked down the driveway to the gate. He inserted four numbers, the gate opened, he climbed inside his Chevy Silverado, and drove off. The exhaust left a sideways-shifting plume as he drove away.

He hit a speed dial number.

"El Cap."

"The money will be there Friday."

"How much?"

"Two hundred."

"Then you saw him."

"I did."

"How was he?"

"I like this man. He is smart."

"Don't call this number again. Throw away the phone."

Juan Carlos rolled down his window and threw his phone against a freeway abutment as he sped past. The phone shattered and skittered across the roadway in pieces.

Juan Carlos smiled.

Everyone wins.

Business, American style.

Chapter 43

On the second day of trial Thaddeus was given the opportunity to cross-examine the CSI team. First up was Nora L. McIlhenny, B.S. She was a matronly woman with thick legs, short blond (bottle) hair, fat fingers, and a great, happy smile. She swung back and forth in the witness chair as she waited for Thaddeus to begin his cross-examination.

He began.

"Ms. McIlhenny, you testified about state's exhibit one-twenty-eight that it was a photograph of the floor around Suzanne Fairmont's desk the morning you visited the crime scene, correct?"

Her eyes met his and were steady. She was quite good at testifying, he saw, always directing her answers directly to the jury. She had been to police testifying school, where all police agents were told to look at the lawyer while the question was asked, then to turn to the jury to give the answer. That was the audience, not the lawyer.

"Correct. That would be the floor."

"And right here--" Thaddeus mounted the blow-up of exhibit 128 on the easel, "right here is a dark pool of fluid. That is blood, correct?"

"Correct."

"Is there anything about that picture that looks out of place to you? Anything odd?"

The witness examined the photograph. She rose up from the chair and said to the judge, "May I?" indicating she wished to approach the exhibit. The judge nodded and she got right up in front of the exhibit and studied it. Then she moved to the side so as not to obstruct the jury's view, and gave her answer.

"There are interruptions in what would be the normal, smooth layer of blood."

Thaddeus handed her the pointer.

"Indicate for the jury what interruptions you're talking about, please."

The witness touched the tip of the pointer to the exhibit several times, saying, "Here, and here, and here, and here. Those are some kind of marks in the blood. Interruptions I call them."

"Could they be impressions left in the blood?"

"They could be."

"As if something touched or poked the blood after it was on the floor?"

"Yes. I don't know if 'poked' is the right word. Something interrupted what I would expect to be the normal layering of the blood. It's a heavy spill. It should be level at the area on the floor. But something has interrupted it."

"You say 'interrupted' and I say 'poked.' That wouldn't make me wrong, would it?"

"No, not wrong."

"Whatever word we use, it's clear something touched the blood and left marks in it, correct?"

"That would be correct."

"And those marks were how big?"

"Those marks were one-point-five inches to two inches in diameter."

"And how do you know that?"

"I measured them."

"Did you get any close-up pictures of those marks?"

"Yes, I did."

"Could you direct us to those pictures?"

She re-took her seat and flipped through the stack of marked photographs.

"One-eight-zero, one-eight-one through one-eight-nine, and one-nine-four."

"Those numbers are the close-up pictures of the photographs you took?"

"Yes."

"I'm going to mount on the easel the first of those you named." He placed the 30x40 blow-up on the easel. "Can you describe this for us?"

"Using the close-up lens, I took that photograph under normal lighting conditions. It's a digital, no color enhancement, no digital effects applied."

"So this is what the close-up of one of the interruption marks looked like?"

"Yes."

"Do you know what left this mark?"

"I do not."

"Viewing the photographs, I see four parallel striations. Like two sets of tire marks, but very small. Do you see those?"

"I do."

"Any idea what might leave four parallel marks like that?"

"Zero idea. The tip of something that touched the blood."

"The tip of something."

"Whoever left that mark, placed something in the blood pool right there."

"What about these other blow-ups?"

She flipped through them again.

"Same thing. Same mark."

"So it's fair to say that each mark contains these striations, these four parallel marks like small tire treads?"

"That would be correct."

"Would it make sense to you that someone using a cane might have left those marks in that blood?"

"Objection! Calls for speculation!"

D.A. Eckles was on his feet, crying out. Clearly he did not want her to respond. Which she didn't.

The judge quickly ruled. "Sustained. Speculative in nature."

"Let me re-phrase," said Thaddeus. "Ms. McIlhenny, have you ever before seen the mark a rubber-tip cane would leave in a blood pool?"

"I have not."

"Yet it wouldn't surprise you if that's what we're looking at in these interruptions, would it?"

"It wouldn't surprise me, no."

"Objection!"

"Sustained. Jury will disregard. Her surprise is irrelevant and immaterial."

"Thank you," said Thaddeus. "Nothing further."

The middle of day two was then spent with the medical

examiner on the stand, describing the cause of death and the general health of Suzanne Fairmont.

The third witness of the day was the lab tech who had found the fingerprints on the gun and matched them. He also testified about the report of DNA evidence and matching. The DNA had been prepared for testing in the CPD crime lab but hadn't actually been tested there, having been sent outside. Yes, those were Ansel Largent's fingerprints on the murder weapon, yes that was Ansel Largent's DNA on the murder weapon.

Thaddeus spent just a short time having the witness confirm that he had no idea when the fingerprints had been placed there or when the DNA from skin oils had been placed there. It could have been before the fatal shot, at the time of the fatal shot, or even after the fatal shot; he had no way of knowing.

The final witness was the crime lab tech who had done the workup on the ballistics. The bullet that had killed Suzanne Fairmont was introduced into evidence and marks were pointed out that compared the bullet to the pistol seized from Ansel's office. The tech explained how she had test-fired the pistol, made all the comparisons, and confirmed the match. It was the same gun. Again, she went through Thaddeus' litany to the effect that she didn't know who had actually pulled the trigger on the fatal bullet, that she didn't know who had placed the gun in Ansel's office, and that she didn't know where the gun had come from.

The state rested its case at the end of the day.

Thaddeus moved for a directed verdict, which was, as customarily, denied.

The defense would begin its case the next day.

Thaddeus and Ansel retreated to Thaddeus' office to discuss strategy and practice Q and A. They split up at nine p.m. Thaddeus advised Ansel to get a good night's rest, that they might get a jury verdict tomorrow. Ansel turned white and nodded in reply.

He is terrified, thought Thaddeus as they parted in the lobby.

Hope he gets a good night's sleep. He's going to need it.

Chapter 44

Trial resumed Thursday at the Cook County Criminal Courts Building on California Street in Chicago.

Thaddeus arrived at court in his two button Armani Collezioni light wool suit and cordovan cap toe lace-ups, a nod to the latest styles of Chicago and to what juries expected lawyers to look like. He might do closing argument today and wanted to look just right for the speech.

Judge Zang got things underway and asked the jury whether anyone had tried to contact them about the case or tried to influence them in any way. No hands went up. Then he asked whether they had discussed the case among themselves or with another person. Again, no hands, though two jurors looked away, hinting that they might have exchanged words. The judge let that pass and pressed it no further. It was common among jurors to sometimes slip up and discuss a witness or piece of evidence. But most judges ignored that and Judge Zang was one of those.

"Counsel, you may call the first witness for the defense."

"Thank you, Your Honor. Defense calls Ansel Largent."

A murmur erupted across the press corps and gallery of onlookers. It was extremely uncommon in a criminal case for a defendant to take the stand and testify.

Ansel and Thaddeus had discussed the dangers and advantages to Ansel testifying several times now.

On the plus side, he had no prior convictions--unlike many defendants--and so he couldn't be impeached by bringing the fact of a prior conviction to the jury's attention. That was a plus. On the downside was the fact he had been inside the building on the night of Suzanne's murder, maybe even at or around the same time period. That could prove to be very difficult.

But the defining factor in the equation was the issue of Ansel's sanity or temporary insanity at the time of shooting. In order to make that defense work, they would have to admit that Ansel had actually done the shooting, and they would then attempt to excuse that action by his temporary insanity. Thaddeus knew he didn't want to go down this road, and so he called for a sidebar before he began the testimony.

The two attorneys gathered at the side of the judge's bench and whispered to the judge.

"I want to put the court and counsel on notice," Thaddeus whispered just loud enough for the court reporter to hear, "that the defense is withdrawing the affirmative defense of temporary insanity. The defense's sole remaining defense will be a denial of the charges."

"Then I assume the defendant will be restricted from presenting psychiatric testimony," said Eckles with a hurt expression on his face, as if the withdrawal of the affirmative defense were a personal affront. He seemed to be almost on the verge of whining, Thaddeus thought, and was visibly upset that the defense was being withdrawn. Why would he care? Maybe he had talked to an examining psychiatrist or psychologist and determined there was something in their workup that was especially helpful to the state's case. Something he had been counting on to help him make the case against Ansel. Thaddeus couldn't think what that might be at the moment, so he let it slide.

"Counsel," whispered Judge Zang, "the court will place on the record at this time that the defendant has withdrawn his affirmative defense of temporary insanity. There will be no testimony to the defendant's mental state at the time of Suzanne Fairmont's death. Is there anything further?"

Both attorneys shook their heads. No, there was nothing further.

The lawyers resumed their seats.

"Mr. Murfee, you may proceed."

"Defendant calls Ansel Largent to the stand."

Libby had insisted on a navy Gant pinstripe for Ansel, plus wingtips, white shirt, and regimental stripe tie. He had lost almost twenty pounds in jail and was still pale and his skin almost translucent under the courtroom neons. His lips had a bluish tint and Thaddeus had to look twice and try to remember his "before" coloring. Jail had definitely taken its toll. Thaddeus redoubled his determination that he would soon have a Not Guilty for the guy.

Ansel took the stand and tapped the microphone to make sure it was on.

"State your name."

"Ansel Largent."

"Mr. Largent, what is your business, occupation or profession?"

"Lawyer. Insurance defense lawyer."

"Are you licensed to practice law?"

"I am licensed to practice in the state of Illinois, U.S. Seventh Circuit Court of Appeals, U.S. District Court, Northern District of Illinois, U.S. Bankruptcy Court, Northern District of Illinois, Eastern Division."

"You need all those licenses in your practice?"

"Pretty much. Bankruptcy not so much, but occasionally."

"What is your area of specialty?

"Insurance defense. Occasional criminal defense."

The last part caused Thaddeus' head to jerk up.

"Did I hear you say criminal defense?"

"Yes, occasionally."

"How many insurance cases are you presently handling?"

"By 'handling' I assume you mean 'defending.' Probably five, six hundred."

"And criminal? How many criminal cases do you have?"

"One."

"Now directing your attention to the night Suzanne Fairmont was murdered. Were you in your law office that night?"

"I was."

"Where is that located?"

"Seventy-eighth floor, Citibank Building."

"Where was Suzanne Fairmont's office?"

"Seventy-eighth floor, Citibank Building."

"Where was her office in relation to your office?"

"Same hallway. I was on the corner; she was two doors down from me."

"Did you know her well?"

"I don't know how well I knew her. We had probably been to a half dozen social events together. Firm get-togethers."

"What was her area of practice?"

"Criminal defense. Exclusively."

"She was running for public office at the time of her death?"

"She was. She was running for District Attorney of Cook County. Primaries were underway."

"Were you active in her campaign?"

"I signed the checks that the firm contributed."

"How much did the firm contribute?"

Ansel leaned back and squinted at the ceiling. "All told, I would guess maybe one hundred thousand dollars."

"So the firm was backing her."

"Big time, definitely."

"How did you get along with Suzanne Fairmont?"

"Just like any other lawyer in our firm. Just fine."

"No arguments with her?"

"None."

"No disagreements with her?"

"None."

"No fights with her?"

"We had nothing to fight about, so no."

"You hadn't recently had a falling out with her?"

"Over what? Not at all."

"How did you feel toward her?"

Ansel spread his hands. "I felt as a partner she was making a significant contribution to the firm's fortunes."

"She was carrying her own weight?"

"Her own weight, plus."

"So the firm was happy with her?"

"Absolutely."

"And you were happy with her?"

"Absolutely."

"Did you shoot her?"

"I did not."

"Do you know who did?"

"I do."

There was a group inhale from all viewers. Breath was held, not expelled.

You could have heard the proverbial pin drop as the gallery and press and participants awaited the next obvious question.

Thaddeus took his time. He allowed the last answer to sink in and command center stage. He appeared to be making notes on his tablet, but in truth he was scribbling, just allowing a full minute to tick by. Then he looked directly at the witness.

"Who did?"

"Who shot her? I can't say."

"Why can't you say?"

"Because that person is a client of mine. The identity is confidential."

"Sidebar!" cried District Attorney Eckles.

The judge motioned both attorneys to step forward.

"I'm going to get it out of him, judge, or we'll wait here all day while I try," Eckles said angrily in an exaggerated whisper.

"That's my decision to make, not yours," the judge reminded Eckles. "Mr. Murfee, is your client serious? Is he really the attorney for the shooter?"

"You can ask him, judge. I'm as surprised as you are."

"I will. Seats, please."

The judge turned and looked down at the witness. He spoke from on high.

"Mr. Largent, the court would like to ask a couple of questions."

"Okay."

"This client, the shooter. Is this someone who has paid you a retainer to act as their lawyer?"

"Yes, judge."

"How much did they pay you?"

"That's confidential, Your Honor. I won't reveal it."

"When did they pay you?"

"They paid me the day after Suzanne was shot."

"Where is that person now?"

"I can't reveal that, Your Honor."

"Tell us the shooter's name, please, for the record."

"I can't tell you that, judge. It's confidential."

"I will put you in jail if you don't reveal the name."

"That's all right, Your Honor. I know my way around there. But I can't give up a client's confidential communications to me."

"Did you witness the shooting?"

"Only the noise of the gun."

"Were you aware beforehand that the shooting was about to occur?"

"Absolutely not."

"Could you have done anything to prevent the shooting?"

"Absolutely not. I was totally shocked."

"For the record, give us the shooter's name."

"No, I refuse. Client confidentiality."

The judge looked down at Thaddeus. "Counsel, as of this moment your client is remanded to the custody of the Sheriff of Cook County. The Sheriff is ordered by this court to take the defendant into custody and hold him behind bars until further order of this court. Deputy, did you hear all that?"

A deputy seated at the bailiff's elbow nodded. "Got it, judge. I'll take him into custody forthwith."

"Forthwith, that's right," said Judge Zang. "Counsel, you may continue with your questions for this witness."

Thaddeus looked up at the witness.

"Now, Mr. Largent. Do you know Jake O'Connor, the detective seated at counsel table with Mr. Eckles?"

"I don't know that I *know* him. I had a conversation with him."

"Where was that?"

"County Jail."

"When?"

"Same date he checked the gun out of the evidence vault."

"I'm handing you that gun, which is now encased in a plastic bag and marked State's Exhibit 104. Do you recognize this gun?"

"Yes."

"Tell the jury all the times and places you have seen this gun."

"Twice. First time in my office. Second time at the County Jail."

"What was the gun doing at your office?"

"It was allegedly defective in a products liability case."

"The gun had been provided to you by an insurance company?"

"Correct. A police officer's son had fired the gun and it blinded his right eye. He sued the manufacturer Sanchi Firearms and I was defending."

"Where was the last place you saw the gun in your office?"

"On my desk."

"Was it in the same state then as now?"

"Appears to be."

"Did you handle the gun in your office?"

"Can't say that I did. It came in as an exhibit in a pending case. I receive tons of things like that. No reason to actually handle any of it. At least not at that point."

"And where did the gun go from your office?"

"Seized by the police, according to the police reports I've seen."

"From your office?"

"Yes."

"Where in your office?"

"Behind a set of books, according to the police report."

"Did you put it there?"

"No."

"Do you know who did?"

"No."

"And the next time you saw the gun was at the jail. Describe that occasion, please."

Ansel drew a deep breath. He shuffled his feet as if making himself more comfortable on the stand.

"All right. Following my arrest for this crime, I was taken to jail."

"By who?"

"Two police officers. I don't know them."

"What happened there?"

"Later that day I was visited by Jake O'Connor."

"The same person seated here in court today?"

"Yes."

"Why did he visit?"

"At the time, I thought he was a potential insurance company client."

"What happened?"

"He came in, told me he had a problem, and put the gun on the table between us. I picked it up, judged its balance--though I'm a novice and actually hate guns. Still, he was a client, I thought, so I tried to demonstrate some familiarity with firearms."

"Why did you think he was a client?"

"I hadn't had my meds that day."

Thaddeus then took Ansel through the list of medications he took on a daily basis, what had happened that morning of the arrest and how the police refused to allow him to take the medications, and his mental state when Jake O'Connor came to see him.

"So mentally you weren't all together when he came in?"

"Not hardly. I was in a psychotic episode."

"How do you know that?"

Ansel touched the side of his head. "Memory. I remember everything that happened. My mental case doesn't affect my memory of things, just my judgment of things. I lose my critical judgment."

"So that's why you thought he was an insurance client?"

"Well, he never did show any ID. Never introduced himself as a police officer. Just came into the little room and plopped the gun on the table. He said something and I thought he was from an insurance company."

"So you handled the gun."

"I did."

"You got your fingerprints on the gun."

"I did."

"And your body oil, or DNA."

"That's correct."

"And you're sure you didn't shoot Suzanne Fairmont? You didn't have a psychotic episode that night?"

Ansel shook his head violently. "No, no, no, no. I had my meds that day. I was stone cold right on. In fact, I was at the office working that night. Doing law stuff."

"So your critical judgment was intact."

"Intact, yes."

"But you do know who did shoot her?"

"I know who had the gun and I heard the shot fired."

"And you've told us that person is now your client?"

"Exactly right. That person is my client."

Thaddeus looked at the judge.

"That's all I have, Your Honor."

"Thank you. Mr. Eckles, you may cross-exam."

Eckles stood, crossed to the podium, and spread several yellow sheets before him. He shut his eyes and appeared to be collecting his thoughts, then began his inquiry.

"Please tell us who shot and killed Suzanne Fairmont if it wasn't you."

"I can't do that."

"Because this person is your client."

"Correct."

"Male or female?"

"I'm restricted from saying."

"Mr. Largent, were you somehow involved with Suzanne Fairmont?"

"She was a lawyer in my law firm."

"Were you romantically involved with her?"

"Romantically? No."

"Physically involved with her?"

"No."

"All right. Had you had sex with Suzanne Fairmont?"

"Definitely not. She was young enough to be my daughter."

"Was the person who killed her, was this person related to you?"

"No."

"Was it your wife?"

"No."

"Was your wife with you that night?"

"Yes."

"Your wife was with you at the office?"

"Yes."

"Is your wife a lawyer?"

"No."

"So if I put your wife on the witness stand and asked her for the shooter's identity, she wouldn't be able to claim attorney-client confidentiality, would she?"

"My wife sometimes works for me. My confidentiality would extend to her as well."

"She couldn't testify because she sometimes works for you?"

"That is correct?"

"Where is your wife right now?"

"At home, I assume."

"Will you produce her at court in the morning so I can call her as a rebuttal witness?"

"No."

"Why not?"

"That's not my job, to produce your witnesses."

"Fair enough."

Eckles then studied his notes and made marks on his papers with his pen. Then he continued.

He asked Ansel about his psychiatric history, his history with medications, his experience at times when he didn't ingest prescribed levels of medication and he brought out that this had in fact happened several times over the last five years. The psychiatric problems were early onset, meaning about the age of eighteen or nineteen, and grew progressively more pronounced in his twenties and at times debilitating in his thirties until the problems were first diagnosed after a complete break with reality following a wine-tasting fete at an artist's gallery opening on the north side of town. He had "come unglued," as he put it, after a glass of wine, and had been taken by his wife to the ER to be checked out. Physical tests revealed nothing and were unable to explain his utter disorientation. He was admitted, a psychiatric consult scheduled, and a day later was diagnosed as bipolar with psychosis. Fortunately the condition was controllable by the use of some pretty common psychoactive medications and Ansel was able to resume a full and happy life thereafter. The only restriction was that he not ingest alcohol or street drugs while he was taking his medicine. He had fully complied and only missed medicating a few times but those few times had been unpleasant and created problems in his personal life.

Ansel testified that the early-morning arrest the day he was taken to jail made it impossible for him to medicate, and that by early afternoon he was seeing things and hearing voices. Was this common for him? Common enough that he never missed his meds, he said; they meant the difference between a life worth living and a life in the shadows of psychosis.

Eckles then tried to bear down on the afternoon-early-evening visit with Detective Jake O'Connor.

"By the time you saw Lieutenant O'Connor you hadn't been without your medications for a long enough period of time that you were disoriented as to place, correct?"

"No, that would be incorrect."

"You knew where you were, correct?"

"It came and went. I--"

"Please answer 'yes' or 'no.' My questions call for a yes or no answer. Agreed?"

"Yes."

"Again, you knew where you were, correct?"

"At first, then--"

"Please, 'yes' or 'no.'"

"I can't answer yes or no. It was like being on a scale of one to ten. It started at a one and went all the way to ten over the afternoon."

"Objection, non-responsive. Move to strike."

Judge Zang peered down at D.A. Eckles.

"No, I think it was responsive. Your objection is overruled."

"At the time you were introduced to Lieutenant O'Connor you understood you were being held in jail, isn't that true?"

"Yes and no."

"Your Honor--"

"Mr. Largent, please restrict your answers to yes or no. If more explanation is required, your attorney can bring that out on re-direct examination."

"Okay."

"You knew you were being held in jail, correct?"

"No."

"You knew he was a police officer, correct?"

"I thought he was an insurance client."

Another objection followed and, when he saw the witness was too agile to be caught up in the cross-examiner's usual 'yes/no' system of attack, Eckles finally shrugged and sat down.

But a point had been made. The witness was very skilled at testifying because he was a lawyer, and therefore not entirely believable. At least that's the impression Thaddeus had when it was said and done. He made the judgment that follow-up would really only be self-serving and, in fact, might open the door for Eckles to come back and grill Ansel again. So Thaddeus declined further questions and Ansel took his seat at counsel table.

Thaddeus wanted to lay more foundation for the psychotic episode at the jail. He needed expert testimony to do that. For that, he called upon Ansel's psychiatrist, Abigail Wurster, M.D.

Dr. Wurster was a 1982 graduate of the University of the Illinois College of Medicine at Chicago. She had completed a four year residency in adult psychiatry at Chicago Lutheran Memorial Hospital. CLMH was a medical provider with a primary outreach to mental patients suffering emotional and mental ailments.

She was tall, nearly six feet in her stocking feet, and pale complected, the result of spending most of her life indoors with books and, as she was assimilated into the practice of medicine, indoors in hospitals. Dr. Wurster wore her gray hair in a bun during the day, and down at night, brushing two hundred strokes at bedtime, as required by her mother from the earliest times on. It was a solid habit, one she wouldn't have admitted to a colleague, as it was compulsive.

She simply didn't have the time--or, really, the inclination--to engage in outdoor activities like gardening or hiking, preferring to spend her downtime reading romance novels in the privacy of her high-rise apartment on Michigan Avenue. Her faves were Rosalind James (she loved New Zealand and wanted to go there) and somebody Freethy. She thought.

She lived alone, her only companion being Sylvester the cat, a tabby accustomed to keeping long hours on his own while his caregiver was off to the hospital. She allowed herself a compulsion or two; hair-brushing was one; another was the study of psychiatry in criminal law. She was accomplished in the first and expert in the second and her testimony was in high demand around Cook County. Fortunately for Ansel, she had been his treating physician for fifteen years and her availability to assist him on the defense of his criminal case was automatic. As in, she couldn't say no.

Thaddeus called Dr. Wurster as the second defense witness.

She was gangly at six feet and made her way from the back of the courtroom down the aisle and crossed in front of the jury, all elbows and knees. She took a seat on the witness stand and folded her hands in front of her. No notes, no patient chart, nothing brought along that might give Eckles the opportunity to nose around. She was a pro all the way and the jury sensed that right off.

Thaddeus smiled at her and said, "Tell us your name?"

"Abigail Wurster."

"You're a physician?"

"Yes, in Evanston and Chicago."

She then told about her education, her residency, her board certifications, and her work experience. All the time the jury was focused and attentive, sensing that she had information that would help them make some very difficult decisions.

"Are you the physician for Ansel Largent?"

"I am."

"How long have you been his physician?"

"Since August 29, 2001."

"Are you treating him?"

"Monitoring his meds at this time."

"Have you performed testing on him?"

"Not really. Psychologists do the testing. I'm a medical doctor."

"How often do you see Ansel?"

"Every ninety days."

"What is your diagnosis of his condition?"

"Bipolar Disorder I. Secondary OCD."

"OCD being obsessive compulsive disorder?"

"Correct."

The doctor withdrew a blue tissue from her purse and wiped her eyes. "Sorry, dry eyes. Makes them water."

"Now tell us about bipolar disorder."

"Bipolar disorder is best described symptomatically probably for what you're asking. Bipolar disorder causes dramatic mood swings--from feeling overly 'high' and/or irritable to sad and hopeless, and then back again, often with periods of normal mood in between. Severe changes in energy and behavior go along with these episodes. The periods of highs and lows are called episodes of mania and depression. It is often not recognized as an illness, and people may suffer for years before it is properly diagnosed and treated."

"Is that what happened to Ansel?"

"Yes, he went untreated for years. That's not uncommon. Peers and friends just see the affected person as odd or strange or, in today's terms, as something of a whack job."

The jurors smiled. They certainly understood that.

"All right." Thaddeus consulted his notes. He wanted to get into the psychosis issues, but first he wanted the jury to understand more about Ansel's treatment.

"How do you treat Ansel's bipolar disorder?"

"With medications. Lamotrigine and Risperidone. Those are a mood stabilizer and an antipsychotic. We used Depakote for a couple of years but that caused weight gain. Almost twenty-five pounds. So we discontinued and added Lamotrigine, also known as Lamictal."

"The Lamotrigine is a mood stabilizer."

"It is, but don't ask me how it works. No one knows that."

"I appreciate that. Some medicines work and medical science has no idea why, correct?"

She nodded. "Exactly." She dabbed at her eyes again. "I'm not crying, really."

"Now let's talk about the Risperidone. You said it's an antipsychotic?"

"It is. Primary use is for treatment of schizophrenia."

"Is Ansel schizophrenic?"

"Aspects of. He can go into psychosis."

"So the drug controls his psychosis."

"Exactly."

"Can withdrawal from the drug trigger acute episodes of psychosis?"

"The therapeutic efficacy of Risperidone for schizophrenia has been well established by several controlled trials conducted worldwide. Risperidone also has been reported to have therapeutic efficacy in major depressive disorder with psychosis, organic delusional disorders, bipolar mania, and schizoaffective disorder. The abrupt withdrawal of the drug can definitely trigger, as you put it, psychosis."

"Even the withdrawal of the drug for, say, six or eight hours?"

"Could, yes."

"In our case, Ansel normally took his Risperidone at five-thirty in the morning before leaving for the office. On the day he was arrested, he wasn't allowed to take that dose and by four o'clock that afternoon he has testified he was disoriented. Is this possible?"

"Definitely. That would be a period of over ten hours. That type of delay in the daily dosage could definitely result in an induced state of psychosis."

"So if Ansel testified he saw a person at the jail and thought that person was a client when, in fact, the person was a detective in plain clothes, would that fit with the type of psychosis you might expect?"

"It could."

"Could or would."

"Definitely possible. That development wouldn't surprise me at all."

"And if that person asked him to handle a gun and he did, thinking it was the gun involved in a products liability case, would that surprise you?"

"Not at all. That kind of misconstruing of data would be very typical of an induced psychosis from the withdrawal of Risperidone."

Thaddeus stepped back. She had just given the full, complete answer he would need to make the argument he wished to pursue in closing argument. The doctor backed up Ansel's story and, truth be told, it didn't get any better than that. He had been around the block enough to know this kind of testimony could also fall apart very easily, so he decided to quit while he was ahead. He told the judge that he was finished asking questions.

"Cross examination?" asked Judge Zang of D.A. Eckles.

"Just one question. Doctor, you weren't there the day Mr. Largent claims he was having a flare-up and so you don't know for certain whether he was psychotic or not, do you?"

"No, I would not know that for certain."

"That is all."

Thaddeus climbed to his feet.

"One follow-up. Doctor, isn't it true within a reasonable degree of medical probability that, given the facts I have given you, Ansel Largent was experiencing a psychotic episode?"

"Yes."

"Yes he was experiencing a psychotic episode?'

"Yes he was."

The doctor was excused.

Thaddeus returned to counsel table. He told the judge he had no more witnesses that day and since it was almost four-fifteen he would ask the court to recess. Judge Zang announced that Thursday he would be away from court on personal business. They would reconvene on Friday. Several jurors looked upset but said nothing. Others looked relieved, and Thaddeus guessed they were the jurors who would have a day off, having been excused from their jobs for the week. They were excused and the judge headed for his office, unzipping the black robe as he went. Two deputies came for Ansel. Thaddeus begged one minute with his client. The deputies said no problem and backed away.

Thaddeus whispered to Ansel.

"That's it for the day. I need you to do something."

"Name it."

"Call Libby. Tell her I'm coming to the house to pick up clothes for you."

"You don't like what I'm wearing?"

"I just want you fresh for tomorrow."

"She can bring my things."

"No, I want to do this. You have to look just right tomorrow."

Ansel gave him a quizzical look and shrugged.

"Okay. You're the boss."

Thaddeus smiled. "That's right, I am."

Ansel was returned to the jail and Thaddeus went back to the office to prepare for the following day.

At nine o'clock that night he left for Ansel's home.

Chapter 45

The drive up to Evanston from downtown took thirty minutes and Thaddeus spent another fifteen locating Ansel's street and house number. His Garmin didn't seem to know east from west and at one time he was about to drive into Lake Michigan when he realized his GPS was acting up. He retraced his path and went west where Garmin said to go east, and found the cross-street. Two blocks later he was at Ansel's gate, where he lowered his window and pressed the intercom. He announced himself and moments later the gate lifted. He pulled up to the front steps and got out.

Libby answered the door. She was wearing grey slacks and a white sweater. A glass of wine jittered in one hand and a cigarette burned in her left. Big band swing was playing from somewhere behind. He looked in her eyes and saw they were glassy.

"Come in, Thad," she said. "I'm having a pity party."

"No need for that. He'll be home for the weekend."

"What makesh you sho shure?"

Thaddeus tapped the side of his head. "Brute strength and awkwardness. Can you take me to his closet?"

"Up the shtairs, second door on the right. Go through the bedroom and there'sh a walk-in. Hish stuff's--well, you'll shee it. I'm shtaying here. Shtairs are too damn much."

"Thanks, Libby."

He climbed the stairs. He passed the second door on the right and went swiftly to the far end of the hallway. Where Ansel had told him Libby slept and kept her clothes.

On entering the bedroom, he glimpsed, on the east wall, a triptych of Canyon de Chelly. He wondered when Libby had found the time to visit this remote place. His eyes moved around the room and he made several mental notes. He went left and entered a massive walk-in closet.

Ansel's side was on the right as some of his things were still kept in this larger, walk-in, closet. Libby's clothes were neatly arranged all along the left side. He made a cursory appraisal of Ansel's hangered suits, chose a hazel winter wool, complemented it with a white button-down, and twirled the necktie wheel until he found a chocolate necktie that would--as the designers were fond of saying on HGTV--pop. The selections were made quickly and almost as an afterthought, because Ansel's wardrobe was not the real reason he had come there.

He turned to Libby's side and appraised her items. The hanging clothes were divided into winter on the right half, spring and summer on the left. He bent and crept to the right side of her half and looked around. What he had come looking for wasn't at that end. He stood up and went to the other end, where he again bent and looked around.

Then he found what he was after. It was a ceramic umbrella stand with a cream glaze, a blue trumpeting elephant raised on its side in relief. It contained no less than eight canes. He pushed aside the hanging clothes and sorted through the canes. A likely prospect caught his eye; an aluminum walking aid with a hard plastic handle, adjustable with a push-lock halfway down the shaft, and tipped with circular rubber that--he turned it bottom side up--and there it was. Four parallel treads etched into the circular rubber foot. With a dark smear of a hardened, thick substance that almost resembled paste.

Except it was red.

Deep blood red.

He tugged the cane out of the umbrella stand and telescoped it down to its shortest length. He inserted it beneath Ansel's coat on its wooden hanger. The handle curled around the top of the hanger and the length of the coat covered it up exactly. He gathered coat and slacks by their hangers in one hand, added the dry-cleaned, hangered shirt to the clutch, and encircled the chocolate tie around the three hanger loops.

Now he was ready.

He silently crept back downstairs.

"Thanks, Libby!" he called back into the house and its inner rooms, and let himself out the front door.

He had the clothes and stolen cane laid out in the back seat of his car before Libby could make it to the front door. Then there she stood, inside the glass storm door, waving weakly as if confused by his sudden disappearance. He tossed her a quick salute and pulled back down the driveway. She must have been watching; the gate lifted and--he was free.

Now he had his answer. Until he had examined it for himself, it had been a wild guess. Well, maybe not totally wild. The pictures of the blood pool beneath Suzanne Fairmont had tipped him off: the round smears in the congealing blood where something had touched and left the print of circles with their inner striations.

It was in the backseat, under Ansel's coat. Not only did it match the photograph with its tread, but it was also caked with blood.

Tomorrow he would go straight to Symatrixx Lab in Niles and have it tested.

But he already knew whose blood it was. She had been visited, just after her death, by Libby Largent.

Now to prove that Libby had been with her just before her death too.

It was all circumstantial.

Thaddeus laughed and slapped the steering wheel.

Like Henry David Thoreau had said, some circumstantial evidence is overwhelming.

As when you find a trout in the milk.

Chapter 46

Symatrixx Lab was a full-service testing laboratory that offered its services to medical doctors, lawyers, police agencies, and anyone who needed a substance analyzed.

He met D.E. Walkerton there, a smallish, hairless man wearing a black lab coat, who measured the cane end-to-end with his eyes, then examined the hard rubber foot Thaddeus had been talking about.

"I see, right there, crusted in the two circles," said Walkerton.

"Exactly. I need DNA testing. Can you do that?"

Walkerton smiled. "We can now."

"Meaning what?"

"We use the Integenx RapidHit testing machine."

"Let's do it."

"And you want me to compare it to what?"

"I'm going to leave you with the complete autopsy report on Suzanne Fairmont."

Walkerton peered through the bottom half of his

eyeglasses, glancing through the report. "Oh, yes," he nodded enthusiastically, "here it is right here, page six. toxicology: sample of right pleural blood and bile are submitted for toxicologic analysis. Blood DNA tested with Integenx RapidHit, markers attached. Excellent."

"Why so?"

"We use the same machine here. We can have the DNA results back in ninety minutes if you'd like to come back."

"Why would the crime lab run this testing?"

"To determine the blood belonged to the victim. That might seem very obvious to you and me, but hey, you're the lawyer. You know it can't just be assumed it's her blood. It has to be proven. That's what the RapidHit testing proved."

"Ninety minutes? Are you kidding me?"

"Welcome to the new millennium, Mr. Murfee. Come back around noon and we'll have everything wrapped up and ready to go."

"Can you testify tomorrow?"

"One of us can."

"Certified operator?"

"Totally guaranteed."

"How much?"

"Five thousand for the testing and one day of testimony."

"I can leave you a check."

"That will be fine."

"Oh, one other thing," Thaddeus said. "About the cane."

"What's that?"

"Do you have a tool marks expert? Someone who can examine the crime scene marks in the blood and compare those to the marks left by the cane's rubber foot?"

"Sure, that would be James Cartwell. He's a Ph.D. in

mechanical engineering and has been qualified as an expert tool marks witness in over a hundred Cook County cases."

"Here are the photographs. My discovery copies, so don't lose them, please."

Walkerton smiled. "Of course not. Consider it done."

"How much?"

"Five thousand for the testing and one day of testimony."

"Do you have any other rates besides five thousand?"

"Ten thousand for two days?"

"I'll take the five. Thanks, Mr. Walkerton."

Chapter 47

Libby Largent preferred flying without Ansel along. That way, if the plane went down, it wouldn't make Winston an instant orphan. Besides, Ansel had insisted she fly out ahead of him. He told her there would be money waiting at the other end. He told her that if something went wrong, he loved her.

Always did love her, he said.

But she knew that. He was a fool--a damn fool--but in spirit he was always beside her.

Thank goodness for the O'Hare Airport Courtesy Cart, she thought, as she plopped down on the plastic seat and seized the grip. The cart lurched and she shot a dirty look at the back of the young driver's head. Butthole, she thought. Don't you know there are people here? She watched up ahead as they scattered and scurried like free-range chickens in a driveway.

He had told her: one suitcase and one carry-on. She had checked the suitcase at the counter.

For the umpteenth time she unzipped the carry-on.

Latest Grisham novel. Check. Two-cheese sandwich, no mayo. Check. Sleeping mask. Check. Motion sickness patch (box of four, prescription strength). Check. $9,000 cash. Check. Emirates Airlines tickets--straight through to Dubai, changeover, straight through to Hong Kong. Check.

The cart narrowly missed flattening an older woman whose limp slowed her. Libby reached forward and punched the driver's shoulder.

"What!" he tossed over his shoulder.

"Shlow the hell down! Theresh people here!"

"Don't want you to miss your plane, lady."

"Oh. Well, run them over, then."

"Can do!"

She boarded at 7:45 a.m. Poor Ansel, she thought, last day of trial. But he seemed to be in high spirits.

And he seemed to know what he was doing.

He always did.

So she settled back in her First Class seat and accepted a glass of champagne.

A dribble escaped the corner of her mouth, which she dabbed with the linen napkin placed on her tray.

It was getting better, the stroke stuff. One day at a time. She looked out the window and realized they were moving to the end of the runway.

Then the engines were run up, the howling of the Pratt & Whitney's deafened her and she pressed her head against the linen headrest.

Close the eyes. Say the prayer.

Another champagne now that we're airborne?

Thank you, believe I will.

Chapter 48

Early Friday morning Thaddeus took Ansel's clothes to him. He then arrived early at court and advised the receptionist he wanted to make a *motion in limine*. She buzzed the judge, he okayed it for eight-thirty, and she then called D.A. Eckles and told him he would be needed at eight-thirty too. He confirmed.

"What's the motion?" she asked, and held out her hand for the paper motion.

"Motion to withdraw contempt citation."

"Your guy is ready to tell us who shot the lady?" Her voice was pleasing and playful.

"There will be no need for that. Please read my motion."

She lowered her eyes and began reading. Thaddeus backed out of the office and rode the elevator down to the basement cafeteria. He loaded up a plate with scrambled eggs, sausage, English muffin, coffee and OJ, and paid the cashier.

The place was packed. He found an empty chair along

the far wall, at a four-person table already occupied by three women who were having an animated discussion about *The Voice*. He eavesdropped and caught the gist of it. Evidently some female vocalist had clicked with two of the women and hadn't clicked at all with the third. The songstress had been added to the stable of one of the judges and so on. Thaddeus tried not to listen.

He cut a link of sausage and stuffed it in his mouth. It was eight-seventeen. In thirteen minutes he would forever change the direction of the Ansel Largent trial with the bombshell he was about to explode. He smiled. Not literally, of course, a bombshell more in the nature of solving the Whodunit the jury was faced with.

He glanced at the manila file as he spread grape jelly on the muffin. Ten thousand dollars of Ansel Largent's money sitting there. Two experts' reports and two experts scheduled to testify at trial. Along with a motion to amend the defendant's list of witnesses. The state would scream bloody murder, but the defendant would prevail, because barring of defense witnesses was anathema to all judges. It was serious grounds for appeal and almost certain reversal not to allow one of the defendant's witnesses to testify at trial, no matter how late in the case they were added to the witness list. Besides which, there was no reason to keep them from testifying. The state couldn't claim surprise because the state would be allowed to interview the witnesses before they testified. Moreover, the defense wouldn't and couldn't object to the state adding new witnesses to its list to refute what the defendant's new witnesses had said.

Which were all arguments Thaddeus was making in Judge Zang's office fifteen minutes later.

When he was finished the judge addressed the motion to withdraw the contempt citation.

"I have no problem withdrawing the contempt citation, given what you've just explained to us," said Judge Zang. "While I don't believe you're proven one hundred percent that Ansel wasn't the shooter, you have definitely placed his wife's cane at the scene of the crime. Does that mean the wife was the shooter? Did the husband use her cane to entrap her? The jury will have to decide these things. But I'm going to call over to the jail and have your client released now. We'll put it on the record in court when we get in there. Now, what about the motion to amend your witness list to add two additional witnesses? Why weren't these witnesses listed prior to the beginning of trial, Mr. Murfee?"

Thaddeus tugged at his shirt sleeve. He straightened his tie, all the while considering.

"Your Honor, maybe I'm just dense. But it took me all this time to realize the marks in the blood pool might mean something. When I finally realized they had actually been put there by some object and weren't just random patterns, it still took me hours and hours of thinking and sleeping and dreaming about it to put two and two together. I even spent a week in Mexico with Ansel and Libby and so I was quite familiar with her use of the cane. But honestly, it just didn't occur to me. As soon as it did, I had my theory tested by the experts and you've now seen those reports. I'll call the experts if I'm allowed to present their testimony and admit the reports through them. But as you can see, they leave little doubt that at least the cane itself was at the murder scene. Why it would have been taken there by Ansel just makes no sense. The circumstantial evidence that I'm going to present will set him free. For this reason the testimony and the amendment is absolutely critical."

"Mr. Eckles? Would you like to be heard?"

Eckles leaned back in his chair and crossed and uncrossed his legs. He jiggled his foot, obviously anxious.

"Judge, this whole thing reeks of prejudice. We haven't been allowed to prepare our case in anticipation of what the defendant could have known weeks ago when he and his counsel first saw the close-ups of the blood pool. Why didn't it occur to him then, what had made those marks? Or did it and he just sandbagged? Frankly, now that I look at the prints left by the cane in the blood and look at the prints left by the cane when it was tested by Dr. Cartwell, this whole thing gets pretty obvious. The state wants to see justice done and certainly doesn't want to convict the wrong person, but it would only be fair for the state to have the opportunity to have this newly discovered or newly revealed evidence tested by its own experts. The DNA evidence, I have no trouble with that. But the tool mark--the marks left behind by the cane--I can't just agree the expert is correct in saying the cane testing is one hundred percent accurate."

"So what you're saying is you would like additional time to test?"

"I would at least like great leeway in cross-examination of the defendant's expert, Dr. Cartwell. I don't think the District Attorney's office wants to actually delay the trial, there's been such close coverage by the press. Off the record--

"Speak freely," said the Judge. "We are off the record."

"To be very frank with the court, the D.A.'s office is looking at a huge public relations gaffe if some reporter questions the state's own competence in not noticing the marks and having them examined more closely in the first place. I don't think I want to walk across that hotbed."

"I understand that," said the judge. "Look, let's do this. Let's have the witnesses testify, and then, at the close of the defendant's case, if you still feel like you want additional testing, we'll adjourn the trial until you can get that done. By then, it's early afternoon and the jury would love to go home early. That would ease some of their disappointment with having to come back again next week."

"How long could I get to test the marks?"

"You have the crime lab with its jillion experts just down the block from here. Let's get the testing done by Monday night and get the jury back to hear your rebuttal expert, if you decide to call one, on Tuesday. Then we can instruct the jury and give them the case."

"Works for me," said Thaddeus.

"Sounds fair," said Eckles.

Everyone took a deep breath and sat back.

Then the judge said, "Five minutes. See you guys in court. Let's put all this on the record then I'll call the jury in."

"Judge, one more thing," said Eckles. "The state will stipulate to the DNA report. The blood on the floor is Suzanne's, the blood on the foot of the cane is Suzanne's. Pure and simple."

"Fine," said the Judge. He was already slipping into one of three black gowns hanging behind his desk. "Mr. Murfee?"

"Sounds great."

"Five minutes, gents."

———

THE TESTIMONY of James Cartwell went swiftly. He told the jury he had a Ph.D. in mechanical engineering from Purdue and that he had worked for Ford in Detroit until he got his MBA but still couldn't get promoted into management. At that time he had taken on his role at Symatrixx Lab and was an equity owner of fifteen percent of the company. His specialty was tool marks. He testified about the marks left by screwdrivers on screws, the marks left by hammers on human skulls, the blade marks from hacksaw blades, the Vise-grip marks left behind when a doorknob was torqued off--any and everything where an impression is made by what was generically known as a "tool." Walking canes for the handicapped qualified as one of the types of items he tested.

His testimony was curt and to the point. When asked what he had done to examine the cane he said he had prepared a blood print and a cane print for observation under what is called a stereoscope. The marks were analyzed, measured and compared. The cane had its own peculiar tread and the trailing edge of the cane foot was worn down more than the leading edge. He demonstrated with photographs enlarged to 30 x 40 how the marks compared, where the worn edges were exactly alike and how, in his expert opinion, the tread marks left by the cane were the same as those seen in the blood pool photos.

All this time Ansel was absolutely still. He stared straight ahead, neither acknowledging nor reacting to what Dr. Cartwell was saying. It was as if he knew it all beforehand and now it was just a matter of producing it in open court. Thaddeus watched him out the corner of his eye and when the expert was done with cross-examination by D.A. Eckles, Ansel Largent had been consciously gone from the court-room for two hours, though his body was still there. He had just disengaged from the trial, was how Thaddeus would describe it later to Katy. He had vanished.

Ansel's reverie was interrupted when Thaddeus called him back to the witness stand.

The cane had already been marked as an exhibit during Dr. Cartwell's testimony, and now Thaddeus picked it up and looked it over. The foot of the cane was now wrapped inside a plastic bag to preserve the remaining blood inside the pattern. Then he held the cane up in front of Ansel and asked, simply, "Whose cane is this?"

Ansel spoke so softly only Thaddeus heard. "Elizabeth Largent's cane."

"Louder, please."

Judge Zang looked over. "Mr. Largent, please speak up so the jury can hear you. And so I can hear you too. You were asked who the cane belongs to. What is your answer, sir?"

"It belongs to my wife. Elizabeth Largent."

"Libby, she's called," said Thaddeus. "Correct?"

"By her friends and me, yes."

"Do you know how it came to be that her cane left the marks in the blood pool?"

"I didn't see. I can only assume."

There was no objection by the state to an answer based on assumption. Such an answer would normally be highly objectionable, but this time Eckles said nothing.

So Thaddeus asked, "What is your assumption?"

"I can only assume Libby was at the scene. At some point, anyway."

"Well, let's consider that."

"Was she with you the night of the shooting?"

"Yes."

"Did she shoot Suzanne?"

"I don't know."

"Well, was she with you when you heard the gunshot?"

"No."

"Do you know where she was?"

"She said she was going to the restroom."

"Is the restroom near Suzanne's office?"

"Across the hall and down maybe twenty feet."

"That would be the women's?"

"Yes."

"Did you ever ask Libby about the gunshot?"

"No."

"What did you do when you heard the gunshot?"

"Me? I got up to walk into the hallway, then I reconsidered."

"Why?"

"Because I didn't want to get shot. If there was a shooter loose in the law firm I didn't want to be the next target."

"Were you concerned about Libby's safety?"

"Yes."

"Still, you didn't go to investigate?"

"It happened so fast, then Libby was back in my office."

"What did she say?"

"Let's go."

"What did you think?"

"I thought it was time to go."

"Why?"

Ansel looked down at the floor. "I didn't want to think about it, to tell the truth. I didn't want to ask what had happened. I guess I already knew."

"Why would Libby shoot Suzanne?"

"She knew we had been intimate. Were intimate. We were having a torrid affair, is the only way I can describe it. I had asked Libby for a divorce."

"What?"

"I told her that after the election Suzanne and I planned to be together."

"When did you tell that to Libby?"

"The night before. We were lying in bed and I turned my back to her and shut off my light. She sat straight up in bed and turned her light on and wanted to know why the hell--her words--I didn't touch her any more. So I told her."

"You told her about you and Suzanne."

"I did. The night Suzanne was shot I had gone to the office to start drafting a separation agreement. We have a form bank on our office computers and I was going to use one of those. Libby wanted to come, so she came with. I didn't care. The last person I expected to find there was Suzanne."

"Did you know Suzanne was in her office when Libby went to the restroom?"

"I didn't even know Suzanne was in the building. I hadn't talked to her at all that day. Don't forget, this was on a Sunday night. You wouldn't expect anyone there on a Sunday night."

Thaddeus stepped back to counsel table and found a yellow pad. He had written a few more questions there while in with the judge.

"Let's cut straight to the chase, Ansel. Where is Libby now?"

"Home, I suppose."

"That would be at the address you previously gave on direct examination two days ago?"

"Yes."

"That is all, thank you."

The judge looked at District Attorney Eckles, who was falling all over himself to get up to the podium and start asking his own questions.

He began, "Did you ask Libby whether she fired the gun?"

Ansel looked at the judge. "I cannot answer that on the

grounds a spouse cannot be made to testify against a spouse. Second, that answer would require me to breach the confidentiality a lawyer owes a client."

"So Elizabeth Largent is your client."

"She is."

"And she has told you about the shooting."

"Again, I claim the privilege."

"Judge?" said Eckles. "Will you just jail him again?"

"Not at all. He can claim client confidentiality. We know his wife is his client and that's as far as this goes. What she has said to him is absolutely privileged. Ask your next question, Mr. Eckles."

"Has she told you she was the shooter?"

"Privileged," said Ansel, "I will not answer."

"Judge?"

"It is privileged. Ask your next question."

"Your Honor, if I can't ask him these things, then I can't continue."

"Then you can't continue." He looked at Eckles and shrugged. Then he turned to Ansel. "Mr. Largent, you may step down."

Ansel didn't hesitate. He took his seat next to Thaddeus.

The judge looked at Eckles. "Does the state need a recess as we discussed this morning in chambers?"

"I think not," said Eckles. "We'll pass on that."

A ten minute recess was taken. Following that break in the action, both attorneys gave their closing arguments. This ate up two hours of court time and lunch was fitted in between the state and the defense. Finally Thaddeus sat down, the state had the last word, then both attorneys had had their say.

"Very well. Ladies and gentlemen, it's almost noon. The state has rested, the defendant has rested, and now is the time for me to instruct you. First we'll take a five minute recess. Counsel, may I see you in chambers?"

The jury was led out and the two attorneys joined the judge in chambers. Ansel didn't go, saying he was off to the restroom. He waited for Thaddeus to leave the courtroom and then reached inside his jacket. He pulled out a brown plastic bottle that was labeled RISPDERIDONE. He unscrewed the white cap, made a quick note on a piece of yellow notebook paper, and placed it inside the bottle. Replacing the cap, he smiled. He pushed up from the table, taking care to leave the brown bottle in the seat Thaddeus would occupy when court resumed.

The press was wise. They knew jury instructions were nowheres-ville. They ran for their offices and the promise of a fun weekend. The gaggle of spectators likewise had dissipated.

Unseen by anyone, Ansel wandered into the hall and sat on the bench across from the courtroom. He opened his iPad and logged into the firm's trust account. He pressed buttons for several minutes then looked up. He shut the iPad and checked the time. 11:51. He had kept his word to Juan Carlos. Winston's head would not be sent to him in a box. As nonchalantly as possible, considering the terrific excitement he was feeling, he sauntered off to the bank of elevators. The doors whooshed open and he found the car empty. He pressed L.

Three minutes later, the judge had shrugged out of his robe and was taking a drink out of a frosty Diet Pepsi can. He wiped his mouth with his hand. He focused his gaze on Thaddeus.

"Where is your client?" the judge asked Thaddeus.

"Restroom. I'll waive his presence."

"Very well. Gents, let's go over the jury instructions and

Defendant's Proposed Instruction Twenty-three. Mr. Eckles you previously objected to the court giving this instruction when we reviewed instructions. I said I wanted to read the case law, which I now have done. Do you wish to be heard further before I rule?"

District Attorney Eckles launched into his reasons for objecting to the defendant's instruction. Thaddeus wanted to go find Ansel and bring him in for the argument, but decided against it. Which left him feeling uncomfortable. He had the oddest premonition that Ansel had left the building. Why he felt that way, he didn't know. But his premonition would prove reliable.

Court resumed ten minutes later. Thaddeus found a brown pill bottle in his chair. The judge already was calling court to order, so he just tucked the bottle inside his coat pocket. Probably Ansel's pills, he figured and gave it no further thought. He turned and looked around. Still no Ansel. The judge sent the bailiff to the men's restroom to look for him. The bailiff returned. No Ansel. The judge looked at Thaddeus and then asked him to explain his client's whereabouts.

"Judge, I really can't answer you," Thaddeus said. "But I will waive my client's presence at the reading of the jury instructions. I don't think it's necessary for him to be here during."

Ever so slowly, Judge Zang leaned forward and nodded. "It's unusual, but it's not in error to proceed. The court will take note that defense counsel has waived his client's presence."

Judge Zang then droned on for thirty minutes, reading the jury instructions.

At long last the reading was completed.

The jury stood, came back to life and was promptly led

from the courtroom to begin deliberations. It was two-forty in the afternoon.

Thaddeus pulled out his cell phone and called Ansel's cell.

No answer.

Chapter 49

Emirates Airline Flight 4477 departed O'Hare at exactly two-forty-seven p.m.

As 4477 went airborne and turned west, the courtroom and its inhabitants seemed tiny and far away.

Flying first class in seat 1-A, Ansel happily received the first glass of champagne just after takeoff. He drank it down. Another came when they were still climbing.

He looked down at himself. Still wearing the suit Thaddeus had selected the previous night. He had made no effort to hide where he was going because a new identity awaited him, along with another packet of airline tickets. New passport, new driver's license, new identity, same wife.

When it was all said and done, he was happy with her. She had stood by his side and never once complained about his horrific hours at work. She had stood by his side and never once complained about his dalliances. She had stood by his side. And then some.

What he had with Suzanne--that had been love. True love.

Or was it?

Because at times it had felt like true lust. All he had wanted was to be alone with her, watching her undress or undressing her himself. It didn't really matter, as long as the clothes came off and as long as they clung to one another and dreamed their dream of spiritual reconciliation. Soul mates, that's what they had called themselves. Mated at the level of the soul.

He pressed his head against the linen headrest and drained the glass. Instantly the dark-skinned stewardess came with the towel draped over her forearm and poured it full again. He thanked her and reclined his seat. He sipped and closed his eyes.

Soul mates.

Which left him and Libby--where did they fit together, exactly? Certainly not at the soul level. Neither had ever felt a cellular union. A social union, maybe, a mating that worked to produce children and a lifestyle and a sense of familiarity, maybe. But bonded at the level of the soul? He winced. Never was, never would be. No, what he and Suzanne were--that was gone forever. And he thought it true: there was only one true love in a lifetime. Now his, due to a collision of circumstances, was gone.

Of course it was Libby's cane that had accompanied him to the office that Sunday night. He doubted she even missed it, the aluminum job, so seldom did she use it.

It had been difficult, shooting Suzanne, but it had demanded doing. She was running for District Attorney and she had laughed at their folly. She had belittled him, even. He was ridiculed and she threatened to tell Libby if he ever called her again. Now that was drastic. And there was no cause for it. One thing he couldn't abide was a threat. He just wouldn't stand for it. So he went to his office and sat there, in the dark, thinking about her. The more he thought, the more abused he felt. He moved the mound of papers that he had gone to the office already knowing he would move. The papers slid off the .38 revolver that had blinded the police officer's son. He picked it up and studied the cylinder. Damn thing was loaded, but he already knew that.

He had known this would happen.

Which was why he brought along Libby's cane.

He clutched the cane under his left arm and hefted the revolver in his right. The weight was solid, the metal cool in his grip. When he took the first step toward the door he knew that he wouldn't stop. He knew that it was done.

Silently he stepped into the hallway and looked east and west. Nobody around.

Except Suzanne.

He knew her habits. She was a creature of habit, always had been. And Sunday nights were catch-up nights. So she would be in her office.

At her door he paused and sucked in a massive chestful of air. Then he turned the knob with his left hand and entered.

"What?" she had said. Then she saw the gun.

"Hello, darling Suzanne. I've come to tell my side of it."

"You crazy bastard. Have you had your meds today? If you think you can threaten me with a gun, you have another--"

The roar of the gun interrupted the meter of her speech. She had been rocking along when it was cut off. Just winding up. She was going to give it to him good. Dress him down and make him feel the fool for showing up in her office brandishing a gun. She might even have called the cops. Worse, she might have made a complaint to the law firm steering committee. A complaint lodged against the managing partner for sexual harassment would have meant the end of him.

He entertained these thoughts while she sat slumped to one side. He watched her blood drain onto the floor as if emptying her mind of thoughts.

So he took the cane and pushed it into the blood four times. Each impression was clean. Each impression showed the tread of the rubber foot.

Then he was done there and he drove himself home and returned the cane to Libby's umbrella stand.

The stewardess raised an eyebrow.

"Again?"

He smiled and nodded.

One thing he knew: you weren't supposed to ingest alcohol with those meds. All manner of bad things could happen if one drank alcohol on top of those psychoactive drugs.

What drugs?

That was then, this was now.

He seriously doubted he would ever take one again.

The wire transfer had dislodged two-hundred-forty-five million dollars from the trust account this go-round. Two hundred for the Mexicans, forty-five for him.

Him and Libby.

They would meet in Dubai and from there they would fly away.

Joined at the hip, surely. Joined at the soul, never.

But it was enough, brother. When you were fifty years old and too beat up to give a damn anymore, the familiar was a priceless and a wonderful thing.

Give him Libby any day.

Familiar won out.

Chapter 50

The judge was steamed and he issued a bench warrant. The cops set off to find Ansel and drag his butt to court--the judge's words, in chambers, when he had exploded at Thaddeus. The jury was back with its verdict and there was no Ansel.

The absence of the accused meant nothing insofar as the verdict. It would stand, whether for or against.

But it steamed Judge Zang, who assessed Ansel's failure to show as a personal affront. After all, hadn't the judge gone out of his way to set Ansel loose on bail in the first place? And now this? Now he just disappears?

State had been notified.

A No-Fly was in effect.

It went in effect when Ansel was over Oklahoma. Libby, who had gone ahead on her earlier flight, was over the Pacific.

The No-Fly was in effect only in the U.S. It would mean nothing when their 777's touched down in Dubai after twelve hours and they changed over to Airbuses for the seven hour haul to Hong Kong. Those countries freely accepted the travelers' American dollars and expedited their journey.

State be damned.

Judge Zang glared across his desk at Thaddeus, who was clueless. He had no idea where Ansel was or why he had left.

But the judge knew he couldn't keep the jury waiting forever. If he stalled more than another ten minutes their post-verdict questionnaires would not be at all complimentary to their care and feeding while under the aegis of the court. No, they would take a swing at him and the judicial conference would get wind of it and it would become part of his permanent record.

Ever so slowly, he began the four foot travel of the robe zipper from bottom to top. The lawyers watched. The wait was over.

"Ladies and gentlemen," Judge Zang smiled at the jury when everyone was reassembled and in their seats, "have you reached a verdict?"

The carpenter in the center of the second row spoke up. "We have, your honor."

"You are the foreman?"

"I am."

"Please hand your verdict form to the bailiff."

The carpenter did as directed.

The bailiff carried the verdict form to the judge, who read it, turned it back over to the bailiff, who returned it to the foreman.

"Mr. Foreman, how does the jury find?"

Thaddeus felt a sharp intake of breath. It never failed. The mean-spirited fear traveled through his bowels and shot up his spine. Just for that moment he was all fear. Head-to-toe fear.

"The jury finds the defendant, Ansel Largent, not guilty."

A clamor shot up among the press and gallery. Thaddeus looked around for a hug or a hand to shake--common and expected at such moments. But there was no one there.

Ansel was a free man.

The judge dismissed the jury and asked the attorneys to remain behind.

"Gentlemen, just so you know, the court is quashing the warrant previously issued for Ansel Largent. His bond is exonerated. He is a free man. Good luck to both of you."

Ever so slowly, Thaddeus climbed to his feet. As usual at the conclusion of a jury trial, he felt fatigue. Not exhaustion, just a pleasant fatigue. He looked around the courtroom, empty now save for a few stragglers and press.

He placed the *Illinois Evidence Manual* in his briefcase.

He touched his pockets out of habit, checking for car keys.

Which was when his hand felt the pill bottle. He extracted it from his pocket and gave it a once-over. Ansel Largent, it said. RISPERIDONE. The antipsychotic.

But there was something inside, something besides pills. A scrap of paper.

Thaddeus pressed down hard on the cap and turned it. He spun it free and opened the paper.

On the scrap was scrawled, in Ansel's unmistakable chicken-scratch:

Thank you, Thad. Didn't need these before. Don't need them now.

Signed: The Mental Case.

Chapter 51

Assignments were never-ending in the Chicago FBI field office.

Special Agents Freyer Smothers and Kip Honeycomb were perplexed over the latest one. They weren't sure if they were seeing an earlier assignment for a second time--a mistake--or whether it was a brand new assignment.

The complainant was James MacDevon.

Now where had Agent Smothers heard that name before. He backed up four months on his calendar. There it was, James MacDevon, Senior Partner at the law firm of MacDevon Largent. Wasn't that what-was-his-name-crazy-person's firm? Ansel--Largent. Ansel Largent.

Smothers punched an outside line on his desk phone and dialed the number on the assignment sheet.

"James MacDevon's office, may I help you?"

"Mr. MacDevon, please. Special Agent Freyer Smothers calling."

"Please hold."

The line pulsed. It pulsed again. Waiting, waiting.

Smothers twiddled a ballpoint through his fingers. Baton twirler in college.

Then a vaguely familiar voice came on.

"James MacDevon, Agent Smothers. Thanks for calling so quick."

"I'm a little confused. Is this the case we already handled, the missing trust funds?"

"This is phase two, I'm afraid. We've been cleaned out again."

"Trust account? Cleaned out?"

"Two-hundred-forty-five-million dollars, vanished."

"Suspects?"

"Who else? Ansel Largent."

"Wait. Didn't he get the money back for you last time?"

"Same guy. But now it's gone again and so is he. We're nuts around here with his caseload. Clients are jumping ship like a dead dog's fleas. We're in deep doo over here."

"Well, I can't help with that. But I can look into the missing funds. Were they wired out again?"

"Uh-huh. Hong Kong."

Smothers made a note. He drew a line and an arrow pointing --> Hong Kong.

And so it went.

That day and the next.

Until the trail went cold. In Albania. After the Albanian Banka Kombëtare Tregtare, the money had vanished.

Pssst, gone.

THE END

Afterword

Mental illness has too long been in the closet. This book presents a hero who suffers from a mental illness--or at least seems to. Or uses it to excuse his funky behaviors.

As a writer and a human being I am extremely sensitive to the plight of the truly mentally ill. This book does not make fun of them and is in no manner a commentary on mental illness. Instead, it's a fun book, a book about a character who maybe does and maybe doesn't need the psychoactive medications prescribed for him.

You will have to read it to find out which it is.

Next in the Thaddeus Murfee series

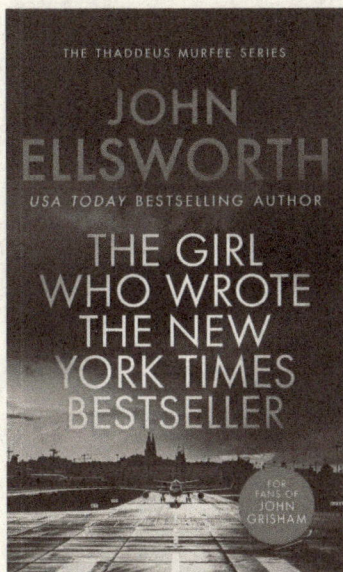

Skyjacked alongside an ambitious journalist, Thaddeus Murfee must navigate a treacherous political landscape.

Turn the page for a free preview.

The Girl Who Wrote The New York Times Bestseller

CHAPTER 1

They were head hunters.

Twenty-first century head hunters.

They wanted the jihadist's head, severed from the body, lifted to the lens on *Al Jazeera* network.

So they summoned her, Christine Susmann. She appeared as ordered. They deposited her in the waiting room while they conferred.

The sudden, overwhelming threat posed by MESA was the topic late that afternoon in Langley, Virginia. Outside, the maples and oaks—leafless—looked stunted, birds flitted among the branches, securing shelter in the deep winter, and men and women in peacoats and watch caps scurried around in CIA spy school, hopeful of making the grade and grabbing choice field assignments. But inside the conference room, long-ago graduates huddled around the broad curve of cherry conference table at one end of the Assistant Director's office. Coffee was poured, pastries were plucked from silver trays and cigarettes set to burning. Notes were exchanged, viewpoints aired, and then came time to vote. Or almost. Two more files to be passed around the huge table. One file was yellow, addressing civilian matters. One file was olive-colored, addressing military matters.

The Assistant Director was a man of rigid bearing, ex-Army, a West Pointer with the required ruby class ring, crewcut, and proud of the thirty-two inch waist he had maintained since college thanks to daily workouts and weekend hundred-mile-bike rides. He plucked the first artifact from the olive file and passed it to his left.

"News clipping, *Chicago Tribune*, 2005," he said into the system that recorded all conversations in the room. The four intelligence officers did quick reads and handed it around the table. The ten-year-old military news clipping reported:

Sgt. Christine Susmann, a military police officer in the Illinois National Guard, was awarded the Silver Star for her role in thwarting a Taliban insurgent ambush, the military said Thursday.

In a two-hour firefight, Sergeant Susmann and two other soldiers fought off more than 35 insurgents armed with AK-47s, machine guns and rocket-propelled grenades after the force attacked a supply convoy southeast of Kabul, Afghanistan. The Americans killed 30 and wounded or captured 3 others. Sergeant Susmann, 23, received her medal on Thursday in Kabul."

Heads nodded and looks were exchanged. She was an American patriot, which elevated the conversation. They could work with her.

The Associate Director next passed around a single sheet from the olive file—bullet points from her military jacket.

Papers were flipped, read, and re-read. Assent was by silence: so far, she was their choice for the assignment.

A second set of papers came from the yellow file. Her FE—family/education sheet. The father was Afghan and the mother was French, both medical doctors, both naturalized U.S. citizens. The genetic admixture produced a dark-skinned woman who could pass for Middle Eastern. She would require no makeup, no disguises for the role. Her father had raised her proud of her heritage, and daily conversations with him in Arabic were required. As a young soldier serving in Afghanistan, she interpreted for the MPs. She spoke perfect Arabic to Arabs who didn't know she wasn't a local. So the language skills were in place.

Against her parents' wishes, she had enlisted in the Army straight out of high school, so she was headstrong and independent, two traits required of spies.

The Assistant Director prepared to close the deal. He strode to his desk, unlocked a drawer, and carried four final files to the table. They were identical in content and pinned inside red covers. He passed the files around the table and waited, contemplating while the officers read.

The AD drummed his fingers on the table while the red files were finished off and evaluations made.

Then the last file was closed. All eyes turned to him.

"Vote?" he asked.

Four heads nodded.

"Afghanistan?"

"Yes."

"Syria?"

"Yes."

"Terrorism?"

"Yes."

"Military?"

"Yes."

"And I'm a 'Yes' too. It's settled, Christine Susmann is selected. Now to find out if she'll serve."

They had voted she would be the operator sent to Syria to behead the leader of MESA. His name: Abu Nidal al-Zaqari.

"Have you contacted her?" Syria wanted to know.

"We have. She's in the outer office as we speak."

"You were very sure about her," said Terrorism.

The AD smiled wryly. "She was my choice all along. I've actually met her. It was ten years ago, but she impresses, as you'll see."

"Family?" asked Afghanistan.

"Husband, two kids. The husband is a problem."

"He objects?"

"He doesn't know the specifics, of course. But when we sent for her he fiercely objected."

"She told you this?"

"Of course. Availability interviews were completed and it surfaced at that time."

"What was her feeling about him?"

The AD spread his large, thick hands.

"You can ask her that yourself. Let me bring her in."

He buzzed and a receptionist opened the door to admit a young woman in her early thirties. All eyes were watching her. Christine was five-five and average weight, but that's where "average" ended for her. For one thing, she was beautiful. She had won a county beauty pageant in the summer of her senior year, right before enlisting. For another thing she was built like an NFL safety: broad, heavily muscled shoulders and upper arms, muscular thighs and calves. Physical Eval reported she could bench press 275 yet she only weighed 145.

The AD smiled at her. He waved her to a chair halfway down the table.

"You are Christine Susmann; we've met before."

She wasn't smiling. She wasn't frowning, either. She had slipped into military-ambiguous-affect.

She pulled a wave of hair from her forehead. "Have we?"

"At the military academy, 2004. You had just completed basic and were partway through your advanced MP training in leadership."

"All right."

"Following Basic Training, you served in Afghanistan, correct?"

Christine's dark eyes narrowed. "Am I confirming what that red file says? Or do you really not know?"

The AD looked at his assistants. One gave an approving smile. That was Syria.

"Touché. So let me get right to it."

"Yes, please. I'm on the seven-thirty back to Springfield."

"Sure. The people you see seated around this table all hold commands inside the Agency."

"CIA. That's what the big gold seal said out in the lobby."

He smiled. "We brought you here to ask for your help."

"I did my tour. I will help with anything I can. Just don't ask me to serve in Kabul again."

"Why's that?"

She all but spat it out.

"Shit hole."

"Your opinion seems to be a majority one."

"Whatever. So how I can help my country other than going back to Afghanistan?"

"What we're going to ask you to do is allow us to put your military training and experience to one more use."

"You want me to arrest someone?"

"We want you to kill someone."

"Okay, well, thanks for the trip back here, the luxury hotel, the great steak last night, and the chauffeured tour of the city. But I'll be on my way now."

She stood and began to turn away.

"Please. Sit down and at least hear me out. You will be able to catch your flight in plenty of time, I promise."

"That's a must. I have a very upset husband at the other end."

"We appreciate that. Please try also to appreciate our quandary. Your government has underestimated the consequences of allowing the Middle Eastern State Army to fester and spread."

"MESA."

"MESA. All over the news, in everyone's mind, people are nervous about getting on subways or flying—it's much more of a perceived threat than we expected."

"Which is worse, the perceived threat or the actual?"

"Both, I would say. Both are equally unacceptable. So your President has decided to declare war. Starting with the top down. Cut off the head and the body will wither and die. That's the administration's best thinking."

She shook her head. "Which we all know is nonsense. Cut off the head and the organism will instantly grow another. That's the reality of terrorism."

The AD raised an eyebrow. "Maybe, maybe not. Cut off the head and immediately address the body and you just might prevent that prediction from coming true. There can be no head without a body."

"There can be no efficacious head without a body, you mean."

"I stand corrected. Yes, that's true. Which is where you come in. We want you to take off the head. Give them some of their own medicine: a public beheading."

"You mean literally? You want me to take off his head?"

"On TV."

"TV. This is your best plan?"

"It's a world stage."

"And how do you see me pulling off this act where the head of MESA disappears?"

"You will gain admission to his inner circle."

"And I would do that how? You still haven't answered my question."

"We would smuggle you in-country. You would use your military skills and great beauty to get close to him. You would prove yourself worthy of his utmost trust."

"And after I have terminated his command, how do I get home to my family? I'm sure my husband will want to know."

"We haven't got that far. We thought we'd ask your help there."

She slowly shook her head. She blinked hard. "Got it. I was afraid it would be something like that. Long story short, I probably don't get to come home."

"We'll have a plan for that. We'll have helicopters, S.E.A.L. teams—whatever is needed, you'll get. We can promise that. No one has to die there. Except their leader."

"But the chances are good that I will die. In that event, what does my family get?"

"The usual assassin's package, ten million cash, full ride

for the kids to any university, college, or other post-high school training desired, paid mortgage."

"Sounds like they're better off financially if I don't make it back."

"Then you'll do it?"

"I didn't say that. No, I won't do it. I'm leaving now. Your Middle East strategy needs to change. It's wrong. Wrong approach."

"I'm sure you have recommendations in that regard."

"No, actually, I don't. I'm a paralegal, not a political scientist. And I'm no longer a soldier. I was a soldier once and I killed my share of bad guys. But I was young and hung then. Now I'm a mother and lots wiser. Gotta go."

She stood to leave.

"Wait. Ten million cash if you come back, as well. Plus the paid mortgage and education perqs. Now what do you say?"

Christine settled back into her chair.

"That's my family's economic future you just guaranteed, either way."

"True. One million today, balance on your return or confirmation of your death. Either way."

She squirmed in her chair. It was getting very difficult to keep saying, "No."

"You people are real assholes, you know that, don't you?"

The Assistant Director allowed a small smile. He wasn't totally against acting human. Just mostly. "Your opinion is noted. Now, suppose you give us some account numbers. You will find the money in your account before you even leave here."

"What about training?"

"Don't have time for that. Besides, you're ready for this. You always were."

"Leaving when?"

"Sunday night."

"What? This is Friday. I get one day with my family and then I'm gone?"

"This can't wait, Christine. It will take you probably six months to make your way inside the castle walls. Time is of the essence."

"You people amaze me."

The AD smiled. "Then it's mutual. We're glad to have you on-board."

She unzipped her bag.

"Here's a check. Routing number and account number."

"And here are plane tickets out of Chicago. In your name."

She accepted the packet. "Pretty sure of yourselves to buy these in advance, weren't you?"

"Sergeant Susmann, you have an asthmatic daughter who visits the ER at least once a month. Your son has been treated for cerebral palsy since birth. He's going to need a lifetime of medical care. Your husband drives a dump truck and you earn sixty-five-thousand as a paralegal working for Thaddeus Murfee. Meaning you make more than your husband, but even if your salaries were doubled you still wouldn't be able to guarantee the health care your son will need after you're gone. So the airline tickets sounded to us like a solid investment."

She opened the packet and studied the tickets.

"My name is Ama Gloq? I'm flying Chicago to Zurich? Then what?"

The AD touched the side of his head. "Need-to-know."

She shrugged. "I find out when I get there. But I'm certain it's Turkey then Syria. Correct?"

He smiled.

He extended his hand. She stared at it. Then shook her head.

"I'll shake it when you cough up the other nine million. Or won't."

"Fair enough."

"And Gloq? What kind of name is that?"

The AD crossed his arms on his chest. Slowly, right before her eyes, he made a pistol of the fingers on his right hand. He pointed it at Christine.

"Glock. You code-named me after the most popular gun in history."

He lowered the thumb hammer and said, "Bang."

"Is that it?"

The AD sighed. "Not quite. We need cover for you in case you're recognized. So we've made arrangements for Thaddeus Murfee to fly on the same flight. But he'll be turning around and coming home once you land in Zurich. You will part ways."

"Does he know about this? He hasn't said anything about it to me."

"He was called this afternoon. Thaddeus Murfee is a patriot. He didn't hesitate to commit to riding along to provide cover for you. Good man."

"Yes, he is a good man. He won't be in any danger, will he?"

"Of course not. Milk run. Chicago-Zurich-Chicago. One and done."

"I'll talk to my husband. I'll let you know."

"Uh-uh. Too late for that. In or out?"

Her chest heaved in a heavy sigh. "We need the dollars. I'm in. Stupid, but in."

"Excellent. Then, away we go!"

"One last thing. What is my nationality?"

"See the passport. It says you're Afghan. Do you have a problem with that?"

She grimly shook her head.

"Would it matter if I did?"

"Not in the slightest."

"There you are, then."

"Yes, here we are."

CHAPTER 2

They operated out of a converted lube shop in Grozny, Chechnya. There were three of them, plus two PC's that still accepted floppy disks, a blue-eyed Bassett hound and four feral cats living in the windows.

But they were well-funded. They spent a stack of cash and received an untraceable email that listed all Swissair pilots age sixty-three or older. They filtered that list to those who flew to Zurich and of those they chose the one who was sixty-four. His name was Royal Evans and his was the perfect profile: mandatory retirement in six weeks, happily married, no criminal record, retirement fully funded. The seats were confirmed and Zurich was confirmed. They knew they had their man.

The Chechens entered the United States and made their way to Chicago. They set up housekeeping in a downtown Hilton suite and went to work.

The pilot, Royal Evans, had to be taken down. Only then would he be useful.

First order of business: they made sure Evans caught his

wife with another man. The other man was one of them, name of Maritan. He was a physician and handsome. Mrs. Royal Evans was swept off her feet in just three days after a chance meeting at the Starbucks she visited every weekday morning. He was wearing scrubs and he wore the requisite stethoscope around his neck like a Hollywood producer sporting gold chains. He reeked of status and riches like lounge lizards reek of Musk.

Maritan was several years Mrs. Evans junior, a surgeon trained at America's oldest hospital, Bellevue. He told Mrs. Evans he'd never known love before. It took her all of seventy-two hours to fall madly in love and phone her sister in Poughkeepsie to tell her so. The man wanted her to come away, she told the sister, but he insisted she first confront Royal Evans and tell him she wanted half of everything. Including his Swissair retirement.

Her sister asked, would she do it? Would she demand half of everything?

Mrs. Evans didn't equivocate. Maritan was the nicest man she'd ever known. He was considerate, caring, and soft-spoken. He wanted to know everything about her, hung on every word she uttered. Two blissful nights with a youthful, virile, intelligent doctor—what woman in her fifties could resist? Especially when Royal Evans was distant and growing angry in his advancing years. He hated the kids crossing the lawn, he hated dark skins, he hated Europe, and he hated her family. When he was home he refused to shave and their time together consisted of white whiskers and regret. The thought of it: that she had thrown away thirty years. It came down to an easy choice for Mrs. Evans.

"Go for it," her sister encouraged. "You only go around once."

Mrs. Evans told Royal Evans there was no way she

could ever turn away from Maritan the surgeon. She demanded half of everything. Including his Swissair retirement. He imagined himself living in a studio with a foldout bed above a butcher shop, the victim of a sack and pillage.

He decided to dig in and let it blow over. But she was having none of that.

Mrs. Evans demanded he leave the house that night. He tossed down two scotches and refused to leave. She dialed the police while he watched and listened to her report a domestic disturbance. Taking the scotch bottle, he grabbed his flight bag and left. Now the Chechens had them separated. They followed him and checked into the room next door in the Palmer House in Chicago.

The following morning, the Chechens noisily settled around the next table as Royal Evans ate breakfast in the hotel cafe. Evans couldn't help but overhear. The topic was an upcoming flight to Zurich. The Chechens erupted into a violent argument about flying times and time zones. Evans was astonished, because it was his flight and he would be flying their plane, so he interrupted their argument and offered his thoughts.

Ayub, the younger of the two, eyed him with bristling suspicion as he spoke.

"And you know this how?" Ayub said sharply.

Evans smiled his friendly, Welcome Aboard smile, hiding from them the fact he actually loathed them because they were dark and spoke with accents. "I know it because I have been the pilot on this trip probably two hundred times. To make a long story short, your friend is right and you are wrong."

Ayub relaxed and let the pilot see he was warming to him. "Well, this is unexpected help. How can we thank you?"

"Not necessary. Call it serendipity. Just let me finish eating in peace."

"I shall call it that. And I shall buy your breakfast as well, if you will allow it. Then you won't hear us again. Not one single peep."

"No need for that."

"We insist. Please—join us for coffee."

"I'm fine over here."

"Are you on a layover?"

"No, I live here as of last night. Problems at home."

Ayub winced. "Aniji, he knows all about that. He had an American wife once."

The older man, Aniji, shook his head sadly. "Never again. No American women."

Evans nodded and found himself oddly sympathetic. "I hear that," he said.

"And what is your name, captain?"

"Royal Evans. And you can forget about the captain stuff. I'm off-duty."

They traded stories. They were petroleum engineers visiting Russaco's home office two miles away. They explained they were from Russia and they found America inspiring and wonderful. Which pleased Royal Evans. Everyone likes to hear visitors admire their home. They asked if he had ever toured a petroleum refinery and he laughed and said no, he actually had not thought about visiting a refinery. One thing led to another and he agreed to accompany them on a tour of the local plant. It just might help take his mind off the problems at home. And for Russians, they weren't so bad after all, thought Royal Evans. And who knows, the Chechens said, maybe Mrs. Evans will have come to her senses in a day or two. Evans said he doubted that, that she hadn't strayed even once in thirty years. No, this was serious and he dreaded the worst.

They toured the refinery. They gave him a Russaco hard hat to keep. Little stuff, including buying his dinner. That night they drank together and they spiked his scotch. When Evans woke for a bladder call at five a.m., he was horrified to find with him in a bed a female who couldn't have been more than fifteen. His two new friends were at the foot of the bed, video recorder in hand, stony-faced as he regained consciousness. It swam into view for him and he realized.

He had been had.

They played the video, showing him the hard drive version of the *Kama Sutra*. Evans ran to the bathroom and threw up. By the time he came back he was shaken and ashen. A quick look around. The girl had disappeared. But his new friends were still there. In fact, they had just ordered up a carafe of coffee and six Danish. They wanted to talk. Man to men. For they had a proposition.

They held tickets on his next flight. A thousand miles out over the Atlantic he would turn over control of the plane to his co-pilot and go to the restroom. When the cabin door came open, they would rush the cockpit and take control. The 777 would be diverted to Moscow and he would fly it there. His reward: $1 million. He did the math: his 401k was at $1.3 million after thirty years of toil. Mrs. Evans was in for one-half, her community property share. The Chechen's deal looked better to Evans. Plus they would destroy the recording of the sex-with-a-minor incident and he would not have to spend his retirement behind bars. The math worked top-down and bottom-up, so Evans agreed.

Two days later his flight came up.

They took one cab to the airport. One big happy outing, at that point. Royal Evans rode in back, sandwiched between them. It turned out they had British passports, good as gold in the U.S.

Captain Evans moved from back seat in the cab to first chair in the 777. In the cabin of Swissair Flight 3309, Chicago to Zurich nonstop.

In a cockpit lockbox, Captain Evans kept a small pistol. He always swore he would use it to prevent a skyjacking. But this time, when they breached the cabin doors, he was busy in the restroom. When he emerged, he played the victim role and immediately assented to re-program the autopilot and head for Moscow. After all, there were 324 civilians onboard his flight and his first thought was for their safety. The co-pilot and First Class stews all heard the threats to kill the two pilots and crash the plane in the Atlantic. Captain Evans couldn't—wouldn't—allow that.

So Moscow was dialed in to the autopilot. No announcement was made to the passengers.

The first skyjacking since 9/11 had just been committed. Not a shot fired, not a throat cut. Just a sickening video recording on a cheap camera starring Royal Evans and a street teen. Jail bait wasn't even the right term. *Prison* bait was more like it.

Captain Evans looked into the dark night at stars above and pitch black below, diamonds tossed at velvet. At 450 knots and slipping into the northern hemisphere polar jet stream, there was no stopping the Moscow-bound aircraft.

Captain Royal Evans was out of good ideas.

At that point, he was just driving.

vinci-books.com/thegirl

About the Author

For thirty years John defended criminal clients across the United States. He defended cases ranging from shoplifting to First Degree Murder to RICO to Tax Evasion, and has gone to jury trial on hundreds. His first book, *The Defendants*, was published in January, 2014. John is presently at work on his 31st thriller.

Reception to John's books have been phenomenal; more than 4,000,000 have been downloaded in 6 years! Every one of them are Amazon best-sellers. He is an Amazon All-Star every month and is a *U.S.A Today* bestseller.

John Ellsworth lives in the Arizona region with three dogs that ignore him but worship his wife, and bark day and night until another home must be abandoned in yet another move.